Readers react to

"How does a heart grow strong?
Read this wonderful book and find out. The characters
charmed and surprised me, and I found myself a willing
companion on their journey, caring deeply for them."

– Kim Heacox, author of
RHYTHM OF THE WILD and **JIMMY BLUEFEATHER**
(Winner of the National Outdoor Book Award)

"...masterfully captures the essence of a teenage girl, lost
in the world, and trying to believe in herself when most
others don't believe in her at all. Sarah's narration was both
captivating and enigmatic. I don't think I've ever read about
a girl like Sarah before, and I find myself contemplating her
character long after the story's end."

– Onlinebookclub.org

CHARLIE SHELDON

IRONTWINE
P R E S S

For

Those whose greatest pleasure is curling up with a book
on a rainy afternoon;

and to contrary girls everywhere.

May each of you find your own short face bear.

Published by Iron Twine Press
www.irontwinepress.com

Cover design, book design and illustrations by Sonja L. Gerard
© 2017 by Iron Twine Press

Cover photo by Charlie Sheldon

Photo of the author at the Royal Museum by Randa Williams

Printed in the United States of America.

ISBN 978-0-9970600-5-8 (pb)

10 9 8 7 6 5 4 3 2

We shall not cease from exploring,
And the end of our exploring
will be to arrive where we started
and know the place for the first time.

T.S. Eliot (1888-1965)

Your vision will become clear
only when you look into your heart ...
Who looks outside, dreams.
Who looks inside, awakens.

Carl Jung (1875-1961)

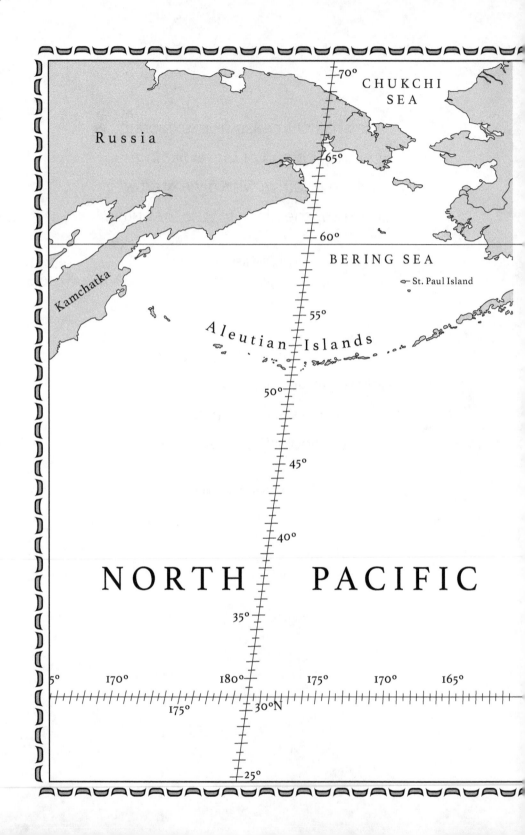

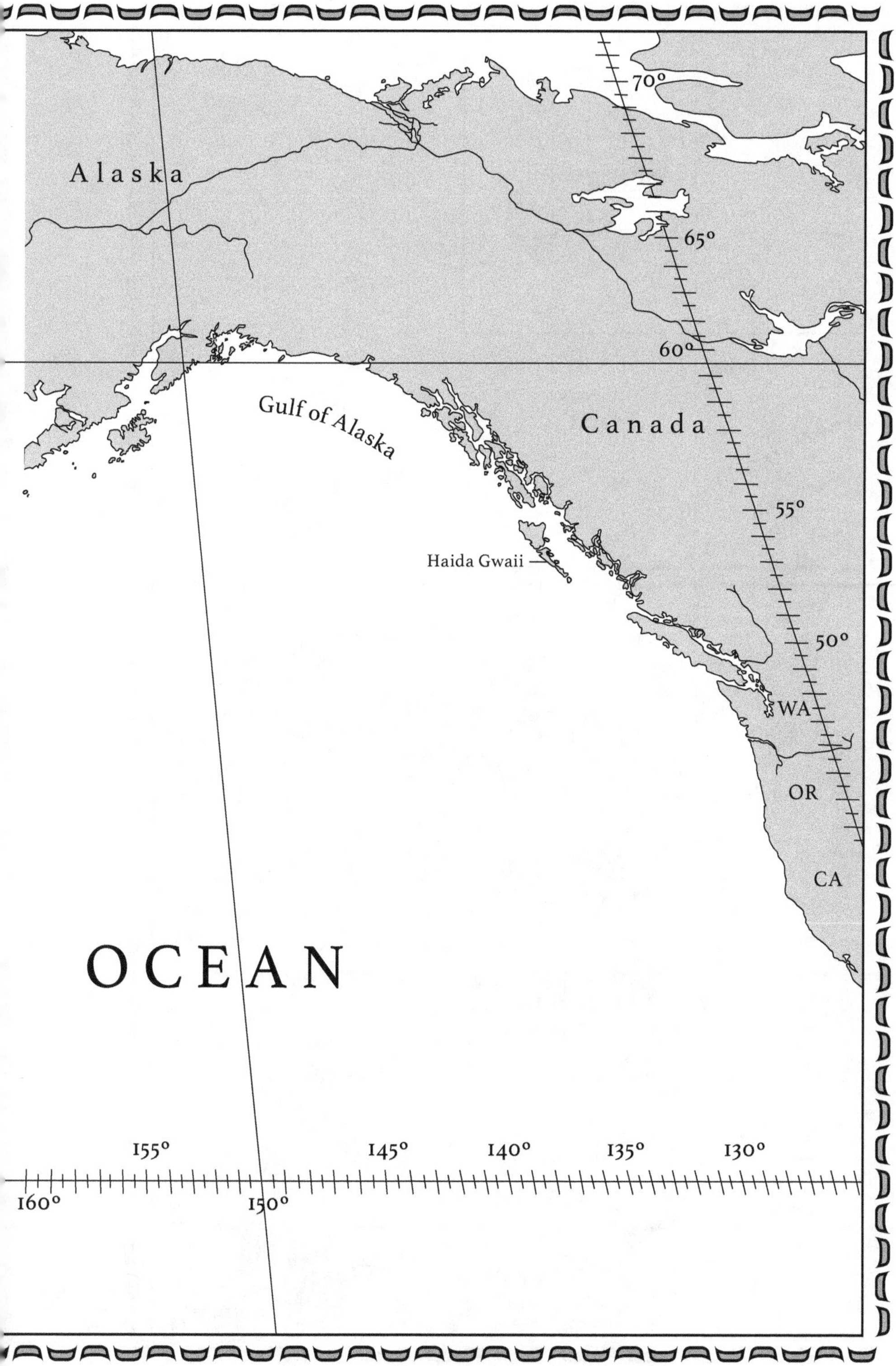

Alaska

70°

65°

60°

Gulf of Alaska

Canada

55°

Haida Gwaii

50°

WA

OR

CA

OCEAN

155°   145°   140°   135°   130°

160°   150°

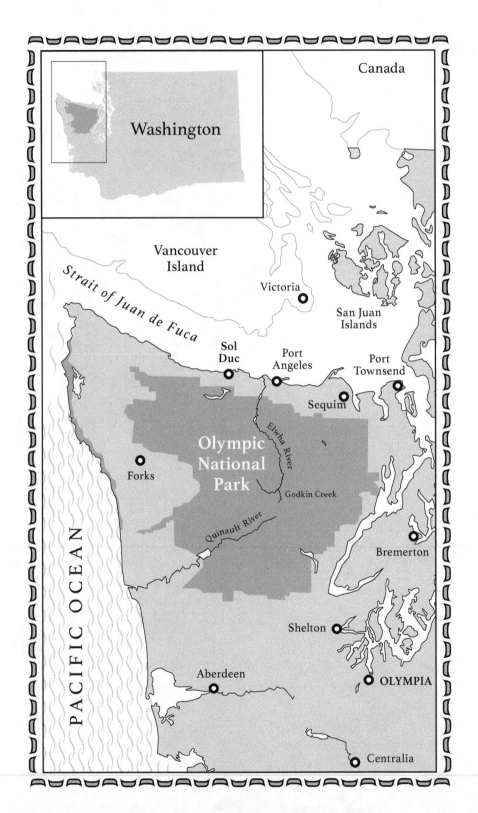

The wind shook the house, roaring like a great animal. Rain thundered on the roof. William imagined ancient spirits, awakened and angry, searching, grasping.

Three harsh blows struck against the front door, followed by three more, urgent.

"See who that is, Walleye." Tom waved down the hallway. He and Myra, William's daughter, were rolling one of the tents.

William opened the door to see before him a woman in a dark coat, vaguely familiar, older than William. A child shivered next to her, almost hidden beneath a soaked sweatshirt and hood. The woman had a tight grip on the child's upper arm. The child held a wet travel bag. Beyond, past the porch, through a driving rain, he saw a jeep, headlights on, facing back down the driveway.

William sensed Tom and Myra coming up behind him. He stepped aside. Tom saw the woman and stiffened. "Long time since we spoke, Ruth." Now William recognized her. This was Ruth, Tom's ex-wife. William had met her many years earlier, back when he had been fishing on Tom's boat.

Ruth pushed into the hallway, dragging the child. "May we come in?" Tom, William and Myra backed up. William guessed the child was a girl, 12 or 13 years old, thin as a stick, less than five feet tall, mouth determined. Beneath the hood, dark hair fell over a narrow face. A metal pin gleamed on one nostril. Ruth pulled at the girl's arm. "This is your granddaughter. I just found out five days ago. She's Becky's child."

The girl, wincing as Ruth held her arm, dropped her bag to the floor.

Tom stared at Ruth, then the girl. His glasses glinted. He swallowed. "You told me our Becky, bless her soul, had no children, Ruth, when you last called, five years ago, to tell me she was dead."

"Becky ran away when she was 15, Tom. I lost touch, all right? When I heard she died, I didn't know she had a child." Ruth eyed Myra and William, then Tom. "Five days ago her father called, out of the blue. He's taken a job in Europe and he sent her out here for the summer. He said she needed a time out from the family. Coming out here was her idea, he said." Ruth's mouth tightened. "She's been with Fletcher and me four days. That's enough. It's your turn. This is your granddaughter, Tom. Her name is Sarah."

Tom looked closely at Sarah, trying to see past the dripping hood, the hair, the metal pin. He squatted, eye to eye with Sarah. "Sarah? Do you have a last name?"

The girl twisted her arm free of Ruth. "Cooley. Sarah Cooley."

Tom stood, keeping his eyes on Sarah. "Ruth, you could have told me about this when you first heard."

"I'm telling you now. Here she is. You can deal with her drinking, her bad attitude, and the skateboard trash she somehow met. Have fun." Ruth then turned and marched through the open door to the idling jeep. She started down the long dirt driveway, not looking back. Tom reached past Sarah, closed the door.

Sarah was shivering. "This is the total boonies. Now I'm going to stay here?" She noticed the camping gear scattered in the hallway. "Your house is a mess."

"Could this be true, Tom?" Myra seemed delighted. "You have granddaughter?" Sarah's teeth were chattering. "I think Sarah needs a hot shower, some dry clothes, and hot food." Rain drummed the roof.

"You have food?" Sarah's voice trembled.

"Elk stew," Tom said. A big pot was bubbling on the stove.

"Elk? Gross."

Myra took Sarah's bag and led Sarah through the living room to a bathroom to show her towels, where she could shower, and where she could change into some dry clothes from her bag. Then Myra returned through the living room to the kitchen. Tom and William were standing, packing forgotten.

"Tom, suddenly you're a grandfather?"

Tom glanced toward the bathroom, then at Myra and William. "This isn't funny, Myra." He was pale. "But she's Becky's twin. Talks just like her. Looks exactly like Becky did at that age. It's uncanny. I have no doubt she is Becky's child."

"What are you going to do? Obviously we can't go camping. Maybe it's for the best. It's only early May." Myra eyed William doubtfully, then Tom. Tom was 10 years older than William, not quite 70, wiry and tall. William was even taller but carried way too much heft. Myra shook her head. "It's over 30 miles, the last six or seven off trail. It would be safer later in the summer."

William wasn't in shape for this. Tom had asked him to come along and William had asked Myra to join them, because he knew he might need help. Myra was skilled in the woods, had some of William's height, much of his strength, and none of his girth or looks.

They could hear the shower running. Tom removed his glasses and wiped them on his sleeve. "Dammit. I wanted to get up there before Buckhorn starts their work, see that valley before it changes. Make sure Bob-Bob's grave is secure. Now is when 'Eye, here, is off his ship. And he told me this is the only time you can get away from the tribe." Tom glanced toward the sound of the shower. "Dammit. This trip wasn't easy to schedule."

Myra placed her hand on Tom's forearm. "It's barely May, Tom. You told us you buried your grandfather Bob-Bob up there over 45 years ago. Bob-Bob isn't going anywhere. Surely a few more weeks won't matter. By then Sarah will be back at Ruth's, or with her family."

Tom's lined face caught shadows. "Maybe you're right. It's a long way in there. Probably not the best time to leave work, either." He pulled bowls from a cupboard, spoons from a drawer. "My God. I'm going to have to set up one of the bedrooms for her. See about getting her in school. She hates it here, that's already obvious. Who's going to watch her between the end of school and when I get home from work?" Tom leaned on the counter, facing the cupboards. "Hell. I can't do this."

Sarah, in dry clothes, appeared from the bathroom. She was carrying a sketchpad. She stopped in the living room, studied a small Haida war canoe William had carved and given Tom years before. Then she followed her nose past the seating counter to the kitchen.

Tom handed Sarah a bowl of stew. She took a taste. Then she took a big spoonful, followed by another. Tom gave bowls to William and Myra. They all sat at the kitchen table. They ate but they watched Sarah. She finished her stew fast.

Tom refilled her bowl. "You and Ruth and Fletcher, you didn't get along, did you? At least, you and me, we have that in common."

Sarah was spooning stew. "There was nothing to do. He's mean. She's all about rules. I don't think I have anything in common with you."

"You're the spitting image of your mother."

"I am? Ruth didn't believe me. Not really."

"We'll take you to the hospital for genetic testing, of course."

William saw the sparkle in Tom's eye and knew he was kidding. Sarah's eyes grew wide. "You'll come to understand your grandfather's sense of humor," William offered.

Sarah relaxed. She placed the empty bowl on the counter. "Where's your television?"

"No television," Tom said.

"There was a television there. At her place."

➤

"Well, not here. Read a book."

"This is absolutely the boonies." Sarah returned to the living room. She slouched in a chair by the woodstove. She opened her sketchpad and began drawing, head down, intent.

Tom pulled Myra and William further into the kitchen, beyond Sarah's sight. He lowered his voice. "What should I do? Ruth's dumped her on me."

"After a week or two she and Fletcher will take her back," Myra said. "Or you can send her to Europe, back to her father."

Tom shook his head. "I know Ruth. She wouldn't have taken her to begin with if there was any way to avoid it. That girl's out here for the summer, minimum." Wind buffeted Tom's house. Tom gathered the bowls and washed them in the sink. Nobody spoke for several minutes.

"You can call Family Services and put her in foster care," Myra eventually said.

"Foster care? Are you serious?"

"Or she stays with you. You're her grandfather."

William noticed Sarah standing at the entrance to the kitchen, listening.

"What about school, Sarah?" Myra asked, seeing Sarah.

"I'm done, this year."

"Here in Washington, school doesn't end until the middle of June, more than a month from now."

"I went to a special school. For problem kids. We finished five days ago."

"And after that you came right out here?" Tom was wiping the bowls dry.

"Well, duh. I didn't know my grandmother was a tight-ass or my grandfather cooked elk. Yuk."

"You ate a lot of elk, Sarah." Tom was grinning. Sarah said nothing. Tom watched his granddaughter. Then he asked William, "What do you think, Walleye?"

"What kind of stupid name is Walleye?" Sarah refused to look at William's wayward eye.

"His real name is William," Myra said. "He's my father, and the biggest, ugliest Indian I know. See how his eye wanders? My dad can be a good friend. Don't let his looks scare you."

"I'm not anyone's friend. There's nothing here. This is the end of the earth, this place."

Myra crouched before Sarah, reached out, and touched her shoulder. "No, Sarah. This is the Olympic Peninsula. This is a land of magic, history, and legend. A place of myth, ancient stories, ancient people."

"Where? All I see is water, mud and trees." Rain rattled the sides of Tom's house.

Sarah was thin and short but William already knew her spirit was hot and strong. Sarah was not much bigger than Myra had been at age nine, 20 years earlier, when William had taken her camping on the Pacific coast. Myra had survived that trip, even learned how to build a fire with wet wood. Now William watched Tom, perplexed, facing his granddaughter. Sarah stared back, watchful. Tom looked past Sarah at all the gear in the hall. Tom had been about to leave to visit his grandfather's grave and now, William realized, he was responsible for a grandchild he never knew he had. Sarah had the same straight thin nose as her grandfather, the same air of careful deliberation. Maybe those traits had come from Bob-Bob, who was Sarah's ancestor, too. Suddenly, William knew what Tom should do.

"Sarah," William said. "Tom here was going to take Myra and me with him to visit his grandfather's grave." Tom caught William's eye, frowning. Tom started to shake his head. William went on, "That's your great-great grandfather, Sarah. We were going to leave tomorrow morning. You should come, you can meet his spirit, too."

"I don't believe that spirit stuff, 'Eye,' and it's not your business to ask her to come." Tom frowned, lips tight. "Bad suggestion."

"What, Tom? We cancel the trip, and you stay here? Why not, we take the trip, as planned, but with Sarah, and you both honor your ancestor?"

"Dad's right, Tom. I'll have someone to help me watch you geezers. Sarah will get to know you, and us. She can see this country herself, make up her own mind about what sort of land this is."

Sarah's mouth was open.

Tom was still shaking his head. "She's a green kid, Myra. Put a pack on her back and head off into rough country? Off trail, maybe snow? Are you serious? 'Eye, you can't be serious."

William pictured Sarah, whining, spitting, a profane bundle of rage, buried beneath a pack, being hauled down the trail. At least, with her along, his fat-ness and suffering wouldn't be so obvious.

Tom was definite. "This is a very bad idea." He glared.

Myra laughed. "I'll need some help making sure you old warriors don't cripple yourselves. Seeing you get fed and have plenty of rest. Sarah will be a big help."

Tom snorted. A branch scraped the roof under the wind.

"You guys are going camping? That's what you're doing?"

William eyed Tom. "Better that than leaving you loose and homeless here in Sol Duc."

"This is a mistake." Tom was still glaring at William.

Myra pulled out her car keys. "I have extra gear, Sarah, from when I was your size. We'll run over to my place on the res. I can get you outfitted in an hour. My dad and Tom can add food for the four of us here, we have plenty. The rain should stop by morning."

"A hike? Seriously? Seriously? This is child abuse."

The heavy clouds blew east. The next morning a bright sun rose. Tom's muddy driveway steamed. They made the short drive to the trailhead, heading south from Sol Duc to Route 101, then into Olympic National Park. At the Whiskey Bend trailhead, the parking lot was empty. Outside the car, the air was cool. Sarah leaned against a car door, pack at her feet, sullen. William knew it it was going to be a long day when he lifted his pack. His pack was heavy.

Another vehicle appeared, scattering gravel. Four men emerged from a white four-seat pickup with a company logo on the door. The men were all dressed in dark green pants, light-colored laced boots, tan vests over green long-sleeve shirts, and bill caps. They weren't park rangers, but they weren't casual hikers, either. Without much talk or discussion they pulled big packs from the bed of the truck.

Myra, returning from the trailhead rest room, passed them. William saw the men staring at her, the way men always did. She stopped, saying, "It's nice the rain stopped. Where you headed?"

"Up a ways," said the youngest. He pointed toward the trail.

"Going all the way through over Low Divide to the Quinault? That's 50 miles."

"Let's go, Pete," A square-jawed man wearing sunglasses gestured toward the trail. Pete, who seemed Myra's age, about to say something, shut his mouth. The four shouldered their packs and headed out. Within a minute they were gone.

"Trail maintenance crew, maybe?" Tom shivered. "It's cold."

Myra helped Sarah mount her pack. William's pack felt huge. Tom pulled a capped, rigid tube from the car and carefully strapped it to the side of his pack. The tube was just over three feet long, four inches in diameter.

"We going fishing?" William asked. The case resembled a rod holder, but shorter.

"Not fishing," Tom tightened the tube straps. "Something else, for when we get back in there. We ready?"

"This sucks." Sarah hitched her pack. "This really sucks."

Tom led, followed by Sarah and Myra. William brought up the rear. As soon as they left the parking lot, they were in forest. The trail was covered with needles and leaves. The trees here grew close, and, despite the sun overhead, they walked in shadows. The trail, along a side hill, twisted and curved, passing tumbling freshets. The forest was quiet but for the sound of their thudding feet and the cry of an occasional bird. Myra followed Sarah, now and then encouraging her. They'd kept Sarah's pack as small as possible, but it still rose over her back like a misshapen hump, swaying.

William overheard Myra. "You'll get less tired if you swing your feet around the rocks, instead of stepping up on each one."

Tom was leading, carrying a long walking stick. As the trail curved, Tom would disappear around a bend, then reappear as they made the bend themselves. William started swinging his feet as Myra had suggested. Within 15 minutes he was sweating, despite the chill day. For Sarah's sake they walked 20 minutes, then stopped to rest for five. William had learned with Myra years before that 20 minutes was a time span a child could understand, and the promise of knowing there was a short rest ahead helped.

The first time they stopped, Sarah sat on a big stone

beneath a beam of sunlight poking through the trees. She leaned back and her pack was braced against the rising slope. Sarah had instinctively picked the one place where she could relax without removing her pack. William caught Myra's eye, nodded.

"This is so lame," Sarah's eyes were closed.

"Have you ever been camping, Sarah?" Myra adjusted her pack belt.

"I hated it."

"Back east?"

Sarah opened her eyes. "My parents sent me to this camp last summer in Quebec." She spat. "I know about sailboats and canoes. I was sent home."

"A total waste of time?" Myra was smiling.

"We tried to cross this huge lake in our canoes and a storm came up. We almost sank. At least out here we won't be in canoes, right? Then a week later we got caught in a bigger storm, and two sailboats sank. One girl broke her arm." Sarah paused. "They caught me opening the drain plugs in one of the sailboats the next day. That finally got me out of there." Tom wiped his neck with a handkerchief, then checked his glasses. "I don't think you're my grandfather. Jailer, more like."

"Have you been in jail?" Tom put his glasses back on.

"Juvie."

"This is like juvie? Being out here?" Myra asked.

"Worse." said Sarah.

"When I was eight, I was sent to a place like your juvie." William's wandering eye roamed up and away. His voice rumbled.

"Where?"

"I was born on Haida Gwaii, off the mid BC coast, home of the Haida people. My tribe. When I was eight, my dad took off after my mother died. The government sent me to a school on the mainland, in Kamloops. For native people, to make us like white people." William's loose eye landed on Sarah and held. "I forgot my language and I almost forgot my people, too. I ran away, at 15, and came down to the States. If your juvie was anything like that place in Kamloops, you know this isn't worse than that."

Sarah said nothing. She lurched forward and rose to her feet. She was ready to leave. They'd been stopped for three minutes.

After an hour they came to a stream that crossed the trail just before an abandoned cabin. The stream was rushing over rocks. They could cross without removing their boots, but the rocks were slippery, covered with racing water.

Sarah began to cross after watching where Tom stepped, but she had no walking stick for support. Her foot slipped. She fell, hard and fast. She grabbed for a branch but she missed. She landed face down in the stream. The water poured against her. Her pack had ridden forward as she fell. She struggled to raise herself. By the time Myra and William reached her and pulled her up, she was soaked through. Even her pack, which had remained on her back, was partly soaked.

Sarah stumbled from the stream, dripping, flinging her pack. "That's it. I'm outa here." Soaked, she marched back down the trail, fast. She disappeared around the bend, head up, arms swinging. She was exactly the whining, spitting bundle of rage William had foreseen.

"Get a fire started. A big one."

Myra turned and went after Sarah. William gathered wood and started a fire. Tom opened Sarah's pack, strung a line, and hung what was wet. Half an hour later, Myra returned. Sarah, feet kicking, was slung over Myra's shoulder. She was sputtering and her teeth were chattering. She was moving clumsily. Myra found dry clothes in Sarah's pack. Sarah changed in the cabin with Myra's help.

William built up the fire and arranged a place for Sarah to sit. Tom pulled out the stove and brewed hot water for tea. When Sarah sat down by the fire, Myra draped her own sleeping bag across Sarah's shoulders. Sarah shuddered, holding the bag, lips quivering. Her bare feet, alabaster white, were covered with pine needles. Tom set up the tents with Myra's help while William fed the fire, tended the hanging clothes, and gathered more wood. Sarah now held a mug of hot tea with both hands. She remained silent.

"We'll camp here," Tom said.

"Duh." Sarah's teeth clacked.

"Ah. You can talk even while shivering. We aren't that far from where we would have camped anyway, at Lillian River, but it's not as gloomy here."

"Not gloomy? Everywhere here is gloomy. I'll report you to the state. Child abuse. Grandfathers don't torture their grandchildren. This is torture."

➤

"I had to chase her halfway back to the car, Tom. She took some convincing to return."

"Convincing? That's what you call it? Carrying me?"

"You were becoming hypothermic, Sarah. It's less than 50 degrees today. Look at you, you're still shaking." Sarah drank tea, then held out her cup for more. Her legs were steaming, as were the hanging clothes. She pulled the bag tighter over her shoulder.

"I should have given you my walking stick before you crossed," Tom said. "That was a mistake."

Sarah looked into the fire. She finally stopped shaking. When she took a breath she shuddered. "This place is cold. Cold. I froze at that skate park. I froze at Ruth's. I'm freezing here." Sarah scratched her nose. "I froze back east, too. Everywhere I go it's cold. I mean, this out here? This is the sticks. Why am I here, anyway? Oh, that's right. I'm on a time out." A tear rolled down her cheek. She sniffled, then straightened. "I'm hungry."

"We'll have dinner at sundown," Tom said. "First we need to get your sleeping bag and clothes dry."

Myra made a place by the fire next to Sarah. Sarah moved away. Tom was looking at his granddaughter, then William. William knew Tom was thinking Sarah coming along was a huge mistake.

"Sarah." William squatted across the fire from her. "Your first time ever with a big pack on your back was today, am I right?" Sarah scowled. She huddled close to the fire. "Four miles we came, today. You didn't complain, not really. The first time I took Myra out, she complained, every single step."

"She did?"

"He's mellowed plenty since he took me out." Myra glared at William. "He was a lot meaner then and not half as old. Or fat.

But, it's true. I complained."

For an instant, Sarah was proud.

By late afternoon Sarah's clothing and sleeping bag were dry. They had seen no one all day since the party of four had started up the trail before them. Once Sarah's boots were dry, she and Myra wandered together down to the broad meadows by the river. Along the winding river bottom, maples and alders clustered along old empty channels. Here, 15 miles back from the strait and the sea, and 1,000 feet higher, the trees were bare of buds. Across the river, through the empty branches and the scattered firs, steep slopes rose to high snowy ridges and rocky peaks.

"You going to be okay, 'Eye? You seemed to be suffering a little back there."

"I'll be all right, Tom, once I get a few miles under me. It hurts plenty right now but it will pass." William could see Sarah down on the meadow. She had a stick and was poking some old elk dung. Myra basked in the sinking sun. "Sarah's ornery. Being ornery can help, out here."

"I don't know," Tom said. "She's small. This is a mistake. It was a bad idea, 'Eye, to bring her. We're keeping her from school. I don't formally have permission to have her with me, and if anything happens, Ruth will sic the authorities on me, that's for sure. What kind of father sends his daughter across the country, alone, to live all summer with a stranger anyway?"

"I'm not surprised Ruth didn't want to keep Sarah, Tom. Fletcher surely wouldn't want your granddaughter to be living in his house. He's had it in for you forever." Tom had once told William that after returning from Vietnam he got together with Ruth, unaware she was spoken for by Fletcher Lynch. She became pregnant. Tom tried to do the right thing, and married her. Gone fishing for months at a time, Tom rarely saw his daughter, and before Becky was three years old Ruth left Tom and moved in with Lynch.

Tom prepared the food. Through a gap in the trees, William could see the Elwha, flowing fast and dark. Across the river, in a distant meadow, three big elk looked his way.

By the time Myra and Sarah had returned to the fire, the distant meadow was in gloom, the elk gone.

They ate dinner, sitting around the hot coals, bowls in their laps, feet braced against old sections of cut logs they'd pulled around the fire pit. The western sky, above the ridges, glowed dark red, then faded. The coals shimmered. Sarah pulled out her sketchpad and pencil.

Myra settled down not far from Sarah. "This cabin here?" Myra waved toward the dark. "People came way out here, homesteaded, over 100 years ago. Before that, this valley and river belonged to the tribes. Before they built the dams to power the logging mills, salmon in this river were 100 pounds apiece. Now, after 100 years, the dams are out again."

Sarah was bent over her pad. Now and then she'd raise her head and look across the fire at Tom and William. Heat throbbed from the coals. Thin smoke rose to smudge stars overhead.

William leaned back against his log, felt the heat. How many thousands of years had people sat before fires just like this, quiet, staring, lost in their thoughts? How many hundreds of thousands?

"A story," Myra said.

Sarah closed her pad. She was finally looking warm. William was stiff. Only four miles and he felt crippled. Tom sat relaxed, opening and closing his pocketknife. Myra was looking at Tom, expectant. "Come on, Tom. Tell Sarah where we're going, and why. Tell me and my dad, too."

"You mean, aside from kidnapping?" Sarah scowled at Tom, Myra, then William.

Tom closed his pocketknife with a snap. "You haven't been kidnapped, Sarah. You're not really a child, either. You made it across the country alone, found the bus to Port Angeles from the airport, found your grandmother."

"Big mistake," Sarah said.

"Maybe so, Sarah. Jury's still out on that. I'm having a hard time seeing you back at Ruth and Fletcher's. They'd put you in school; the law requires that. Either that or, what? Homeless in a strange town?"

"I'd be fine."

"I was older than you, but when I came back from Vietnam I bet I was as miserable as you are today. Back then, my grandfather, your great-great-grandfather, took me into these woods when I had nowhere else to go. Not so different than you, actually. My last trip in with him, where we're going now, he was going to show me something. He died up here. I buried him." Sarah blinked. "I have some unfinished business, and I asked 'Eye to come with me, and 'Eye asked Myra. Now, with you, we're four. Here you are, and as 'Eye said, you did pretty well today."

"What unfinished business? You said you had unfinished business."

"Ah. I'll answer your question only if one day you tell me about yourself and your mother. Will you do that?"

"Maybe. Depends."

"Fair enough." Tom tossed another thick log on the fire. Sparks rose. Sarah backed into her log, side against Myra. Myra adjusted herself to fit with Sarah.

Tom began.

"I grew up in Port Angeles. My father worked in the logging woods like his father before him, but when he returned from the Navy, after World War II, he got hurt, so he took a job with the postal service. My mother was a grade school teacher. I was pretty wild when in high school, rousting around. I had no interest in college, or money for college, when I graduated from high school. It was 1965. That summer I was drafted."

"What's that?" Sarah brushed needles off her ankles.

"Back when I was young, we had no choice about military service once out of school. There was a war over in Asia and the army needed bodies. We'd be sent a letter, told to report to military training. One day I was stuffing grocery bags and the next I was on a bus headed for basic training. Six months later I was in a war. I flew home in January, 1968. I landed in Los Angeles, flew up to Seattle, finished my duty at Fort Lewis, and mustered out that spring. I was 21 years old. My mother died while I was in Vietnam and my father, your great-grandfather, disappeared into the bottle, got fired from the post office." Tom stretched. His back cracked. "It was my grandfather who came to see me down at Fort Lewis every other weekend before I mustered out, even though it was a long damn drive. His name was Robert Olsen, but his friends called him Bob. I'd called him Bob-Bob since I was three. Bob-Bob's grandfather, Henry David Olsen, came into the west in 1855. Henry David was, let's see, Sarah, your great-great-great-great-grandfather. He was here just after this place was first settled by whites. He hunted game for the logging camps. He had a native wife whose brother showed him the ancient trails into the high country."

Myra and William exchanged a look. It was news to William about Tom's heritage.

Tom went on, "Having a native wife meant he was shunned in settler communities. His three children, though, passed for white. By the time Bob-Bob came along, the family had buried our native heritage, as people did in those days. Bob-Bob, though, learned of his heritage from Henry David Olsen, his grandfather. Bob-Bob first went into this country, maybe the same trails we're on now, as a boy with Henry David before 1910, back when these trails were ancient Indian paths."

"Did Henry David kidnap Bob-Bob the way you kidnapped me?"

Tom thought. "Maybe he did. I don't know. That's what Bob-Bob did with me, though. A month after I mustered out from the army, Bob-Bob told me to get my drunken ass off his couch. He took me into the Olympics."

"So this grandparents kidnapping grandkids is, what, an Olsen family rule?"

William, seeing Sarah's expression, laughed.

Tom studied his granddaughter. "Maybe it is, Sarah. Anyway, Bob-Bob showed me the secret places, the high tarns, basins, the lost valleys. He'd spent his entire life logging the peninsula, plus he'd ranged all the creeks and streams looking for minerals. He even had a mining claim in what later became part of the national park. He knew these million acres as well as any man. He had close friends in the Sol Duc Tribe. They taught him something of this country. The settlers here thought that the native people were afraid of the interior, and had never explored it, but Bob-Bob knew that was untrue." Myra nodded. Tom reached for a stick, pushed coals. "Once you get up high, back in here, in addition to peaks, glaciers and snowfields, there are miles and miles of open alpine terrain, basins, lakes, and fields of heather, blueberry, paintbrush. It's beautiful." Tom shifted against his log. "In August we came in here, same exact route we're taking now. We spent a week lugging in huge packs of food and stores, building big caches up where Godkin Creek drains into the Elwha. We were preparing for a long September trip. Bob-Bob wanted to take me back to his old mining claim. He told me he wanted to show me something up there, something his grandfather, Henry David, had found years and years earlier. We made two trips up to Godkin that week, maybe 100 miles of walking. I was in pretty good shape; young, able to run like the wind if I wanted to. Bob-Bob, he was 74 years old, but he kept going."

"Snowfields? Snow in July? That's summer."

Myra waved toward the ridges. "You saw the snow across the river, up high, earlier? These mountains start at sea level. There's lots of moisture coming off the ocean."

"September is the best month, here, for weather," Tom went on. "The bugs are gone, the nights are cool, the days, hot. Back then, the late '60s, we had the place to ourselves. A week later we brought huge packs a third time up to Godkin Creek."

By now fully dark, the glow to the west was gone. The coals glimmered.

"Where was he taking you?" Myra asked. "Did you know?"

Tom shook his head. "All he said was, 'I have something to show you that Henry David showed me.' We reached our cache, big sacks hanging from trees beyond the reach of bears. We camped there and the next day started ferrying food up into Bear Creek, off Godkin Creek. Coming up from Whiskey Bend we were on a trail and the walking was clear and unobstructed.

Now we were off trail, working through the forest.

"It would have taken three or four days to get everything ferried up there. It's not that far, maybe six miles from the mouth of the Godkin to the camp on Bear Creek, but we were in no hurry and it was a little far to make a round trip in one day lugging a big pack. Bob-Bob had anticipated this; we brought along our tent, sleeping bags and cooking gear. There was a level area on a bench above the creek in that high valley, away from a cliff. We set up our tent and he pulled out his ax and went to chop wood. I explored east toward the head of the valley. There was a huge slide slope beyond the cliff and I climbed high on that, several hundred feet, over boulders. I found a place to sit, facing west, down the valley.

"The sun was strong. Dragonflies buzzed. This was a remote valley, far from trails. I could see, on the slide slope below me, two huge boulders, they could have been two people standing, and embracing, with a space between them. High above, an eagle circled. I could hear Bob-Bob down by the campsite, hidden in the trees, chopping wood, and then it was silent. I was tired, my seat was comfortable. I was sleepy in the sun. I must have slept, but then I heard the eagle cry, twice. I started back, surprised that I didn't see smoke, because Bob-Bob always started a fire when he made camp. When I reached our camp I knew something was wrong right away. It was silent. A distance away I saw a log with a deep new cut, smooth and almost perfect. He must have paused for some reason, swinging the ax into the log, because it rested there, standing, stuck in the wood, one blade of the double-bit pointing at the sky. Bob-Bob was on the ground."

Coals settled with a whisper.

"Was he alive?"

"No, Sarah. Heart attack? Stroke? I couldn't just leave him there, but I couldn't carry his body out either. Not 30 miles.

I found a place further down the shelf where he could be buried. The biggest tree that had gone over, pulling up its roots, leaving a deep hole. I used that. I covered him with rocks so bears or cougars couldn't dig him up. I took his pack and stuffed it deep in one of the clefts below the cliff. Then I returned to the mouth of the Godkin and spent a few days ferrying the food we'd brought in back to Bob-Bob's truck at Whiskey Bend. I reported his death to the park rangers and the Port Angeles police when I finally did come out. At first they wanted to go in, retrieve him, maybe see if what I'd said was true, but it's a long damn way. That September, the weather turned early, brought cold rains, wind, flooding. Nobody wanted to travel back in there to exhume a body. "

"What was he going to show you?" Sarah was leaning forward. "What did Henry David Olsen find?"

"I'll never know, not for sure."

"What?" Myra sounded disappointed.

Tom reached for one more log. "Let's finish this tomorrow. It's late."

"How about, you carry my pack, William?" Sarah wasn't going to call William Walleye.

"I don't think so. I was hoping you'd carry mine."

Sarah almost smiled. She scrunched closer to the fire. "Was that hard, suddenly alone with Bob-Bob that way?"

"What do you think?"

So their first day ended, with Myra and Sarah in one small tent, Tom and William in the other. William could hear Myra and Sarah's voices, but then Tom started to snore. William always forgot Tom snored.

The next day they were on the trail by nine. William was out of shape. He knew it, and he knew Myra knew it. She was worried about him, much as she tried to hide her concern. Again, they walked for 20 minutes, then stopped for five. Sarah trudged along under her pack. She had found a walking stick. After passing the Lillian River crossing they climbed 400 feet and spent the morning following the trail high above the Elwha, through thin scrubby trees perched on scarce soil. Where the trail rejoined the Elwha, four miles further, they came upon a smoking fire ring, scattered wood, and live coals. William could see the impressions from two tents. The other party had spent the night here, 10 miles in from the parking lot. Three miles further, where the interior valley widened, they stopped for the night. William was happy to stop.

Sarah helped Myra pitch their tent. She then pulled her sketchpad from her pack and asked if she could go forward past the meadow, see what lay around the next bend.

"Not too far," Tom said. "We'll eat in two hours."

They watched Sarah walk across the meadow and disappear up the trail.

"Smart to let her go off?" William didn't want to have to go hiking after Sarah. His feet hurt.

"You're hovering, dad."

They started a fire. Tom assembled food for dinner. Tiny flies swarmed. William pitched their tent. Then he joined Tom and

➤

Myra at the fire. He sat down, trying not to grunt.

"How you doing?" Myra asked.

"I'll be fine. Who's hovering now?"

Myra faced the way Sarah had gone, then turned to Tom. "What are you guys at the port going to do with your pier?" Myra's work for the Sol Duc Tribe meant she sometimes came to port meetings. The tribal fishermen used the port pier to tie up their boats.

Tom shifted against his backrest. "Eye, didn't you train your daughter to get out of the truck? This is supposed to be my vacation."

"You know how well I control Myra, Tom," William said. Myra laughed.

"Funny you should ask me that, Myra. Tuesday I realized the commissioners were hell bent for that proposal by Buckhorn International to lease the pier for their mining operation. Fletcher Lynch even had that Buckhorn woman, Victoria Oldsea, come in to our executive session, talk to us. Totally improper, in fact, illegal, but Lynch is the longest serving commissioner and the rules don't apply to him. I got pissed. I think I'll be fired when we get back."

"That pier's critical to the tribal fleet. The Sol Duc marina's got room, but it's too expensive. That port pier's the only place we have."

"I know that. I said that. Usually there's a permit needed, because any in-water work requires tribal approval, but in this case the company wants the pier as is, without work. No need for any permit. Hence, no tribal approval necessary."

"Tom, if Buckhorn wants to do something on this peninsula, they better have their story straight. There's all the people desperate for jobs, they'll agree to anything. Then there's the environmental groups. They're religious about preventing any new mining or resource extraction work, jobs be damned.

Our poor little tribe's stuck in the middle."

Tom was nodding. "I agree. It gets worse every year, Myra. It's like two different religions. The jobs-at-any-price sect, and the go-back-to-the-past sect. They're both jihads, actually."

"It's ideology-driven zealotry, Tom. Zealotry is the eighth deadly sin, if you ask me." Myra turned over some coals with a stick. The fire flared.

Tom leaned forward, stretching. "These Buckhorn people are smart. They're leasing the upland behind the pier. They've offered to build this conference center Fletcher Lynch has been promoting for years, about the first people who came here after the ice age. We've also been trying to get someone to use that pier for years. Buckhorn said they'd take the pier, lease the upland, and pay for the center Lynch wants. Lynch, with Buckhorn's support, has arranged this big conference in Port Angeles late this coming September, the Human Dispersal Conference."

"I've heard about that conference." William was surprised. He shifted his position. He was stiff. "My Russian friend, Alec Dujin, over in Petropavlovsk, and his son, Sergei, are both speakers. Alec will talk about his migration ideas, his son about genetics." William glanced at Myra. Sergei was a tall, whip-smart geneticist, single, someone who could stand up to Myra. Few men could. He smothered a smile. When those two met, sparks would fly. "Alec plans to ride back to Seattle with me in August on the ship. We'll go in the woods for a bit, and then he can join his son."

"The conference is the big kick-off for Lynch's dream, the Human Dispersal Center, or Clovis Center, as we call it at the port," Tom said. "I'm sure he thinks this will get him re-elected this fall, for the fifth time. "

"Clovis Center?"

Tom was cleaning his glasses. "Devoted to the first people

who came to North America, 'Eye. Most archeologists think these were the Clovis people, so named because their distinct spear points were first found in Clovis, New Mexico. They've been found all over North America, all appearing suddenly about 12 thousand years ago. Lynch is a serious hobby archeologist. He found some Clovis spear points in Sequim a few years ago, not that far from where we are here. These were supposedly the first people to visit the New World. Across the Bering land bridge.

"That's in dispute," Myra was peeling a twig.

"I know, Myra. Almost all North American tribes have legends saying they've been here forever. This center and conference will be Lynch's crowning accomplishment for the election this November. He needs an accomplishment. All he's done for 20 years is get staff fired and try to turn our industrial land into real estate parks. The Fletcher Lynch Human Dispersal Center. That's his dream."

William recalled his grandmother's stories. Myra was staring into the fire. She'd heard the stories, too, that time he'd taken her to Haida Gwaii when she was 12.

"We've always been here," William said to Tom, remembering the legends. "Always. Our stories say so."

"Lynch's big moment." Myra was disgusted. "Why is Buckhorn spending money like this?"

"Buckhorn wants a mineral out here on the peninsula, erbium. They need it for their labs, so they can fabricate a similar substance from abundant materials in huge quantities. Buckhorn says they will commit to Sol Duc and Port Angeles for the fabrication facility. First, though, they need to take some of this mineral, ship it to their existing facilities in Los Angeles, and test it."

"What does this mineral do?"

"That's the thing, Myra. Very hush-hush, by the way.

We've been sworn to secrecy, but the word's already out. Apparently erbium, mixed with other rare elements, helps precipitate out all the toxins in coal. All of 'em. You can imagine how valuable that would be, if true. Buckhorn would make billions. Trillions."

"They're trying to buy the community," said Myra.

Tom nodded. "They're succeeding, too."

Sarah reappeared across the meadow, walking stiffly in the lengthening shadows. She sat down by the fire, holding her sketchpad tightly, a strange expression on her face. She was pale.

"Sarah?" Myra asked. "What is it?"

Sarah shivered. She finally spoke. "The next meadow beyond, I sat on a stump. I was going to draw the river. I never heard a sound."

Her sketchpad was six inches by nine inches; the pages bent from being carried in her pack. She opened the pad and passed it to William.

Sarah had drawn a bear. Huge, facing forward, standing, enormous wide head cocked, peering, curious, long forearms hanging, the bear, staring out from the page, almost seemed human. Although extraordinarily realistic, the coat was too mottled, the fur too long, and the face too wide. William showed the drawing to Tom and Myra.

"This looks like a grizzly, sort of, but there are no grizzlies on this peninsula, so this must be a black bear," said Tom. "You drew this? You actually saw this?"

"Swimming the river. I saw it. Then it climbed out, stood there. Looking at me. I drew it. Then it dropped to all fours, went straight up the slope past the little meadow. It stopped three times, looking back at me."

"This drawing," Myra said. "I can smell him. Hear him."

"Not a sound. It was almost as if it wanted me to follow.

Right up there." Sarah pointed to the slope that rose beyond the meadow where they sat. If there had been a bear up there, they should have seen something.

"They always look big when you see one face to face," Tom was holding the drawing close, glasses off. "Sometimes black bears are light brown or even albino. It just stood there?"

"The next meadow."

"Myra? 'Eye? You see anything?"

"I didn't see a bear, Tom," William said. "Sarah saw the bear."

"Weren't you terrified?" Tom asked. He kept peering at the drawing. "What you drew, that's the biggest black bear I've ever seen. You got some of the details wrong but I can see how you would, facing something like that."

"What, you don't believe me? Think I made it up? He was close to me. Close. I was able to finish before he moved. I can show you where he was. Come on, I'll show you."

"Why? You said he went up the ridge. There'd be nothing to see."

"You mean, there was nothing to see." In her anger at Tom, Sarah had regained her color.

William looked at the steep slope, now in shadow. Then he looked at the river. The river here was narrow and fast.

"Let's have dinner," Tom said.

After they ate dinner, washed up, and gathered wood, they settled down by the fire. Myra had taken Sarah's sketchpad and she examined the drawing for a long time before returning the pad to Sarah. Something was troubling Myra. William could see it in the set of her face. Sarah hugged her knees.

"OK, Tom," said Myra. "We've had dinner. Now finish your story from last night."

William was sitting on the ground against a section of stump. The fire crackled. Beyond them the meadow flickered in the firelight.

Tom moved over and settled by Sarah. "Sarah, I've been coming in this country a long, long time; seen dozens of bears, dozens. Your second day, you get closer to one of those animals than I ever have. I'm jealous."

"You don't believe me. None of you do."

"None of us like to be shown up." Sarah sat, arms over her knees, stiff. "Okay, Sarah, have it your way." Tom made himself a new cup of tea. "Logging made a living but it was tough work. Bob-Bob, like some others, filed a mining claim way up the Elwha in the early 1930s, but was unable to work the claim when the 1937 depression hit and he got behind on his house payments. He would have lost the house except he was able to sign over the mining claim to the bank to cover missing payments. His banker was the then very young Fletcher Lynch Senior. When Senior died in 1980 his son, Fletcher Junior, inherited his estate, which included that mining claim."

"That claim must be in the middle of the park, if it's in the Elwha watershed," Myra said. "When the park was created in 1938, all mining claims were wiped out. Weren't they?"

Tom shook his head. "Mining claims in force at the time

➤

a national park is created are grandfathered, or were in 1938 when Olympic National Park was established. This is something few people know, even today. Bob-Bob's claim, which Lynch Senior refused to sell back to him when he had some money, is still a valid claim." Tom paused. "Even today."

"Let me guess." Myra shook her head. "That's the claim Buckhorn now has for this erbium, right? Lynch sold the claim to Buckhorn. Now Lynch gets his Clovis Center. Hell."

"I don't care about mining. Here." Sarah opened her sketchpad. She handed it to Myra. Myra began to laugh. She passed the pad to Tom. Tom raised the pad so William could see it.

Sarah had drawn William's face. He remembered when she'd been drawing the previous night. She'd caught his huge domed forehead, wayward eye, the wild black hair, and the chin that could drive spikes, as his ex-wife used to say. Sarah had drawn him in the middle of saying something.

Myra was beaming. "You really caught his mug. First bears, and now portraits? How long have you been drawing?"

"They put me in an art class in school, but the teacher wouldn't let me draw the way I wanted to. So I stopped. In school, anyway. What's the second reason you're dragging us up here?"

"She's persistent," Tom said.

"Relentless, Tom. Your granddaughter is relentless." William began to laugh. His laugh boomed.

Tom rose, went over to his tent, and reached inside. He pulled out the tube he had brought and carefully unthreaded the plastic top. From the tube, he pulled something wrapped in soft cloth, gently tied. He laid it across his knees and unknotted the ties, then carefully unrolled the cloth. He stopped just before the final turn.

"That day Bob-Bob died I saw Bob-Bob's hat down in

the hole by the fallen tree he'd been cutting, next to some big stones that had been pulled free by the roots. I thought, why would Bob-Bob leave his hat there? I lifted the hat and discovered something lying beneath it, beneath the leaves. This."

He pulled away the cloth. The object was almost three feet in length, like a long shoehorn, two inches wide, an inch thick. One end was slightly wider, ending in a carved figure three inches across. The last inch of the other end, on the side opposite the carved figure, and bent 90 degrees, held a small post half an inch long pointing inward. It was a carved socket, made to hold something. The piece was pale yet discolored. William could see it was bone.

Sarah reached and Tom handed her the piece. Sarah cradled it in her hands, turning it over. Then she passed it to William. It felt cold, smooth. Mostly, it felt old. The carved figure was an animal, defined with incised lines, lines as perfect and smooth as those Sarah had drawn when sketching the bear. The piece felt perfectly balanced. There were carvings along both sides of the shaft, dots in a pattern, lines.

"Was this what he wanted to show you? Is this what great-great-great-great grandpa Henry David Olsen found?"

"We'll never know, Sarah, will we? Did Henry David find this and give it to Bob-Bob? Did Bob-Bob find it under the stones beneath that tree, or find it somewhere else and place it with his hat in the hole while he cut wood? Was this what Bob-Bob was going to show me?"

William noticed a deep nick near the carved end. The nick appeared recent.

Myra took the object and peered at the carving. "It's a raven. See the bill and the crown of the head? And aren't those wings?"

"I didn't bury this with Bob-Bob," Tom said. "I brought it

back out with me. I stored it in my garage where it was mostly forgotten. Then Lynch started with his Clovis Center scheme, talking about the artifacts he had found and how old they were. At one commission meeting he had a professor in from the university to talk about dating artifacts, and it occurred to me to try to date this." Tom glanced at Myra, who had been silently listening, stone-faced, staring at the nick. "I took a nick from the piece after the professor gave his presentation. I kept meaning to have it dated."

"Jesus, Tom." Myra was angry. "This is an artifact. This could be 100 years old or 100 times that. Removing it and taking it home, that's illegal. Cutting a piece out, that's unforgivable. You've had a good relationship with the tribes. How could you do this? Hell, we just learned yesterday you've got native blood yourself."

Sarah was startled by Myra's anger. William was not. He knew what Myra was feeling. It was an invasion and a betrayal when people removed artifacts from ancestral sacred lands.

"Myra, you're right," Tom said. "I was only 21 when I brought this piece out. I knew nothing from nothing. I didn't know as I do today how sensitive this subject is. How could I? I was fishing, then fixing engines in a maintenance shop. It was only later, after hearing those speakers Lynch brought before the commission, that I saw the problem."

"How old is this?" Sarah asked. "How can you tell?"

Myra turned to Sarah. "You can measure the radioactive decay of carbon in formerly living things. It takes 50 thousand years for the radioactivity to completely decay. Depending on how much is gone, you can determine the age within a few hundred years. You need to be sure your samples are not contaminated by other materials." Myra glared at Tom, then continued. "Unfortunately, to do carbon dating, you need to destroy a lot of material, hence the need for a terrible gouge in this piece."

Sarah wrinkled her brow, sly. "Contaminated? You mean, like adding water to a piss test for drugs?" When Sarah saw their expressions she grinned. It was the first time William had ever seen her really smile. "What is this thing, anyway?"

Tom took back the piece. "This, Sarah, is an atlatl. A spear thrower."

Tom held the carved end in his right hand. His hand fit perfectly around the carving. He held it so the piece extended forward parallel to the ground, with the socket-like end furthest from him. Then he swung his hand and arm overhead to stretch behind, also parallel to the ground. The piece was at shoulder level, the socket end behind his hand. He spoke as he demonstrated.

"These things use darts, a type of arrow. Their shaft might be three, five, even seven feet long, straight, with a stone point at the tip and feathers mounted on the back. You place the dart on the atlatl, feathered end held against the socket behind me, deadly point stretching ahead, balanced. Then you throw, holding the thrower, releasing the dart." Tom swung the piece, as if throwing, but he held on to the atlatl. "The extra length adds velocity and power to the throw. Something about the physics of the throw causes the dart shaft to bend while in flight, increasing the force. These things can be thrown twice as far as an Olympic javelin. They may look flimsy, but the darts can go through hide, skin, and bone. See how it works?" Tom pretended to throw again. The atlatl extended the length of his arm three feet. William saw how the increased leverage would accelerate the throw. "These have been used for thousands of years, all over the world, since way before bows and arrows. These darts have more penetration power than an arrow shot by a bow. Atlatls were used against the Spanish when they fought the Aztecs in the 1500s. The Aztecs' shafts went right through the Spanish armor. This is a perfect hunting weapon, capable of killing any game."

Sarah took the spear thrower and stood, extending her arm, practicing.

"How old is this?" Myra asked Tom. "Do you still have that sliver you cut free?"

"In my desk at home. How old would you guess?"

"I'm not an archeologist, Tom. I took a few courses in school, that's all. Bone can fossilize fast in the proper conditions, in a few hundred years. But this could be really old. Thousands of years old."

Sarah was practicing. Then she handed the atlatl back to Tom. "People have been living out here that long? Here? Yuk."

"Longer, Sarah," Myra said. "Here in this park they found an old basket melted out under snow up on Lillian Ridge, just above Port Angeles. It was estimated to be 2,500 years old. When they widened the parking lot up at Hurricane Ridge, at over 5,000 feet elevation, they found fire rings, 4,000 years old. People have lived here at least 12 thousand years, ever since the ice age ended and all the big animals died out, mammoths, mastodons, saber tooth cats."

Tom took the device back from Sarah. "Myra, I knew it was wrong to take that nick, just as I eventually came to understand it was wrong to take it from Bear Valley over 45 years ago. Whatever else, this spear thrower was one of the last things Bob-Bob touched before he died, and possibly a direct link to his grandfather, Henry David Olsen, if Henry David was the one who found it." He tied the cloth loosely, slid the spear thrower into the case, and closed the cap. "So, to answer your question, Sarah, we're going in there to return this piece to that valley and to Bob-Bob. So it can rest with him forever."

Myra said to Sarah, "Of course, now this company Buckhorn

is going to desecrate that place anyway with its mining." Myra suddenly paused, then grabbed Tom's arm. "Of course. The pickup that drove to the trailhead yesterday? You see the doors, Tom?"

"No, I was cinching my pack." Tom was confused.

"Those four guys? That truck? The logo on that truck was a rock with the initials BI over it. Those guys are surveyors for Buckhorn International. If Buckhorn's surveying your old claim, they're headed to the same place we are."

"Bob-Bob's," Tom said. "That was Bob-Bob's claim, more than 75 years ago."

Later, after Sarah and Tom had turned in, Myra and William remained by the fire. The river rushed by. The sky above the meadow was deep cobalt.

"You were pretty ragged today, dad."

"I'm a little out of shape. It'll pass."

"Just be careful, OK? You aren't 30 anymore."

They watched the fire.

"What was bothering you, Myra, this afternoon, after Sarah drew that bear?"

Myra poked the fire with a stick. Coals lay black on one side, red on the other. Myra took a breath. "Dad, you and Tom think Sarah saw a black bear but drew some of the details wrong." Myra turned to William, touched his arm. "She doesn't know it but she's an extraordinary artist. She drew exactly what she saw."

"What did she draw, then?"

"The largest bear that ever lived, dad. Ever." Myra's hand tightened. "I remember from graduate school. A short face bear. That's what she drew. And, dad?" Myra hesitated. "Short face bears have been extinct since the end of the last ice age. Almost 12 thousand years."

William turned his head and studied Myra. He saw that

his scientifically trained, degreed daughter was dead serious. "Then she must have seen a drawing in a book somewhere, Myra."

Minutes passed.

"And, dad? Sarah wasn't frightened. Look, she's sleeping in her tent. If that had been me, Sarah's age, I'd have been by this fire all night." Myra paused. "It's almost as if that bear befriended her." Myra huddled closer to her father.

William put his arm over her shoulders. He pictured Sarah's drawing. "What did you say to Sarah back at Tom's house, Myra? After she said this peninsula was the end of the earth?" Myra was silent. He hugged her shoulder. "You told her, this is a land of magic...."

Myra sat straight, remembering. "A land of magic, history, and legend." She gazed over toward the tents. William felt her shift against him. Sarah had drawn what she had seen, yet what she had seen no longer walked this earth. His feet ached, throbbing with the beat of his heart. The night sky blazed with stars. He wondered if the star positions were different in the time of great ice and great bears.

"Myra, we think we brought Sarah on this trip, but maybe it is she, who is taking us."

He faintly heard Tom's snores, rising and falling. They sat for a long time.

The next day they hiked 10 miles up the Elwha to Camp
Wilder near Godkin Creek. William knew they were
deep into the park. He had never been in this far. He saw
that Camp Wilder lay on a shelf near the Elwha, a few
hundred feet from the main trail. There was a small shelter
sagging with age. Myra took Sarah off to wash in the river.
They disappeared downstream. Tom and William heard
shrieks and laughter. When they came back, Tom and
William took their turn. They took longer to wash, and swore
instead of shrieked. The water was damn cold.

Clouds came in from the south, gathering and twisting over
the high ridges. William tied a light plastic tarp over where
they would sit eating their food. If it rained, they would stay dry.
Their packs and gear were in the old shelter. The tents were
pitched nearby.

They ate silently. William noticed nobody dared mention
Sarah's bear sighting from the day before. Tom didn't believe
Sarah had seen such a bear, Sarah was furious he didn't
believe her, and William and Myra didn't know what to think.
Rain fell that night for an hour. In the morning a pale sun rose.
William got the fire going and Tom heated water for oatmeal.

Tom said they had all day to find their way into Godkin
Valley. William was glad to hear it wasn't far. Mist rose
across the river. They decided to dry their tents in the sun
before departing.

"So were those ice ages here?" Sarah asked Tom. "Did those big animals live here, then?"

Tom was holding his tea with both hands. He inclined his head to Myra.

"Yes, they did live here," Myra said. "During the last ice age."

"Last ice age? There's been more than one ice age?"

"Sarah, we live in a warm time, which began about 10 thousand years ago, since the last ice age. The earth has had many ice ages in its history. We're still in the latest ice age period, which began about two million years ago. There's been an ice advance and retreat about every 100 thousand years during those two million years."

"Every 100 thousand years? So there have been, let's see, 20 ice ages?"

"Yes. But during each ice age, even though colder than today, there were many ice advances and retreats, warmings and coolings. There was so much water locked up in the ice that ocean levels dropped by as much as 400 feet. Then, for about 10 thousand years, sometimes longer, the earth warmed, much of the ice would melt, and the oceans would rise. We live in such a warm time now."

"If it's been 10 thousand years already, is it going to get cold again? In school they talked about how the earth is heating up."

"That's what a lot of people think. But, during the cold times the land was very different. A huge ice sheet two miles thick covered much of North America and all of Canada. The ice filled all of Puget Sound and most of the Strait of Juan de Fuca. The ice sheet never got into this park, because it was blocked by the Olympic mountains. Scientists think the strip of land west of the park out to the Pacific Ocean was never covered with ice, and was a refuge for plants and animals."

"And these animals?"

"They were big. Mammoths were the size of elephants. Mastodons, bigger than a huge steer. The American lion was bigger than African lions. Dire wolves stood almost as tall as you at the shoulder. Saber-toothed cats had teeth up to 11 inches long. Bears weighed over two thousand pounds. All these animals disappeared 11 or 12 thousand years ago. No one is sure why. Maybe human hunters, maybe because it got warm and the vegetation patterns changed."

"They didn't disappear after the weather changed during an earlier ice age, did they? Or didn't it get as hot between ice ages before?"

"The warm time before this one, called the Eemian, ran from about 130 to 120 thousand years ago, and was hotter than today. The sea level was almost 20 feet higher than today. And yes, you are correct, the big animals survived the earlier warm times." As Sarah started another question Myra raised a hand. "You have now totally exhausted everything I know about ice ages. No more questions."

"William?"

"Sarah, my daughter here received all the formal schooling in my family. I only know some old legends. The only archeologists I know are Myra, here..."

"I am by no means an archeologist," Myra interjected.

"...and this Russian, a Koryak, I got to know in Kamchatka who has a serious hobby collecting mammoth tusks."

"What's a Koryak?" Sarah asked.

"A people who live in Kamchatka. A native people, like Myra and I are native people. I met him the first time our ship landed there, and we became friends. His son Sergei's a genetic scientist. They've both been invited to this conference in Port Angeles."

"Time to get going," Tom said.

The tents were dry.

"Who put these things on my pack?"

"I did, Sarah." Tom stood with his hands on his hips. "You can carry more weight and these are only the tent flies. The tents still go with me and 'Eye."

"You're a slave driver."

At Godkin Creek they turned and left the trail. They worked uphill, keeping the noise of the creek to their right, until Tom found the game trail, which rose, cresting a steep slope, then leveled off. Occasionally they saw patches of snow on the north side of gullies. They hiked through hemlock, fir and spruce, passing rhododendron, twisting branches not yet filled with buds of shiny green. They found evidence of the party ahead of them: boot prints, a cigarette butt, the torn corner from a plastic wrapper.

Two hours later they crossed a slide area about 150 yards wide. High to the left they could see rock and scree. Heavy snow, pocked with twigs and needles, filled the slope, which dropped to the creek far below on their right. Ahead, the creek burst over a ledge to drop in falls to the foot of the slope. They had to pick across carefully.

Tom led, kicking steps.

Sarah stopped, halfway across. "This look like you remember?"

"Been a long time, Sarah. I remember this gulley, except when Bob-Bob and I were here the snow was long gone."

William sat on an uprooted log emerging from the snow. North, the way they'd come, the Elwha Valley stretched miles and miles. His legs and hips hurt.

A few minutes later they left the slope, entered forest, and met Godkin Creek. The water was clear, icy, and high from melted snow. A gravel bar lay in the sun. The sun felt hot.

"We'll have lunch here." Tom dropped his pack.

Sarah found a depression in the gravel and sat, leaning

against her pack, face in the sun. Myra wandered ahead and peered into a pool. Tom pulled out the stove. He filtered some water from the stream. He started a pot to boil. William sat by his pack.

After lunch they followed the creek. The walking was easier along gravel bars beside the creek than through the trees. Around a sharp bend they discovered two tents pitched on a wide flat area, wood stacked by a circle of stones, water bag hanging from a nearby tree. Four empty camp chairs surrounded the fire pit. Smoke rose.

"They must be off surveying," said Tom.

William could see four sets of boot prints headed upstream.

Sarah wandered close to the smoldering fire.

They left the creek. Tom led the way, moving through the trees to the base of the saddle leading up to Bear Valley. The slope was thick with alder and brush. They kept the sound of Bear Creek to their right as they climbed, thrashing through alder.

As soon as they reached the top of the rise they crossed another big avalanche chute filled with deep snow, branches, and entire trees. This was a wider slide than the one they'd crossed below. William could see, a mile ahead, an even wider slide, toward the head of the small valley. They crossed the piled snow and headed up the valley. They walked for 20 minutes. They were on a bench that followed Bear Creek.

"About here," Tom said. They dropped their packs.

They were in a grove of firs, tall and straight, mixed with birches not yet budded. William could see the creek below the bench, 200 feet away, turning toward the ridge opposite, south. North, behind them, a vertical cliff rose like a pillar, framed with trees growing on both sides. The face of the cliff was streaked with water and tiny plants. At the base of the cliff boulders lay scattered, tilted, piled one on another. Beneath the cliff's overhang the ground was more open, filled with brush, warm in the sun. Many fallen trees lay across the bench, each with a root ball at its base.

"This is it, right?" Sarah sounded hopeful.

William watched an eagle circling, high above.

"This is where Bob-Bob and I camped." Tom pointed to a circle of stones, half buried in cedar fronds. He walked over to a fallen tree and root ball. Young trees grew from the depression left by the roots when they'd pulled free years before. The shallow hole was filled with leaves, ferns and moss. An old ax-cut was notched in a thick, moss-covered log stretching into the forest. The notch was smooth and clean. "This is where he died. Right here."

"Where is Bob-Bob buried?" asked Sarah.

"West, back the way we came in. Not too far." Tom led the way. They followed him. Several fallen trees lay clustered together. "Here." Tom was standing by a large tree, one of six that had come down, opening the forest to light and sun. Maple and birch grew in the open area. The root ball of the fallen tree had left a hole. A mound of stones rose from the center. Tom dropped into the hole and brushed leaves and brush from the stones. "I made a cross with big forked sticks, mounted it on the grave."

"He's shaded by the maples in summer," said Myra. "Falling leaves insulate him in the winter."

Some of the stones from the mound were scattered.

"We'll just place more stones here tomorrow, neaten it up, make it nice," Tom said.

Sarah walked to another fallen tree some distance away. She reappeared with a big stone in her arms and walked back, both arms around the stone, staggering. She dropped the stone with a thump by the edge of the hole. Then she headed away.

"She thinks the sooner we get more stones placed, the sooner we can leave."

"She's helping, Tom," Myra said.

Myra and William, then Tom, joined Sarah. They gathered more stones: white, mottled, black with veins of white quartz, many covered with moss. In a short time, they had enough to cover the grave the next day.

Before dinner, William washed in the creek around a bend from the camp. The water here was even colder than the Elwha. William was glad to get back in front of the fire.

The first insects of the season were swirling, catching the sunlight. Myra was braiding her hair. Sketchpad on her lap, Sarah drew a spider web slung between the branches of a low bush. Tom had water on the little stove for tea.

When Sarah finished the spider web she rose and walked over to Tom. "Can I see the thrower?"

"Sure." Tom untied the tube from his pack and removed and unwrapped the atlatl, handing it to Sarah. She touched the marks on the shaft.

"Where will you put this? In Bob-Bob's grave?"

"I haven't decided. Tomorrow we'll pick a place, how about that? Not in his grave, though. Leave him in peace."

"You think he knew he was going to die? He was pretty old. Was he sick?"

"When you're 13, Sarah, 74 is old. When you're almost 70, like me, suddenly it's not so old. He wasn't sick that I know of. He'd had a lot of injuries over the years; logging does that to you. I'm not sure, maybe he did know he might die. I never thought of it. He was peaceful when I found him."

Sarah inspected the spear thrower.

"You're really going to leave this spear thrower here?" Myra asked.

"You're the one who yelled at me the other day," Tom said.

"'This is an artifact,' you said. 'How could I do it?' Remember?"

Sarah held the atlatl close to her eyes, turning the shaft.

"Buckhorn wants to extract erbium, Tom," said Myra. "This land may be a national park, and 30 miles from the nearest road, but no way can a few small tribes stop a corporation from mining a mineral that their experts claim can clean up coal. They'll argue they can do this safely. The mining won't last long. Not much volume, just a few thousand tons. They'll tell everyone they can build then decommission a road, return everything to the way things were. I can hear the arguments now. We'll get screwed again, like always. But this artifact, Tom, this could stop them."

"I've heard their logic," Tom, leaning forward, was shaking his head. "We had a briefing in executive session last month. No roads. Minimal impacts. They plan to use helicopters; two seasons only."

"That's ridiculous."

"No, it isn't, Myra. Ever seen a freight helicopter, two big rotors, looks like a banana? They use them to do selective logging in California, haul whole trees."

"So, great, people come in here hiking, have to listen to those damn things clattering overhead?"

Tom pointed south to a ridge barely visible through the trees. "They'll run the ridges. No roads, no damage, and they'll work far from trails. Heck, helicopters already come up here for search and rescue, firefighting, to haul out containers of poop from backcountry privies. You ever see one? I didn't think so." Tom leaned back.

"You think these marks mean anything?" Sarah was tracing the dots and lines inscribed on both sides of the atlatl shaft with a finger.

"Tom," Myra said. "This is an artifact. Very old. I think it's fossilized."

"I don't even know if Henry David or Bob-Bob found this here."

"Come on, Tom. Obviously it was found here. Point is, it's already been removed from wherever it was resting. The damage is done. If you leave it here, never seen publicly, Buckhorn will get their permit. But if we take the thrower back with us, inform the park service you found it here, then this place becomes an archeological site. All sorts of different regulations apply, regulations that could stop Buckhorn in its tracks."

"These dots look like landmarks." Sarah was sketching the atlatl. "An outline."

Myra, I'm going to leave this spear thrower here. It's a promise I made to myself and Bob-Bob."

Myra straightened. "You think this mining can happen without causing harm, don't you?"

"Maybe. Hell, I don't know, Myra. I just know this thing needs to be left here, and that's what I plan to do."

Sarah pointed at one side of the atlatl. "I think that's the sun, between some mountains." Suddenly, she took the atlatl and her sketchbook and thrust both beneath her sweatshirt.

"Nice place for a camp, but why not be under the overhang back there?" The voice was low, steady, calm. Without looking, William could tell this was the same man who'd told the younger surveyor to get going back at the trailhead. Now he emerged with another man from behind some trees. They carried tiny flags and complex sighting scopes. Both wore sunglasses. Myra was rigid next to William, alert.

Tom rose, relaxed, friendly. "Little late in the day to be up here working, isn't it?"

The two men stopped a few feet from them, looking around.

"Thought we'd stop by. See how you were doing. There's just us few up here, nobody else in miles and miles. Early in the season to be up here." The man speaking was about 50, fit, tall, in command. His companion was nearly as tall, with a weak chin and the hint of a tattoo above his collar.

"I've been here before," Tom said, still friendly. "We're just showing my granddaughter here some of the back country."

"Anything happens, long ways for help."

Even with sunglasses hiding his eyes, William was sure the guy with the tattoo was staring at Myra. Now the man in charge addressed Sarah. "You having fun, little girl? You don't look too happy to me. I'm Roger. This here is Raymond."

"What do you know?" Sarah would not look up at Roger.

"Well." Roger smiled, cold. "We won't trouble you folks further. We need to get back before we lose the sun. Just wanted to say hello. I expect we'll see you around tomorrow. We'll be running sightlines to the south for a bit, then we'll be headed back. You stay careful. This is a long ways in, people your age."

They walked away, their boots rustling leaves and snapping twigs. Raymond lit a cigarette. Then they were gone.

Sarah removed the atlatl from under her sweatshirt and handed it to Tom. Once wrapped and back in the tube, he placed the thrower in his tent.

"Tom, this is now your grandfather's home," Myra said. "If we brought back that artifact, we could insure that nothing happens up here, ever."

"I'll think about it."

"I sure hope I didn't get your stubborn gene," said Sarah. "Yours either, Myra."

After dinner, Tom and William washed the bowls in the stream.

"What's the plan, tomorrow, Tom?"

"We'll pile the stones on Bob–Bob's grave, find his pack, burn it. I'll have Sarah help me pick a place to leave the atlatl. We'll head back after lunch tomorrow."

"You think bringing her was a mistake, don't you?"

"This was your idea, 'Eye, and a bad one. But we couldn't leave her in town, and I wanted to make this trip, so here she is. She hates this. She hates me, too."

"Tom, it was not a mistake to bring her. Bob-Bob had his grave tended by his great-great granddaughter. How can that be a mistake?"

"Don't go all shaman on me, 'Eye."

When they returned to the fire, Sarah had built herself a seat from stones and logs. She was sketching Myra, who sat leaning against a log.

"What did your mother tell you about growing up out here?" asked Tom.

Sarah stopped drawing. "Not much. She ran away from

Ruth and Fletcher when she was 15. She went to San Francisco, tried to be an artist, got married, was there a few years, no kids, got divorced, then moved to Miami, met my dad. My real dad, I mean. That's what she told me."

"I thought your dad was in Europe."

"My stepdad is in Europe. My real dad got killed in a car accident when I was eight months old. My mom met Mitch later. Mitch and his creepy kid Little Mitch. Little Mitch is 17 now. I put a lock on my door, a big one, when I was eight, soon as my mom died."

"When did Becky get sick?"

"I was six. First grade." Sarah bit her lip as she worked on the sketch, shading Myra's cheeks.

"I should have done more for Becky," Tom said. "I could have done more."

"She said you'd take her for ice cream; let her have whatever she wanted, as much as she wanted. She was real sick, at the end. Thin. Mitch put her in some kind of place, wouldn't keep her home. I snuck over there to see her and she told me, then. Told me she'd run away, told me about Ruth and Fletcher, said she hadn't talked to them since she left, said they didn't even know about me. When big Mitch got this job in Europe he was going to send me to his nasty sister, that's when I told him about Ruth and you. Maybe I should have gone to my step-aunt's."

"Why'd Becky run off?" asked Tom.

"She told me Fletcher acted wrong and Ruth wouldn't back her. She said I'd understand some day. I understand now. That's when I learned Fletcher wasn't my real grandfather. That's when she told me about you. About the ice cream. She liked you." Tom fiddled with a pocketknife. "She told me your name, Ruth's name, where she was raised. Said you were thin and kind of nerdy. She was right. She didn't tell me you were a hard-ass. I had to find that out for myself."

"We could have taken you back to Ruth's, Sarah," Tom said.

"What, so Fletcher can chase me like he did my mom?" William realized Sarah was an orphan—both parents dead, her stepfather moving to Europe, travelling to a grandmother she had never met, unwanted at her grandmother's, and now in the wilderness. Sarah turned the pad and held it toward William. The sketch was Myra. "After tomorrow we go back?"

Tom rubbed his eyes. "We go back. We'll get Bob-Bob's grave well covered. Find his pack, burn it. Place the spear thrower in a safe spot. Then we'll hike back out. This hasn't been so bad, has it, Sarah?"

Sarah said nothing.

Myra moved over to sit by Sarah. "I wasn't much younger than you when I met my great-grandmother. My dad here took me. Going up to see her wasn't that different for me than you coming all the way out here to see your grandparents, I bet. We drove to Prince Rupert, up in British Columbia. Then we took the ferry out to Haida Gwaii. The whole trip from Sol Duc took three days. Once on Haida Gwaii, dad called his grandmother and then we drove 40 miles north to Massett, where we stayed."

William remembered that trip. He'd never been back since he'd left as a boy. When he saw the scattered and rickety buildings as they approached the ferry dock he'd started to cry. It had been years and years, yet the smell of the old pilings, the dead fish and salt brine, was exactly the same as the day he left for Kamloops with one other desperate, confused small boy.

"When we arrived in Massett, dad's grandmother stood in the rain, waiting for him, a scarf over her head, chin high, holding a carved wooden staff. When dad got out of the truck, she said 'This was your great-grandfather's staff. His father's father before him carved it. I have held this for you ever since you were taken as a boy. Now that you have returned with your child I can give it to you.' She handed him the staff. Then she said to me, 'You are my great granddaughter.' She was bent over, eyes clouded. She was 103 years old. As a child, she knew elders who had been alive before 1850, before white men came, before smallpox killed thousands, when life there was as it had always been. She said to us both, 'Welcome. You are welcome.' She says to me, 'I am Mary.'

"That entire evening people appeared, cousins, friends of relatives, strangers, to see us, to see my dad, to pay respects. They brought gifts, as people do. I felt as if I was at the absolute end of the earth. My great grandmother's old dog started to bark softly in his sleep. Then Mary fixed me with her old eyes. She had no teeth and she was almost blind, but her voice was strong and clear.

"She said, 'I have waited for you. Your father almost waited too long. I hold stories. As a girl I was trained as girls have been trained forever. This story is short. This is the story from the time before there were people as we are people. The first story, this tells how we became people.'

"'In ancient times, the land grew cold, the sky dark. Living beings suffered. Nearly all died. Those animals remaining gathered in small places where water flowed, fish swam, where there was food to eat. The killer whale sang and hunted, close to shore, always able to sing, always able to kill. The great bear on land, thoughtful, could not sing, and hunted alone.

"'In those times the animals were close together, on land and in the sea, in those small places. If a bear was seeking salmon, a killer whale would charge the beach, tear the bear away. After so much dark time the bears were few. One day, a foolish young bear walking the shore saw a young female killer whale waiting for fish to come to the river. He began talking to her, as animals did in those days, being careful to stay back from the shore. She was hungry. He, being foolish, boasted how he could sweep fish from the river and gather them on the riverbank. The killer whale walked from the ocean and joined the bear on the land. Fish came to the river. The bear swept them onto shore. When the bear had caught many fish, the killer whale, being a killer, fought with the bear for the fish. The whale admired the bear for ignoring her sharp teeth. The bear admired the whale for withstanding his great blows. They fell in love. They formed a family, and in that small place under the dark sky they had children. In time other bears and killer whales met on the riverbank, fought, fell in love, and had children. The children were different, not whale, not bear, but both.

"'While the killer whale could sing and kill, and the bear could think but could not sing, their children could hold their thoughts and memories with song, tell stories, and so learn how to become people. They sang their lessons, they sang their memories. They sang their stories. Long ago, this is what made us people.' Then my great grandmother began to sing. When she finished she raised her hands, palms up." Myra paused and glanced at her father. "That visit, I received a great gift. Hearing her stories, that story especially, feeling her love, though we had never met before, being with my cousins, my people, my dad, taught me something."

"Taught you what?"

"That I was someone able to hear truth, and to understand. In my great grandmother's house I was made to feel like a full person among wise people. That was my gift. Now, that bear you saw the other day, Sarah, perhaps that was your gift."

Tom said something under his breath. Sarah turned on him.

"You don't believe I saw anything."

"You think you saw something. I know that."

"It was there. Close. I drew it, exactly."

"But that's the point, Sarah. It looked like a bear but no bear looks like that. Not a black bear, not a grizzly. No, Sarah."

Myra faced Tom. "Sarah drew a short face bear, Tom. I'm sure."

"What the hell is a short face bear?"

"Bigger than a brown bear. Bigger than a polar bear. A

short face bear could run 40 miles an hour; a total meat eater. Sarah's drawing, the huge head, the long arms, exactly the same. For two million years, that bear was the biggest predator on land."

"I saw it," Sarah said.

"I've never heard of this bear." Tom was irritated. "There's only black bears in this park."

Myra spoke carefully. "The last short face bear died 12 thousand years ago, Tom. When the ice age ended. They're extinct. Yet, that's what Sarah drew. I know that's impossible, but that's what she drew."

"I saw it. Right there. Real." Sarah opened her sketchpad. The bear loomed, peering, terrible. Tom glanced toward William for help. William said nothing, just grinned, wide. Sarah moved away from Tom. "You don't believe me. You'll never believe me. I saw that bear. Well, know what? You're not my grandfather. I should have stayed at Ruth's. She's a jerk, but you're an idiot."

"Killer whales walking? Short face bears from the ice age? You're telling ghost stories, Myra. You should know better. Sarah, Ruth is welcome to you." Tom rose and stalked to his tent.

Sarah faced the fire, quivering. She struggled to bring herself under control. Finally her rigid posture relaxed. She took a breath and closed the sketchpad. "If what my supposed grandfather said is true, his grandfather's grandfather had a native wife. Native, like you guys. Right? So I had a great-great-whatever grandmother who maybe knew those stories, too?"

"And if your, let me see, great-great-great-great-grandfather's wife was a member of the Sol Duc Tribe, you and I are cousins."

"I don't want to be your cousin, Myra. You carried me over your shoulder, and your dad's a slave driver like my supposed grandfather. At least you're not totally boring."

Sarah and Myra went to their tent. William heard Tom rustling around, settling down. William stayed out by the fire, removed his boots, tended his feet. The night was utterly silent. Even the creek below them was quiet. Coals glowed, hot. Stars filled the sky. A fat moon had risen. The fire hissed. The air was cold. His feet, naked before the heat, ached. Tom began snoring. William could hear Myra telling Sarah another of his grandmother's stories. He heard her low voice from their tent. Either he lost a lot of weight or he would have to give up wandering in the woods. This had been too difficult. It seemed so easy for Myra, Tom, even Sarah. It wasn't easy for him. At least the next day they would head back, mostly downhill. The walking would be easier, he told himself.

Before breakfast, they went looking for Bob-Bob's pack. Tom handed Sarah the headlamp to search among the rocks and crevices at the base of the cliff.

Sarah turned on her headlamp and crawled in to the first niche.

"Nothing here, " she said as she backed out. "Dust and animal poop. Old." She wouldn't speak to Tom directly.

After more empty cavities, Sarah crawled in one until just the soles of her boots faced them. She said something, then backed out of the hole, emerging with a canvas pack, rotten, filled with holes.

"That's Bob-Bob's," Tom said.

Myra gathered debris that had fallen from the pack. It still contained a sleeping bag, some clothing, a knife and a hat. Tom carried the pack to the fire. William added wood.

Tom pulled the tube holding the atlatl from his tent and placed it beneath his overcoat. Then he took some water from the water bag, filled the pot, and started the stove.

This time they heard the surveyors approaching. The pack was on the fire, smoldering, throwing heavy smoke. It was the two other men from the Buckhorn group, Pete and a stout man, slightly older than Pete.

"Morning," said Pete "Heard you were up here. Saw your smoke this morning. I'm Pete." Pete was speaking to Myra. "This is Bernie. We're running a transit line east, from the saddle. Other guys are running one on the south side. We'll be out of your hair by this afternoon."

By now the pack was burning and smoking.

"Burning your gear?" Bernie asked.

"Old pack, left up here long ago," Tom said.

"You up here for long?" Pete asked Myra.

"Until tomorrow."

"We're heading out tonight, we get done in time," said Pete. "We've had decent weather this short trip. Been lucky. You guys are pretty far back in, pretty early, right? Looks like you know what to do, though."

Pete kept hoping Myra would say something. William felt sorry for Pete.

"Well, back to work." Pete and Bernie headed east up the valley.

"He, at least, had manners," Tom said, watching them go.

"You didn't get creeped out in those dark ledges?" Myra had gone over to join Sarah.

"Dirty in there. Dark. Smelled."

The place Bob-Bob was buried lay 100 yards west of their camp. It wouldn't take long to pile the stones on his grave. On their way there they passed a tiny red marker Pete and Bernie had tacked to the trunk of a tree. Sarah reached up and pulled the tag off.

As they stood around the pile of stones, Tom tried joking with Sarah.

"Those crevices you explored, none of them were big enough to hide a big bear, were they?"

Sarah stiffened. "You mean, like the bear I thought I saw but didn't see? The one I'm lying about? That one? You move these stones by yourself." She turned and marched back toward camp. She walked fast, arms swinging, exactly as she had marched down the trail the first day. She disappeared in the trees.

"Leave her be," Myra said, when Tom started to follow. "She's having a tough time. She'll calm down."

They moved the stones, piling them on Bob-Bob's grave. Soon the mound resembled a grave again. Tom found a big branch and piled stones around the base, making an upright post on top of the stones.

High above, an eagle cried, twice.

Myra started back toward camp. "I better go see if she's all right."

Tom finished bracing the post and climbed out of the hole, watching Myra stride between the trees. "Mistake, bringing Sarah, 'Eye. We get back, what then? Her real parents are dead. There's just me and Ruth."

"Maybe you're going to get the chance to raise the daughter you didn't raise the first time around."

"Me, going to parent teacher conferences? Helping her with homework? Me?"

"She'd be damn lucky to have you, Tom."

"Then, in a year or two, boys will come after her. She's going to be a looker, like her mother was."

"You're lucky, Tom. Just after Myra and I got back from Haida Gwaii, my wife threw me out and I joined the merchant marine. I was still drinking, remember? I hardly saw Myra when she was in high school, not until I sobered up, ten years ago. I was just her drunken father, away all the time."

"I'd like to say a few words here for Bob-Bob, but I don't know what."

"How about, 'I brought you your great-great-granddaughter. I hope you will guide her strong spirit in the years ahead?'"

"Well said, 'Eye. You always tell me you're no shaman but sometimes I wonder."

"Well now that I know we might be distant cousins, maybe I'll tell you my secrets."

When they reached camp, it was empty. Then Myra appeared.

"Sarah's missing."

Sarah had left them 30 minutes earlier. Her pack was hanging from a branch. Her jacket still lay by the tent, her hat on top.

Myra waved toward the cliff. "I looked over by the cliff. I called for her. I didn't hear anything."

"If she'd decided to start back to the main trail she'd have gone right by us," William said. "Tom or I would have heard her. I think."

"She wouldn't be stupid enough to walk back to the trailhead alone without a coat or sleeping bag."

"She was pretty angry, Myra," Tom said. "Who knows what she'd do?"

They stopped talking and listened. They heard, very faint, a whistle from up at the head of the valley.

"Sarah?" Tom asked.

"That whistle came from the surveyors, must be over a mile away. Maybe more. Too far," Myra said.

"If she's hiding to punish me I'm going to throw her over my knee when we find her." Tom was staring toward the sound of the whistle.

Myra began tightening her bootlaces. "I'll search out to the saddle, and then hike down to Godkin. If somehow she went that way I can catch her. You two start checking every void, every niche by the cliff, see if she's fallen out of sight. We have no idea how deep some of those voids are. She can't have gone far.

We all have whistles, right? Any of us finds her, three sharp calls, all right? Two hours, meet back here."

It was not yet mid-morning. The sun was fully over the ridge. Traces of high clouds had come in from the southwest, a sure sign of rain. Myra was already gone by the time Tom and William had their boots laced tight.

Tom was grim. "Eye, you start checking the voids, the niches. I'll range up toward the head of the valley, see if she went that way."

William started with the tumbled and piled rocks between their camp and the foot of the cliff. Piled next to and on top of each other, they left big gaps. He called Sarah's name and searched for signs of scuffed rock, footprints, and clothing. He kept hoping Sarah's face would pop out somewhere, satisfied she'd played a good joke on them.

Two hours later they met at their campsite.

"You see the surveyors?" Tom asked Myra. "When I got to the head of the valley they weren't there. I saw some red tags, that's all."

She shook her head. "I saw no sign of Sarah, or the surveyors."

"You go as far as their camp?" Tom asked.

"They've packed but there's nobody there."

"'Eye, you hear them go past you leaving the valley?"

"I heard nothing. I was behind those rocks, in the voids beyond the cliff. I wouldn't have heard them."

"You're sure about the voids and ledges, dad? Sarah's not there?"

"As sure as I can be without rope and ladder. I'll check them all again."

"No, 'Eye." said Tom. "Myra and I will check them. You find the surveyors, see if they'll help in a search. Maybe they have a radio, too. If we can't find her, we'll need more help."

"Same signal," Myra said. "Three blasts if we see her. If the surveyors have left their camp, blow an SOS on your whistle, dad. Maybe they'll hear it. Meet back here in 90 minutes."

When William reached the surveyors' camp on the Godkin, it was abandoned: no tents, no packs, no hanging lines, and no camp chairs. He saw four sets of boot prints heading downstream toward the Elwha. He pulled out his whistle and blew SOS four or five times, as loud as he could. Then he waited. After 10 minutes, he blew again. He did this for half an hour, then gave up. He made a large arrow in the sand, pointing to their campsite up on Bear Creek. He wrote SOS in the gravel and started back to the cliff.

When he saw Tom and Myra he knew at once they had not found Sarah.

"Myra's heading out," Tom said. "She'll chase down those surveyors, if she can, see if they have a radio. We need rescue up here, as fast as we can." Tom gave a tired smile. "Guess we'll see how loud a helicopter is in this valley after all."

Myra rifled the food stores, grabbing energy bars. "You two geezers be careful. You've got enough food. Just save some in case Sarah shows up. Tom, she's an ornery, angry, defiant kid. She can survive for days up here on spite alone. Dad, get off your feet and eat something. I should be able to get as far as Hayes River before dark tonight. If I catch up with those surveyors and they have a radio we can call for help. If for some reason Sarah is with them or I find her down the trail I'll bring her back here. You both take care."

With that, Myra was gone. It was after five in the afternoon. Tom and William were alone, the valley around them empty. William felt a drop of rain strike his shoulder.

"I'll check the voids again," William said, and despite his hurting feet and the rain he spent the next hour peering into niches calling Sarah's name. Tom was further east at the base of the big slide.

When rain began to fall harder, they gathered at their camp.

Tom stowed their gear in the tent. "'Eye. You seen the atlatl tube?"

"It was by your tent. You put it there this morning."

"It's gone. Missing. Do you think Sarah took it? She was furious with me."

"Maybe."

"Could have been those surveyors, too, sneaking back here. Those two guys with sunglasses seemed to be looking for something. I'm sure they overheard what we were talking about last night. But that's for later. Right now, all I want to do is find Sarah."

"You came up here to make peace with your grandfather's spirit. You brought your granddaughter. Now, wherever she is, that spirit will guide her."

They ate dinner in the dark. The night was long. Rain fell hard. The wind blew. William kept listening for Sarah, hoping to hear a footfall, branches breaking, her voice. Dawn brought gray light. A chill fog had settled in the valley. The ridges were lost above. Behind them, water fell from the cliff in sheets.

They unpegged the wet tents and carried them, with sleeping bags inside, beneath the cliff overhang where the ground was dry. They started a fire. They ate breakfast. Then they searched.

They searched all morning, and all afternoon, moving north and south through the valley, checking the creek edges, shouting Sarah's name. By five o'clock that evening they had completed five sweeps of the valley. They trudged back toward the tents.

As they splashed up out of the creek a quarter mile west of their camp, Myra, Pete and Raymond appeared. William was happy to see Myra but saw that Sarah was not with her.

"Talk about a sorry looking sight," Myra said. "You two should be on a veranda somewhere, not out doing this."
Raymond had a sour expression. "The other two went on out. They should reach the parking lot late tonight, maybe early morning. They'll call for help. After a little discussion, their boss, Roger, agreed to let Pete and Raymond come back and help us search."

➤

"You call that a discussion?" Raymond laughed. The tattoo on his neck was a dragon. "Hellcat, you were."

Pete nodded. "Roger wasn't happy, that's for sure. We brought some food, extra blankets, batteries, lights. If she's here we'll find her."

"She's here," Tom said. "And thanks."

"Not where I want to be," Raymond said.

"Sarah didn't want to be here either. The sooner we find her, the sooner we go home."

Pete and Raymond pitched their tent beneath the overhang a distance away. After dinner, they turned in.

Myra spoke to Tom and William quietly. "No sign of Sarah. I found them at Hayes River. Roger's an asshole. He didn't want to help. He was in a big hurry. He could care less about Sarah being lost. But Pete made him realize that if they didn't help find Sarah, things would look bad for Buckhorn. That got Roger's attention. Plus, I was pretty insistent."

"The atlatl's gone," said Tom. "Vanished, like Sarah. At this point either she has it or that survey crew does."

The next day, the fog lifted in the early afternoon. The rain ceased at dusk. They ranged the floor of the valley. Tom and William struggled to keep up with Myra and Pete. Raymond, whining and lagging behind, proved to be useless. Myra drove them all day. No helicopter came.

Nearly three days had passed since Sarah had vanished. The nights had been cold and the rain, icy.

William understood, that evening, Tom was preparing to find a body.

"Never say never," Myra told Tom. "She's probably within 500 yards of us. She may just be hidden. She may be sheltered and dry."

"How long you going to look?" Raymond asked Tom.

"As long as it takes."

That night, the weather cleared and the next day the temperature rose. They kept searching. Tom and William used the line they'd brought to hang their food to lower Myra into some of the deeper voids.

A helicopter arrived early that afternoon. They heard the rotors clattering long before the machine appeared just above the lip of the saddle, landing at the base of the chute on a finger of snow. Four people emerged, carrying packs, bags, and coils of rope. They included the other two surveyors, Roger and Bernie, and two search-and-rescue rangers. The helicopter spent the rest of the afternoon searching from above, while everyone else again combed the valley.

They searched this way for three more days, the helicopter flying back and forth overhead. Finally, the search was called off. Rain and fog were forecast. Sarah had been missing a full week.

The next day, early, the eighth since Sarah had vanished, the helicopter carried away the Buckhorn surveyors and the two rescue specialists. Tom tried unsuccessfully to convince Myra to take the helicopter, so she could return to work. Myra tried to persuade William to fly back because of the horrible condition of his feet. William chose to remain behind with Tom. Before the helicopter left, the lead ranger gave them additional rations and two radios.

"Keep looking," he said. "If she was my granddaughter I'd stay up here too."

"Well," said Myra, after the last sounds of the helicopter faded. "What's it going to look like, Tom, you not showing up at work?"

"Same as for you, I expect. 'Eye, you and Myra should head back. Leave me food, matches. I'll be fine for a while. I have a radio."

"Sarah won't be helped if you decide to die up here, Tom," said Myra. "There's still a chance she slipped down to Whiskey Bend, unseen. Maybe she ran off. She's run off before. Tom, you'll be fired for sure if you stay up here."

"I know, Myra. Lynch will use this to prove that I can't make good decisions, that I'm losing it. He'll say I took a young girl out of school, brought her deep into the wilderness in bad weather with no prior experience. He'll say this whole trip was an effort by me to stop Buckhorn's investment and ruin his legacy, the Clovis Center." Tom rose and rummaged in Sarah's pack. He pulled out her sketchpad and turned the pages: a spider web, Myra, William, the bear, detailed sketches of the two sides of the atlatl. "She hates me, hates this place, all of it. She's the angriest girl I ever saw. But goddammit, anyone that small who could lug a stone that big for Bob-Bob's grave, who could draw like this, it's just not fair." Tears rolled down Tom's cheeks.

"Tom, I'm staying," William said. "I'm not due to rejoin the ship for days. Myra, you walk out, go back to work. We'll stay up here for a bit, Tom and me. All this exercise is great for my figure."

It was settled. Myra would hike out, while Tom and William would continue the search.

"I hope she did get your stubborn genes, Tom," Myra said. "If she got even half of them, she could live out here for a month. You are the most stubborn man I have ever known. Next to my dad, of course."

"Me? Why do you say that?"

For a moment, they were all able to smile.

Myra packed her gear and left, taking one of the radios. She would try to get to Elkhorn by nightfall; get out the next day.

William helped her straighten her pack. "Myra, if the weather really turns, take shelter or even come back here. Okay?"

They watched her leave. Myra was soon lost in the trees. For an hour they searched the voids beneath the boulders, yet again. The sky darkened. They took a break and rested beneath the cliff overhang.

Tom waved an arm. "We could search in here for a month and find nothing. You see some of those tree falls across the creek? Trunks all piled together, with spaces beneath? All the gaps along the base of the cliff? Sarah is small. She could be lying dead in some tiny space none of us can reach. I think she's here. And I intend to find her, put her to rest."

Sarah had been missing eight days. She was unfamiliar with being in the woods. She had no matches, no food, and no protection for the cold wet nights. William put a hand on Tom's shoulder. "Like you I have steeled my heart for a heavy blow, Tom."

They stood beneath the overhang as thunder, black clouds and heavy rain rolled across the Godkin Valley. Soon the storm was directly over them. They remained dry beneath the overhang, but it was hard to see through the downpour to the forest beyond. Out toward the creek the forest floor was nearly dark. When lightning flashed, everything ahead was bright, vivid, yet blurred by the water pouring off the overhang. Between lightning flashes, they were temporarily blinded. Wind raced through the valley. The thunder was deafening.

Tom was shouting at William. All William could see was Tom's mouth, open. Thunder crashed at the same moment a flash of white light exploded. In that instant William saw Tom pointing ahead. William stared but he was blinded by the flash, hearing only thunder, rain, wind, and somewhere close a great crashing as a tree collapsed in the forest.

Tom was still pointing toward the forest when they could both see again. Ahead, to the right, a tall tree smoked, flames licking, a lightning strike. Adjacent stood the jagged broken stump of another tree, its trunk stretching away, smoking.

"I saw Myra," Tom shouted.

In the next flash, in the instant before being blinded, there was Myra, stumbling toward them. She was covered with mud, had lost her pack, seemed, somehow, shrunken, as if injured.

Another sheet of light flashed, twice, again with thunder, instantaneous. William blinked and blinked. Already the thunder sounded more distant, coursing beyond their valley as the storm raced east. Nobody was standing before them when their eyes adjusted. The forest seemed empty. The struck tree smoked.

They both saw her at the same time, lying before them, just beyond the overhang, face down, motionless. They both ran ahead. How did she get so muddy? Where was her pack? She seemed broken. William kneeled next to her.

But this was not Myra.

This was Sarah.

She lay, unrecognizable, filthy.

Tom and William carried her to the fire. She smelled. She was covered in mud. Her hair was tangled, her face scratched and torn, the metal stud from her nose missing, her nose, bloody. Dark shadows rimmed her eyes and her pale cheeks were sunken. She was even thinner than before, a wraith. Her hands were shredded, fingernails broken, palms torn. Half the fourth finger on her right hand was missing. Her pants were torn and soiled, but she still had her boots. She had a badly healed cut on her forehead. She would always have a scar. Her eyes were half-open. She was breathing.

Tom called Myra on the radio, reached her down by Camp Wilder. She said she'd return as quickly as possible. Then Tom radioed the rangers. They said they could get a helicopter out by noon the next day.

They heated water and cleaned Sarah. Her hipbones were sharp. They bandaged her nose. They treated her finger. The cut was clean, no bone exposed, the flesh over the small stump of her finger already healing.

Sarah wasn't unconscious, but she wasn't conscious, either. She mumbled, but made no sense. They got her into dry clothes and tried to make her comfortable in her sleeping bag. She slept.

Myra appeared two hours later. Sarah woke. Her eyes widened briefly when she saw Myra.

They tried to feed her. She ate little. She drank. She remained silent. Myra tended Sarah's nose, hands, and some bad scrapes on her ankles.

"Where was she?" Myra was carefully wiping Sarah's torn nose.

"She appeared right at the height of that thunderstorm. Tom saw her first. He saw her out by our old tent site, thought she was you. So did I."

"But where was she all this time, dad? It looks like she fell. Lost a finger." Myra re-bandaged Sarah's nose. "Sarah? I don't know if you hear me, but you're going to be all right.

You banged your head. You're warm, now. Your cuts are cleaned. You have water, food. We moved the camp under the overhang, out of the rain."

Sarah began speaking in a hoarse voice, asking a question. "Kali? Kali? Saar, kali." She repeated herself twice, mumbled some other words, then fell silent. The recent cut on her forehead was bright, pulsing.

"Maybe she's saying, 'carry, carry, far, carry,'" Myra said. Sarah's eyes fixed on William and for an instant seemed almost aware. Then, in the afternoon sun, she slept again.

Later, they moved Sarah into her tent. She slept heavily. Once she cried out.

"Concussion, probably," Myra concluded, as they ate dinner. "She's had that blow on her head several days. The cut has healed. Same with her finger. Where the hell was she? What happened?"

Tom heated water for tea. "When the helicopter comes we can get her to a hospital. She is malnourished and dehydrated. She didn't eat much today."

They all kept watching Sarah's tent. William moved her drying boots closer to the heat. "She looks pretty good for someone who went through whatever she went through. Some of those nights were damn cold. She should have died of exposure."

"She didn't look very good to me, 'Eye. Half starved to death. You should have seen her, Myra, before we cleaned her up."

"Who...cleaned....me.... up?" The voice from the tent was hoarse, weak, hesitant, almost as if speaking English for the first time.

Myra's smile was huge. "You're awake, Sarah. Welcome back." Myra spoke to the tent. "We were afraid you were unconscious. Are you hungry?"

"Who...cleaned me up?"

"You were in pretty bad shape, Sarah."

"Myra, right? Myra, tell me that was you?"

"No, Sarah, not me. Tom and my dad. I wasn't back yet."

Sarah, after some groans, emerged from her tent, found a seat on one of the log sections, and stretched her stocking feet toward the coals. She peered at the thick bandage on her finger. Her forehead was terribly bruised, the cut deep. Her nose was bandaged. Her hands were badly torn. William had been surprised at the thickness of the calluses on her palms. She drank some water. Then she ate some dinner, prepared by Tom.

They said little, giving her time. She sat by the fire, seemingly alert, but somehow remote. At least she could talk, though she seemed to have little to say. They'd already decided not to press her to tell them what had happened. She would speak in her own good time.

She kept looking around camp, head turning. She gazed up, then west. The sun had set, the sky glowed, and a planet glimmered. She fingered her wool shirt, her long underwear leggings.

"Where's my pants?"

"Burned, Sarah," William said. "I burned them. They were badly torn."

Sarah said nothing. She rubbed her head, careful with her torn hands.

Myra spoke quietly. "A helicopter will be coming tomorrow to get you."

Sarah shook her head. "I'm going back to sleep." She crawled into her tent. Before she closed the front flap she looked back at them. "No helicopter. I walked in here, I'll walk out."

"You should be in a hospital," Tom said. "You might have a head injury."

"How many days was I gone? How many?"

"Eight days. You were missing for eight days."

"You kept looking for me?"

"We did. Plus a helicopter, rangers, the surveyors."

"Where are they? The others?"

"They called off the search, Sarah. They left. Gave up."

Holding the tent flap open, Sarah watched her grandfather. "You didn't?"

"I have a stubborn gene, Sarah, as you once told me. William, Myra and me, we all stayed. We thought, though, if we found you, it would be to bury you."

"You wish. No helicopter. I'm walking with you guys. If I could last that many days I can walk out of here. Besides I have you guys to carry my pack." She closed the tent flap decisively.

"As ornery as ever," said Tom. "Never thought I'd be glad to see it. But I am."

The next day they woke early. Sarah seemed much better and Myra called the rangers, called off the helicopter. They packed up, everything, cleaned the site, and left. Sarah was weak and she moved slowly. So did William. His feet were in bad shape even though he'd lost pounds and pounds.

There was no snow on the lower slide below Godkin Creek. They stopped for lunch. There, sitting in the sunshine, Sarah began to talk, then stopped. Later, when they rested and camped during their four-day hike out, she said more. She spoke slowly, with long pauses, and refused to answer questions.

What she told them was impossible.

fell into a dark space, sliding on mud, a long way. I hit my head. Then I was on rock, by water. I touched the water, feeling around. The water was hot.

Time passed. Later there was cold water running down where I had fallen, then draining below me. My leg hurt. I tried calling for help. I heard nothing.

More time passed. I was not cold, except when the cold water poured down. I could stand only beneath where I fell. I tried to climb back the way I had come, but all I did was slip, again and again. Except for the sound of water dripping, all was quiet. I was very hungry. Then I was not hungry. The dark was so dark I could see light behind my eyes.

Later, I saw the yellow eyes of a bear. The bear was looking at me. I was not surprised to see the bear. The yellow eyes gave light so I could see.

I drank the hot water when I became thirsty.

The bear watched me. We were waiting, together. We waited in the dark, lighted by the bear's stare.

I slept. When I woke I was in a strange place, above ground, cold.

My head hurt. I could see out between lashed, thin sticks. A roof lay close over my head. The roof too was built of sticks. I was on my belly, peering out. I was in a wooden cage, with six others. Like me, they were young, not yet grown, not yet women. Two were crying. I named these two Weeps a Lot

➤

and Weeps a Lot More. A third young woman crouched, silent, eyes cold. She I named Cold Eye. The rest stared out, whispering.

The cage stank. I stank, the others stank. We were crouched in piss. My clothes were rough, torn, and strange. My head ached. I remembered only how I got here. There had been 11 of us at first. I had been the first taken, on the sea of grass, before the new grass grew, when ice still covered puddles and the wind blew cold.

The first of us who died was the second taken. She fled one morning and our captors chased her down. The animals got to her first. Our fear of the animals kept us from running. With men guarding us, and a blazing fire, the animals remained distant. Alone, on the run, life was short.

The second who died stumbled and twisted her ankle. She could not keep up, so she was killed.

After they captured the last girl, we came to some low hills between mountains that smoked. On the other side of those mountains, we came to a shore. I had been taught that the ocean was the sea of grass but here the ocean was water you could not drink. Our captors lived at this place, among trees.

They loaded us into a skin-covered boat, all but two of us, the oldest, who remained behind as wives. Two women, Sami and Than, joined us. Their job was to tend to us, and they were kind and helpful.

The others, the men, treated us like animals, but did not touch us. I named their leader Old Bear because he was the oldest and his hair was ragged and long like a bear.

We traveled in the skin-covered boat, using the many small islands along the coast for protection from the winds and the animals. The boat could be pulled onto the shore at night. The boat was strong and carried much. We huddled in the bottom while our captors paddled.

At first I was sick on the boat. We all were. Many times the boat was in big waves and several times we could see no land at all.

Cold Eye was one of the oldest, 14 or 15 summers, tall, her hair like straw. She hit the smaller girls, but she only hit me once. Her look was always cold. She hated me because I hit her back and hurt her. She was pretty but mean, and she talked much.

I named the other girls. Woman Too Soon had her first moon time just after we left the land of the skin boat people. She was ugly, her eyes were set too close together, but her body was lithe and strong and she knew it. The men began to use her.

Weeps A Lot and Weeps A Lot More were stupid, weak, and answered to Cold Eye. They were twin sisters, not much taller than me, and heavy. They had short dark hair and low brows. They had much trouble accepting they would never see their home again.

Tree Hide and Rock Hide had been taken in the forest after hiding behind a large tree and boulder. Their hair was red and their bones heavy. They were by far the strongest among us. They were not sisters. They talked between themselves and their talking sounded like singing.

Cold Eye and the twin sisters, the weepers, were taken from the sea of grass, like me. We all had the same legends of ice and grass extending all across the world.

The others – Woman Too Soon, Tree Hide and Rock Hide – were from lands of trees, hills and mountains, south of the grass.

I was the smallest and I was the youngest. I knew I was entering my 12th summer.

We always had to bail, with shells. This kept us warm. As the days passed, and the longest day moon approached, the air grew warmer, though the nights stayed cold.

We camped on islands. Once, a bear smelled us and swam out, but we saw its head bobbing in the water and we were able to get away. We travelled for many days, always toward the rising sun.

At first, I could not understand what the skin boat people or my fellow captives were saying, but as we journeyed, I learned much of our captors' language, as did the other girls. In time, we were able to talk amongst ourselves, in this new, common language, when we dared to. When we reached the headland and the trading place, we waited. We whispered among ourselves in the cage, huddled for warmth, sharing what we had heard.

"These men who have taken us have done this before," whispered Rock Hide.

"Old Bear has made this journey five times," Tree Hide said. "Every five summers, they travel east to the headland with women and bone tools to meet the razor stone people. Sometimes when they went east the razor stone people were not there. Then they had to return, empty-handed. But other times they could trade wives and tools for black razor stone."

Woman Too Soon was lying on my other side. "Sami and Than say such trading has been going on since the dark time, the time of no summer, no sun. The razor stone people come this difficult way for wives. They come in canoes formed from great trees."

"We are to be wives to these people," Cold Eye whispered. "This journey will be long."

"At least they feed us," Rock Hide said. Rock Hide and Tree Hide liked to eat.

"That is because we are what they trade for this razor stone they so love," I said. "That is why they give us robes for warmth, and why they don't use us. Except you, Woman Too Soon, because you are now a woman."

"You will be woman soon enough," said Woman Too Soon. She did not like me.

"They must be in a great hurry," Weeps a Lot said. "Some days we travel all night."

"We travel at night when the wind is calm and the moon bright," said Cold Eye. "Than told me after we left the land of smoking mountains that we must reach the trading place before the longest day moon."

When I awoke in that cage, I had only the memory of the journey there. I could remember none of my life before. From hearing the others whisper, I knew I had been part of a small band living on the sea of grass, following herds. The bands gathered every summer for talk, trade and weddings. Except for this gathering, the bands fought each other. Always, we lived with the fear of the big animals, which would take us, in ones and twos, all year.

The longest day moon brought the woman moon time. During this time, the women stayed apart from the men. The men collected seal and smoked meat for the trip back to their home. The women repaired clothing and made tying straps from the tendons of seals.

The skin boat people were afraid of the razor stone people, and only their desire for the razor stone overcame this fear. The skin boat people talked of a time in the deep past when they tried to follow the razor stone people back to their home. They followed them south along the shore to where the ice rose on the mountains and there they learned that their skin boat could not survive the waters and winds. The razor stone people, using a big one-log canoe, continued.

Sami told of legends of the razor stone people coming all the way to the land of smoking mountains and even to the sea of grass. These were ancient myths and dreams, told to children in the night to frighten and teach. These tales were not so different than stories I knew from the sea of grass, of singing brutes and people not quite people who once roamed the earth.

The razor stone people arrived with the sun three days after the longest day moon. Their dark canoe glided to shore, striking the pebbled beach. They were nine. Two men were old, but not as old as Old Bear. Another was over 30 summers, old, but younger than the first two. Of the other two men, one was pretty and one not much older than me; he was not yet a man. Two of the women seemed to be wives. The last two were not wives of men, but of each other. Our captors welcomed them with hand signs and simple speech. The men all shared hot seal flesh. The women who had come in the one-log canoe talked as they could with Sami and Than.

We were led from our cage and stood in a line. The two oldest razor stone men opened our mouths, pulled our teeth, and checked our skin, our bodies, all of us. Then they stepped back and began to speak to Old Bear. They spoke before a fire made with branches from the small trees at the base of the headland.

The new people brought the razor stone from their canoe to the fire. Our captors brought fresh bone pieces and piled them by the razor stone, then gestured at us, the seven captive girls. Then shouting began.

The razor stone people were unhappy we were only seven. They were displeased and becoming angry. The three younger men cast longing looks at those of us girls who were older and knew how to glance at a man like a woman. Cold Eye, Woman

Too Soon, and Tree Hide smiled back at the men.

Old Bear shouted and put us back into the log cage. Sami and Than retrieved the bone tools from near the pile of razor stone.

Seeing this, one of the two older razor stone men, with a long braid, grabbed Sami and Than together. The razor stone women fell on Old Bear. The three younger visitors reached in their canoe, pulling out spears and throwers. Before our captors could reach their weapons, the razor stone men threw. Two of the skin boat people escaped over a ridge toward the headland. The others died. Old Bear's throat was cut. Sami and Than's skulls were crushed.

Blood ran over the stones before us. One of the skin boat people, impaled through the chest, made sucking sounds. Bodies sprawled on the ground. The razor stone women took knives and slashed the skin boat. Three razor stone men ran after the escaped captors.

By the time the men who had chased the fleeing captors returned, laughing, the sun was low in the sky. The razor stone people dragged the dead bodies into the water and pushed them away. They picked through the stores and food of the skin boat people, finding some food, knives, and rope made of bark. Everything else was thrown into the fire – robes, spare clothing, everything.

We spent one more night in the cage. In the morning we were loaded in the big canoe. The razor stone was stacked in the middle of the canoe. We seven were made to sit on slats and furs between the thwarts. The bone pieces were placed in the canoe toward the bow.

After our new journey started I named our captors. The leader, one of the two older men, I named Thin Hair. I could see his scalp when the wind blew. I knew he hated this thing about himself, and the others pretended they could not see it. Thin

Hair was not the tallest but he was very strong. His eyes were black and piercing.

The second older man I named Fat Hair. His hair grew thick and was long enough to braid, and he was vain about this. He was very tall and his flesh was in places soft, like a woman. He had a small mouth and small eyes.

Long Braid was Fat Hair's wife. She was the keeper of medicines and plants. She had beautiful black hair. She was the oldest of the women.

Thin Hair had no wife. With him was his son, Thrower, who looked just like his father except his ears stuck out far. His hair curled and his eyes were black and wide apart. When he smiled, his whole face smiled. Thrower was the youngest and the smallest. I knew he would grow to be a strong man like his father. At the headland, I saw him throw stones at birds and strike them time after time.

Watcher, the third oldest, steered the canoe. He could see far. He was thin and tall, all sinew and cord. His chin was heavy and his eyes were dark and cruel, but he was kind to us. He said little but would hum when steering the canoe. He was husband to Bright Eyes, who among the women could throw stones as well as Thrower. She had heavy lidded eyes, which flashed with laughter. She was fair to look upon and the youngest of the women.

Pretty Face loved himself best, knowing he was pretty like a woman, with beautiful long muscles. He expected us to like him, so I did not. All the captives except me gazed at him. He kept his hair short and trimmed with razor stone while looking at his reflection in the water. He would whisper to Fat Hair. I knew as soon as I saw him that Pretty Face wanted to be leader.

The other two women, Heavy and Anger, were the biggest women. Heavy was almost as big as the biggest man, and her hands were larger still. Her face was covered with bumps and wens, and she had heavy lidded eyes like Bright Eyes. Heavy was kind to us.

Anger was short. She had huge muscles, a thick neck, large breasts and wide hips. She had a long head, huge nose, and her eyes were large and bright green. I soon learned she could sing best of anyone.

Even before we left the headland, I knew these razor stone people had much conflict and disagreement. They seemed in a great rush. I was certain we had far to go.

The day we started our journey, the sun was still high and the day warm.

Beyond the cove at the headland the shore went south, at times exposed to the open sea, in other places sheltered by low barrier islands. The shore was sometimes sandy, other times rocky, rising several feet to a great plain. From the canoe, we could not see beyond the lip of the plain; all we could see was the beach. The wind came from the southwest, steady and gentle.

I had thought the skin boat of the skin boat people was large, but this one-log canoe was huge, as long as 10 men lying head to toe, and wider at the top of the sides than a tall man head to heel. The men and the women each took a place at a thwart, four on one side, four on the other, standing just ahead of where the thwart met the sides. The canoe had room for more to paddle. The paddles were longer than the men were tall. Everyone paddled in unison, chanting quietly, often singing. They took strokes beat by beat, not fast, but steadily, hour after hour. Watcher stood on a thwart at the stern, steering with a long oar, controlling the canoe. When Watcher did not steer, Thin Hair or Fat Hair did. Many times nobody used the steering oar, but when there was wind or when the sail was up, the long oar was necessary and helpful. We were often able to travel in shallow water behind barrier islands. The two paddlers closest to the bow sang out if they saw obstructions ahead.

We seven girls crouched in the middle of the canoe, facing the stern, protected with furs against the wind. Whenever the canoe left the protection of a barrier island, large waves made the canoe rise and fall. The shore slipped past, not far away. The high headland dropped behind, so slowly I was sure we were not moving at all. Yet, by the time the sun neared the horizon, the headland was barely in sight.

We paddled all the short night. The moon was just past full. The wind died. At night, four of the paddlers slept, lying on furs on the bottom of the canoe, while four others kept paddling. They rotated through the night.

The only time we stopped was to get water, where streams or small rivers entered the sea. This too was the time we moved our bowels, always near, in sight of the canoe, because we feared the animals.

As we traveled, we captives listened to the razor stone people talk, trying to understand their speech. Soon we were sharing the new words in whispers among us.

Thin Hair was the leader, his decision the final decision. Everyone accepted this except Fat Hair and Pretty Face. Thin Hair knew they disliked him as leader yet seemed not to care. He was unafraid of anyone.

Fat Hair was the finder, the one who knew the landmarks and the currents and the wind patterns. He chose the route. He would watch the stars just before the rising of the sun.

At the start of our journey, we saw no trees, just shrubs and bushes in protected valleys.

The second evening we stopped at a small island far from shore. Here, on this island, protected from the wind, were trees. Along shore was much driftwood, fuel for cooking and warmth.

As with all islands we visited, two went ashore to check for animals while we waited in the canoe. It took Anger and Pretty Face only moments to walk from one end of the island to the other. We brought the canoe to the beach once they signed all was clear. Seals lay in the sun on rocks. Long Braid killed a seal for meat and oil.

We pushed the canoe onto the beach. The bone tools, razor stone and everything else in the canoe were removed. We rolled the canoe on its side until it leaned against stout branches held by Fat Hair and Thin Hair. We washed the inside of the canoe, using bark buckets to throw water until we had a clean and secure shelter. A fire was built in front of the leaning canoe. We cooked the seal meat and several birds Bright Eyes and Thrower took with stones. We ate well. The meat tasted of fish.

That night, the wind blew. The sea raged between our island and the mainland, white rollers frothing down steep waves. No animals could swim out to us in this weather. A knoll in the center of the island sheltered our camp. While the wind blew and the trees groaned around us, here by the canoe it was calm and warm.

For hours, these razor stone people talked, telling stories. They carefully inspected the bone pieces. I understood they planned to carve the bone into tools.

Always, while they sat talking, some made darts for their throwers. They used branches from small willows collected at our water stops. They debarked the branches and straightened them in the heat over the fire. Using feathers from the birds they had killed and cutting points from the razor stone, they assembled darts. We girls helped as we could. Choosing feathers, lashing points—these were things we knew how to do.

The wind blew all night.

n the morning the sky was gray and still the wind blew. All this day we remained on the island. Thin Hair made a target of seaweed bound together. He leaned the target against a tree north of the knoll and the men practiced throwing darts. They began their practice close to the target, but by the afternoon they were many paces distant, nearly as far back as the leaning canoe. Thrower threw the best, always.

Then the women threw. They were just as accurate as the men. There was much laughter, and the seaweed target was remade many times. Pretty Face threw wildly. One dart he threw flew high, striking near the top of a tree. The others laughed at him and he grew angry. The dart's shaft quivered. Later, a bird flew close and perched on the shaft, watching us.

Our second night on the island, it began to rain. We left the next morning. Long Braid and Bright Eyes placed a hide over the thwarts in the center of the canoe to make a tent where we could stay dry. The wind dropped, but the sea remained rough. We continued along the shore, always paddling.

In the afternoon, the rain stopped. The sky cleared and the air became colder. The wind increased, but now it came from behind us, blowing us south toward the sun. Fat Hair and Heavy mounted the mast and then hung the sail, a sheet of woven bark attached to the mast. The corners of the sail were tied to the canoe with bark rope.

The sail filled and bellied ahead. The canoe flew. We

remained some distance from shore, now passing outside barrier islands, staying in the darker water, which I now understood was deep water. The canoe rode over surging waves. Behind us, I could see a bubbling trail marking our passage. The canoe leaned with the wind and water echoed against its thin sides. Occasionally, a large, splashing wave slopped into the canoe.

We travelled so three days. During this time, we followed the shore, first going south and then west. We spent the nights on small islands, where we watched for animals and gathered food as we could.

On the afternoon of the fourth day, the land before us changed. To the west, toward where the sun sets, lay a large high island. Beyond that, further west, I could see, just above the horizon, another island. Straight ahead, south, gray and blue water caught the sun. To the left, the shore turned east, rising to hills, then mountains. The shore stretched east as far as I could see.

Watcher shouted, and the people all sat up to look. Fat Hair pointed to the left, guiding us toward a barrier island far ahead that held a sharp peak. Beyond this island, I saw only the ocean. We sailed to the south end of this island and put ashore in a small cove against a gravel beach.

As we waited in the canoe, Pretty Face and Watcher checked for animals. This island was larger than others we had visited and was close enough to the mainland to be reached by a swimming animal. I saw a fire pit on the beach and knew these people had stayed here on their way to the headland earlier in the spring.

Pretty Face and Watcher climbed the slopes behind the cove and disappeared into trees. When they emerged some time later, we brought the canoe ashore and they spoke with Thin Hair and Fat Hair. Thin Hair listened, and then nodded.

We did not pull the canoe onto the beach. Instead, we secured the canoe with an anchor stone, so we could quickly depart if we had to.

By the fire pit, Heavy and Anger assembled a lean-to frame from branches and smaller logs. They covered the frame with boughs and our wettest hides, leaving them in the sun to dry.

Long Braid and Bright Eyes started a large fire. Thin Hair, Bright Eyes, Heavy and Anger found seals not far from the cove and took two for meat. They carried the carcasses to our fire and began cutting the meat and blubber into strips. We all ate sizzling fat while waiting for the meat to cook.

Like people everywhere, the razor stone people talked not just with their tongues, but also with their eyes, faces, hands and arms, even their bodies. We understood their gestures, and in just these few days we began to understand their speech.

That night, we all sat before a big fire, we captives furthest from the flames. The watchers on the ridge had small fires of their own. Heavy and Bright Eyes were up on the ridge for the first watching time. Thin Hair and Fat Hair were talking, using sticks to draw in the sand.

"We will now make the turn," Thin Hair said. "We must use this north wind while we can."

"We will get the ice winds," Fat Hair was shaking his head. I saw that Thin Hair was impatient. Fat Hair was patient and careful. They had both made this trip before, Thin Hair five times, Fat Hair three. The last two times the winds had been strong and the ice too heavy. They had never even reached the headland. "If we get too close to land we will have the ice winds and those will stop us."

"You are too cautious to be finder," Thin Hair said. "The places of shelter along shore are disappearing. The sea is higher, the summers hotter, and this causes the ice to move and fill the waters. The animals are more. For all these reasons we must move fast when we have a fair wind, ice wind or not."

I saw that Fat Hair was insulted to be called too cautious. Now he was angry with Thin Hair. "The times before you and I made our trips, six times, there were no wives. Twice, no one returned at all. Then you made two trips, Thin Hair, and could not even reach the headland. Of our three trips together, we brought wives the first time, 15 summers ago, then the next two trips we never reached the headland again."

"Always, these journeys are difficult." Thin Hair cared not that he had insulted Fat Hair. I knew Fat Hair would not forget this insult. "With these seven, if we bring all seven, this is many."

"We have not yet started the difficult passage. That starts tomorrow. We don't know how many wives we will have." Anger was not afraid to speak directly to Thin Hair and Fat Hair.

Thin Hair spoke as he drew. "There is strong ice ahead. We should reach this ice in five days. To pass the ice is two long days' paddle. Then we cross open water to reach The Place People Were. That is half way to our home."

"What is The Place People Were?" I asked.

"You speak." Thin Hair was surprised.

"I have not had to paddle so I have breath to speak."

"You may get the chance, small one. The trip is long."

Long Braid leaned forward. "People lived at that place in the dim times, long ago, when this journey was easier, when our people travelled this way not to find wives but to look, seek, wonder. Some never returned, either killed or choosing to stay. Long, long ago, after the dark time."

Thin Hair drew in the sand. "The Place People Were is sheltered in a deep narrow channel between high steep slopes. The water is calm always. This is a place to stop and gather strength before the rest of the journey."

Above us, smoke rose toward a dark sky. We ate seal.

"Are there no people near you, for wives?" Cold Eye gazed at Thin Hair, warm. She had come to be sitting near him.

"The only people we know of, anywhere in the world," Thin Hair said, "are found where the sun rests each day, where you were found, the land of smoking mountains beyond the great wide plain. Where we live, west is the ocean, north and east is the ice, south the great river, floods, and animals. Between us and the ice lie our mountains and our small land."

Cold Eye moved closer to Thin Hair.

Long Braid, sitting next to me, gazed up the ridge toward where Bright Eyes was on watch. "Men cannot marry their sisters," Long Braid said. "Many women die in childbirth. Our women are few. We have found nobody else on our land. We only find people at the setting sun. But the way is always difficult." Long Braid pointed toward Bright Eyes and Heavy over the ridge. "Even among us here are two who were brought as wives earlier. Heavy is one, she arrived when she was 11 summers old. Bright Eyes is the other, she came then, too, 15 summers ago. They are now of the people." Long Braid shared a look with Fat Hair, then turned to me. "They came to the people when they were young, not yet women. They are happy with the people."

Watcher spoke. "Bright Eyes and I come on this journey as two who have no living children. Our son was taken by an animal when he was two summers, just as Fat Hair and Long Braid's child was taken. If we are lucky, we will both bring home a journey child."

Long Braid's eyes sparkled. "If the man and wife return from a trip such as this and the wife is with child, we call that child a journey child. Such children are most precious and rare. If Fat Hair and I are blessed, we will have a journey child. Bright Eyes and Watcher, they will surely be blessed." Long Braid began to laugh. "The way they have been practicing, I am certain she will be with child."

Everyone laughed. It was good to laugh. Long Braid reached over and touched my arm. She pointed toward Thrower with her eyes. Thrower was at the other end of the shelter, working on one of the bone pieces.

"Thrower is a journey child. He was made 15 summers ago when Thin Hair was Pretty Face's age, young himself, travelling with his wife, Thrower's mother, who has been dead now 10 years. Thrower is the first journey child in many generations. When he came we people found hope."

eavy's scream was terrible. The animal had been utterly silent, stalking. The men seized darts and throwers and raced toward Heavy's fire. Bright Eyes appeared, running toward our camp. A huge bear, with a mottled coat, followed, swinging its head as it charged. The bear was now one leap from devouring her.

Thrower threw. His dart struck the bear's chest. Three more darts struck around the bear's throat, and one struck the bear's left eye. Watcher's dart stopped the charge, a direct throw below the shoulder into the chest. The bear fell, gushing blood. One clawed paw tore into Bright Eyes' calf. The bear thudded to the earth.

Anger ran over the ridge, searching for Heavy. Bright Eyes was bleeding, her calf nearly torn from her leg. The bear lay on its back, a broken dart emerging from one eye. Blood covered its muzzle. Over the ridge, Anger began her loss song.

Watcher and Long Braid pushed Bright Eye's torn muscle back into place and bound it with leather and boughs. Bright Eyes shuddered, her blood seeping. Fat Hair and Anger brought Heavy back off the ridge. Her body was torn nearly in half, her insides loose. Anger wept. We all gathered wood and built a pyre. Anger and Fat Hair placed Heavy on the pyre. Like on the sea of grass, this was their way, to burn the dead, to make them ash and release their spirit. The pyre flamed high. Heavy's body crackled.

Bright Eyes was under robes, by the fire.

Thin Hair pointed at the dead bear. "This bear was here all day, watching. Scavengers will come, now. We must leave at daylight." He faced us captives. "Now you must work for your lives. We have lost two of our paddlers this night. We have far to go."

Watcher, Pretty Face and Thrower skinned the bear. The bear was too heavy to move. All they could take was the belly and chest and forelegs, still a large pelt. Thrower rolled the pelt and tied the roll with leather thongs. We cut meat from the dead bear for roasting. The bear meat was delicious after so much fishy seal. Even Bright Eyes woke to eat her share.

Stripped of its skin, the bear had muscles like a person. We covered the carcass with ash and coals. Now there were many fires: our campfire, the watcher fires on the ridge, Heavy's pyre, and the fire built on top of the bear. Such smoke and heat would keep other animals away. We spent a long night keeping the fires high, tending to Bright Eyes, and rotating watchers. The stars rolled slowly, that night.

When the sun rose, we saw clouds high in the sky, reaching like fingers. On the sea of grass, such clouds meant wind and rain would come within a day. Here I did not know what they meant, but Thin Hair and Fat Hair were in a great hurry. We carried Bright Eyes to the canoe and placed her beneath the tent.

We left that island and headed east, toward the sun. The long shore lay to our north, rising from a narrow plain into mountains of snow and ice. Once we left the shelter of the island we came into waves. These waves were not steep with breaking tops. They did not have ruffled surfaces streaked with foam. Those are waves that rise with the wind. These waves were smooth and long, like hills. They seemed to need no wind, and they marched from the west one after another, silent and powerful.

They moved faster than our canoe, coming behind and flowing beneath us. When we were at the top of these waves, we could see the land to our left. Ahead and behind, we could see nothing but other waves stretching to the horizon. Then we would drop, caught between two waves, unable to see beyond. There was little wind. Clouds in thin streams walked across the top of the sky. To the west, thicker bands of cloud rose.

First, Cold Eye and Woman Too Soon helped paddle. They were placed against the second thwart, one on each side of the canoe. They were told to follow the person ahead, to stroke the paddle as that person did.

Thin Hair instructed them, showing them how to tie in, how to grip. The motion was short and steady, one hand grasping the shaft of the paddle, the other on top of the shaft. Watcher laughed as Cold Eye and Woman Too Soon struggled.

This day, we all faced our turn paddling. Weeps a Lot and Weeps a Lot More had thick bodies and short arms. When pulling the paddle, their hands struck the side of the canoe. They wept. Tree Hide and Rock Hide needed little teaching. Their people lived in the forest and fished in rivers and they knew how to paddle.

When I took my turn, Pretty Face and Fat Hair laughed at me. They thought I would be the worst paddler because I was the smallest and very thin. I wanted to kill them. I was small, but my arms were long enough that I did not smash my hand against the side of the canoe. The paddle soon seemed heavy, and my arms began to ache and burn, but I pictured Pretty Face and Fat Hair behind me laughing and this gave me the strength and energy to continue.

The shore to our north turned into a steep cut face with surf crashing against its base. We had nowhere to land. In places, the ice covering the mountains reached the sea, threading down slopes in thick, long, broken tongues, ending in piles of rocks, dirt, and old snow. On the slopes between the tongues of ice, I saw clusters of trees.

When not paddling, sitting beneath the tent on the bottom of the canoe, I could see little except the sides of the canoe, the legs of the paddlers ahead of us, and what we carried. Although my arms ached, and my hands became blistered, I preferred paddling to sitting. When paddling I could see. The fresh air felt good against my face.

At rest beneath the tent, I listened to Cold Eye's scolding. The others spoke of their home and family and their life before. I could speak to none of that because I had no memory of home or family. My silence made Cold Eye and Woman Too Soon suspicious of me.

My second time paddling, I paddled while the sun crossed four hand spans of the sky. Pretty Face and Fat Hair stopped laughing. I stopped paddling only when Thin Hair spoke. By then, my hands were bleeding.

"Strong Heart," Thin Hair said, and so I was named.

Anger replaced me at the thwart. I handed her the paddle. The shaft was sticky with my blood. When I sat under the tent with the others, Cold Eye said nothing. The weepers stared at my hands. Bright Eyes was awake.

"You will be paddling again, Strong Heart," she said. "For one so small you have strength."

"I wish to live."

"You are not of our people." Cold Eye pointed at me. "You are different. You are not from the sea of grass. We do not know where you come from. The skin boat people feared you." The twin sisters nodded. I did not think the skin boat people had feared me. They handled me and pushed me and tied me like everyone else. Cold Eye and the others had made a story about me among themselves that they now believed. "One of us ran and was killed. Another hurt herself and was killed," Cold Eye said. "All the skin boat people were killed. Heavy has been killed. Bright Eyes is hurt. You bring a curse, Strong Heart. Dark Heart should be your name."

"You have picked up our way of speech fast," Bright Eyes said to Cold Eye. "You are smart, so listen. If you talk about a curse, you will surely bring one on yourself. Everyone has a strength, and a weakness. Your weakness is gossip. Already I know this about you. I wonder, what is your strength?"

"But she is different," Cold Eye repeated, pointing at me.

"She is a person," said Bright Eyes. "The skin boat women told us that this one, Strong Heart, was the first taken. They did not hunt her down; they found her. She was alone and her head was injured. She was found close to strong bear sign, yet she was alive."

"It would have been better if she had died."

"If Strong Heart had died, it would have been you paddling four hand spans of the sun. And then your hands would have been as hers are now." Bright Eyes adjusted her leg.

"How is your leg?" I asked.

"Long Braid placed healing paste this morning. That helps. But we have many days yet, and if the flesh becomes hot I will die. "

Watcher steered, standing, looking ahead, then looking down at his wife. Long Braid hummed as she paddled against the last thwart. I could hear her over the canoe and water sounds.

We continued this way for three hand spans of the sun, maybe four. Thrower, now paddling forward, sang out he could see an island ahead.

A sudden, strong, cold wind came from the ice.

"We must find shelter," Fat Hair called to Thin Hair, who was now paddling forward. "These will be the ice winds and they will cast us away."

The cold wind reached deep into the canoe. Overhead, the sky grew dark.

"Three spans," Thin Hair cried. "Three more. Now is the time to set the boards."

Bright Eyes gestured toward several long planks in the bottom of the canoe. We placed these planks in notched openings located along the top of each side of the canoe, raising the side a hand width and a half. The raised sides kept sea spray from coming into the canoe but made paddling harder. Cold Eye began to whimper as her hand struck the hull.

Thin Hair had us all paddle as the wind strengthened. The island ahead did not get closer. The ice wind came in sharp gusts, and each gust pushed the canoe further from shore. Watcher struggled with the steering oar. A cold wind whistled over our ears.

"We will miss the island," Pretty Face said.

"You speak defeat," said Anger. "By so speaking, so you will bring the outcome you most fear."

The canoe rocked and plunged. Spray blew into our faces. The sky was dark gray, the disc of the sun faint. We all paddled as hard as we could, into the wind, seeking the lee of the island. We seemed to be making no progress at all.

Watcher pulled the steering oar inboard and began paddling with the rest of us. Now all of us were paddling. The canoe crept forward. We passed through foam and tongues of surf surging against the island. The canoe wallowed and tipped; water sloshed aboard. We almost turned over, the canoe heeling so steeply those of us on the downside could touch the water itself.

We reached the beach. Thin Hair, Thrower, Watcher and Fat Hair leapt from the canoe and pulled us ashore. Then the rest of us, except for Bright Eyes, climbed from the canoe. Holding the sides, we walked the canoe east to a place where we could pull the canoe well onto the gravel. We pulled the canoe all the way up the beach, three canoe lengths, on rollers, to the base of a knoll, and leaned it so we were protected from a west or south wind. We took Bright Eyes and placed her on a thick bed of boughs beneath the canoe shelter. Much wood lay on the shore - dead branches, broken logs, old trees that had fallen into the ocean and then drifted to this island. With some of this wood, we built a strong lean-to next to the canoe so all of us could be sheltered.

We built a fire before the canoe at the base of the knoll, out of the wind. The wind was cold.

We killed three seals on the west side of the island. We gathered more wood and secured our canoe and camp. When the rain began we set out baskets to collect water draining off the canoe. The wind started gusting, driving the rain.

Huge, rough waves marched onto the shore. The jagged rocks and shoals protected us from the surf, but occasional surges rose up the beach nearly to our canoe.

We waited four days for the wind to die.

We had leaned the canoe so the bottom faced southwest and protected us. Some of us took shelter beneath the canoe, the rest beneath the lean-to next to the canoe. Anger and Long Braid unrolled the bear pelt and scraped the skin clean of gristle and blood. After stretching the hide on branches, Long Braid and Anger rubbed seal brains and urine onto the skin. Two days later, when they were finished, the bear hide was a soft, clean, warm robe.

Long Braid found some herbs and lichens to keep Bright Eye's leg healing.

At times, dark clouds poured rain. Surf roared. The fire was steady. The southwest wind turned warm. The wind had pushed a large raft of floating ice against the island shore.

On the fifth morning we rose to a clear sky. A few stars still shone overhead. The southwest wind had passed and now a

➤

fresh wind blew from the northwest. Sunlight sparkled on the trees on the peak of the island. Mist rose like smoke. Before we packed the canoe, we spread our robes and the bear pelt to dry. We had 10 seal stomachs full of water but Thin Hair and Fat Hair still frowned, fearing we had not enough for the long passage past the ice.

"These next days, we cannot stop." Thin Hair was inspecting the robes. "Now we will depart."

We rolled the canoe to the shore. I now knew how to help, as did the other captives, and we understood the need for haste. I helped Thrower pack the bone pieces forward in the canoe. Thrower worked hard, not speaking. His ears stuck out like wings. Behind us I heard Cold Eye scolding Weeps a Lot and Weeps a Lot More, acting as if she was already Thin Hair's wife. Cold Eye was fair to look upon, she was strong, and she was smart. She talked, much.

Thrower heard Cold Eye scolding and spoke softly, so only I could hear. "My father is lucky that he is growing deaf. He will need to be deaf if Cold Eye shares his robe." Thrower's smile was wide. Looking at the bone pieces, he set one aside. "These pieces have become wet and this bone is soft again. I will make a new thrower. I will carve a raven on the holder place."

"Will you teach me how to throw?"

"I will show you when we get to The Place People Were."

We set off from the island, pushing the canoe into the sea. When we moved past the shelter of the shoals the canoe rose high, then fell, as each heavy wave passed beneath. The steady wind was strong and chill. Thin Hair, Pretty Face, Anger and Long Braid stopped paddling to set up the mast and sail. The canoe surged ahead.

We went thus all day. People rested by leaving their post for a hand span of the sun, sitting, drinking water, and then paddling again. At the second thwart I paddled when I could, as did Tree Hide and Rock Hide. Weeps a Lot and Weeps a Lot More did not paddle. Bright Eyes had them working with her under the tent sewing and repairing clothing. They did not complain and I had not seen them weep for days. They seemed not so fat, either.

Ahead of us, the ice face extended beyond sight. The ice had come all the way from the mountains and walked into the ocean itself. Against the water, the ice was jagged, dirty, and broken, with fissures and cracks. In some places, the face was high and straight. In other places, the ice was cut by gullies and deep coves. At times, huge pieces fell from the face, collapsing into the water, raining ice and snow, throwing huge waves. We could hear great splashes, even out where we were. A thick field of broken ice rose and fell in the waves at the foot of the face.

"The ice bear is singing," Bright Eyes said. "The ice bear has taken over the world and is singing her triumph."

The ice roared. Birds followed our canoe, calling and swooping. Two landed on the bow. Their black eyes shone and they seemed to be saying, "Paddle hard, paddle hard."

While we had sheltered from the storm my hands had healed and hardened. When my turn came at the thwart, the paddle shaft felt smooth and right in my hand.

We set a steady pace, stroke by stroke, and the canoe flew with the sail and wind. When I stood just ahead of the second thwart, ahead of the sail, paddling, I could see before us. The ocean, blue with white flecks, stretched endlessly ahead. When we rose on the big waves, I could see far - the great ice wall, the ice bear roaring, and the dark peaks behind, far in the distance. Just ahead of me Thin Hair's back worked and twisted as he paddled. In a low voice, he chanted, "Hut-hut-hut."

Bright Eyes pulled a small drum from her robe. With a short beat, she began striking in rhythm to Thin Hair's voice.

With this steady beat we traveled.

The sail snapped in the wind, the mast creaked, Bright Eyes struck the drum, the ice bear sang, the sun crossed the sky.

We sailed and paddled thus for two full days, well out to sea, away from the ice bear. The next-to-autumn moon was approaching and now at night the air grew chill. We ran out of food. We drank very little water.

Just as in camp on the sea of grass, here in this canoe were all the sounds telling us where we were. On the sea of grass we would hear insects, small singing birds, the sweeping sound of the wind flowing across the long grasses, the rapping sounds of people striking stone to sharpen points. The fire crackled if we had wood, hissed if we used dung. In the canoe we heard different sounds: the water slopping against the bone in the bow, the thudding as waves struck the side, the wind sighing with the sail. From beyond the canoe we heard breaking seas, the more distant roar of the ice bear, the harsh calls of seabirds, and whooshing sounds when Tiny Whales surfaced near us and blew.

At night the moon rose, span by span. Close by the moon two bright stars traveled, one red, the other silver. All across the sky stars spread in their uncountable numbers, a bright band overhead. The stars here over the ocean were even brighter than over the sea of grass. To the north, billows of color swept and swung, green and pink, robes covering the stars beyond.

A bird perched on the bow, both nights.

Our robes were damp, our clothing damp. The water in the canoe stank. All we could see to the left was the face of the ice bear, distant. Even at night the ice bear glowed, white.

The second night, after the moon rose, clouds swept in from the south and covered the moon and stars. By dawn the clouds were dark, heavy, thick, and the wind shifted west then southwest. The wind began to increase. Far ahead, the ice bear ended. Past the sudden sheer wall of ice was water, only water.

"That is the passage we must cross," Thin Hair called. "Rain is coming."

Watcher steered the canoe further away from the ice bear. We were forced to sail with the wind coming from the side. The canoe leaned and I became scared. I understood that Watcher was trying to get us far from the ice bear. After that, he would sail before the wind into the open channel, clearing the ice face.

Ahead, the sky was now dark. The rain began. We could not see the sun. The clouds were low and thick. Wind blew rain against the canoe. Thunder roared. Lightning flashed. Under Thin Hair's direction, some paddled, helping Watcher keep the canoe headed in the correct direction, but the wind was too strong and we had to head downwind, back toward the ice bear. We took down the sail and mast. Some of us bailed.

We could see nothing ahead. The seas were steep and breaking. Their tops rose above the sides of the canoe. Somehow we rose and each sea passed beneath us.

We were running before the wind and we were heading the only direction we could head. We could not see more than a few canoe lengths, even between squalls. The ice bear lay somewhere ahead and to the left of us, but we did not know how far.

We bailed. Spray from the seas overrunning us spilled over the sides of the canoe. Water sloshed across the razor stone, swirling robes and clothing at our feet.

I bailed. My arms ached. The canoe heaved one way, then another, and even on my knees in the water I could not stay balanced. Watcher steered and those who could paddle, paddled. Bright Eyes was helping bail but even now she could not kneel, or move, and all she could do was fill buckets for the rest of us to throw over the side.

I saw another squall coming, rain like a cliff behind us, running after us, running over us. The canoe rose and fell, tilted and swung, water poured aboard, spray flew, seas broke.

The wind then stopped. For long moments all I heard was rain. Then I heard a deep roar behind us. A huge black wave, blocking the wind, was coming upon us. The stern rose higher and higher until the canoe almost stood up straight. People grabbed what they could as things began to fall forward. A tumbling wall of foam then fell down the face of the wave, grasping the canoe. I knew we were all going to meet our spirits. We plunged down the great wave but then somehow rose before the next great wave, which passed beneath us. The wave's shoulders were hunched as if a great animal had come from the deep ocean and risen to toy with our canoe before diving again, deep.

We had taken much water. Desperately we bailed.

As the squall passed, we saw to our left the high broken teeth of the ice bear. We were close to the foot of those teeth, only one or two canoe lengths away. I understood then that had not Watcher steered us away earlier, against the wind, we would not have cleared this face. We all stared at these teeth as the canoe wavered and wallowed past, driven by the wind. We were among ice chunks.

We were moving away from the ice bear when a tooth of the bear fell away, collapsing, plunging into the sea. Huge waves rose and raced toward us. This time we could do nothing. Water poured over the sides into the canoe.

Baskets, robes, and paddles floated and drifted in the flooded canoe. Bright Eyes lay in the water, holding a thwart. All of us bailed. The canoe was heavy with water. From the bow, Fat Hair and Thrower tossed over the side some of the razor stone that had slid forward. Water flew from the canoe, throw by throw, and still we could see water in the canoe, little waves, piling to one side or the other as the canoe leaned on the waves.

"I welcome the strength, the spirit of this great tree who gave herself to be our canoe." Anger sang as she bailed, kneeling next to me. She sang to the canoe's spirit, a beautiful song. The wind blew her hair. The rain came again.

The water level dropped. The canoe grew lighter. My arms were numb but I kept bailing. Weeps a Lot and Weeps a Lot More bailed even faster now than they had before. Cold Eye was to the side, knuckles to her mouth, holding a bucket, bleeding from her brow. Long Braid bailed.

The ice cliff behind us faded in the rain. Now that we had passed beyond the face, the wind was slightly blocked by the ice, and the seas smaller.

Pretty Face and Thrower together took the steering oar from Watcher, who was exhausted. Cold Eye and Woman Too Soon began filling seal stomachs with water flowing off the roof of the tent. I helped make Bright Eyes comfortable on top of the wet robes. Rain continued to fall.

We went thus for many spans of a sun we could not see. Two lookouts always searched for land. The squalls continued. We could not rid the canoe of water, no matter how much we bailed, and we realized we had a leak. We would have to continue bailing until we reached The Place People Were. Perhaps there we could repair the canoe. The lookouts saw no land. All we could see was wave after wave, marching before us.

The sun broke through the clouds. The red cedar sides of the canoe glowed. Fat Hair's long raven hair was tangled. Cold Eye's straw hair caught the light and flashed. Tree Hide and Rock Hide's hair was the color of the canoe, a dark red.

Anger began to sing a thanks song, and Tree Hide and Rock Hide joined in. They sang to the sun and the blue sky and the frolicking water, and ahead to The Place People Were.

Thin Hair stowed and tied the bone pieces at the bow. He turned and gazed at us. When he smiled his teeth were brighter than the sun.

"We are people," he cried. "Now we are all of the people."

The seas were still high, but to the west all was clear, the ocean bright blue, the whitecaps many. The ice face behind us was distant, white.

"The Place People Were," cried Watcher, pointing. As the clouds raced away, two sharp peaks rose ahead, so distant they seemed a dream.

"They lead us," cried Long Braid. "They have led us. Their spirits will welcome us when we arrive."

"We will arrive this night," said Thin Hair.

Bright Eyes, from the bottom of the canoe, had found her drum. She tied the drum to the thwart. "These are good wives we have found," she cried, pointing at me and the six other captives.

"Yes." Thin Hair opened his arms. "You are of the people now."

The sun shone. The sky was blue. We dried our robes and clothing on the thwarts and the tent. We even unrolled the bear pelt.

For the rest of that day we paddled, and bailed. Always, the two mountains grew closer. Now we could see their base, wavering in the light. A channel lay between. On each side, steep slopes rose to high ridges. The channel was narrow and the ridges high. The big easy waves beneath us rose higher and curved as we passed into the channel, but they did not break. The curved waves ran a long way into the channel and I could see the white curl of their break against the trees and rocks along each side, both far from us as we entered the middle, now all paddling.

The channel stretched east before us, then turned north. By the time we were halfway to the turn the water was flat and there was little wind. As we continued, the walls of the channel closed, steepened. Two ravens passed overhead. High above, I saw an eagle circling. The tops of the ridges held snow and ice. The trees were thick and seemed tall. All along each side of the channel water fell in straight streams, waterfalls from the snow above.

Out of the wind the sun was hot. We had not been hot for a long time. The water was smooth like fresh ice on a pond. As we took a stroke and brought the paddles back for the next stroke, the water draining off the blades splatted against the water passing beneath. First, the thunk of the blades entering the water, a sucking sound as we pulled, then the draining drops off the paddles. Again and again.

Bright Eyes' drum had dried, and she struck a beat.

"Hut-hut-hut."

We ghosted toward the turn. Anger sang and Tree Hide and Rock Hide joined in. Their song echoed off the walls of the channel. The channel was filled with harmony, and the ravens joined in, croaking.

We made the turn to the left. The sun had been behind us, west, and as we turned we came into cool shadow. Here the channel was narrow, 10 canoe lengths wide, but the ridges were still high, and steep. Here the waterfalls were louder. Here the trees came down to the shore, branches even drooping into the water, hiding big rocks and ledges.

We followed the channel, now turning to the right. The channel widened, and the slopes were less steep. The channel made one slight final turn to the left. As we came around this turn we faced a gentle beach. Beyond the beach lay an open meadow. Behind that, slopes rose gently to a low ridge. Beyond that ridge, I saw one more ridge, then peaks and ice. To the right of the beach, many seals lay, sunning on rocks. They raised their heads as they heard us approach.

We came slowly toward the beach. The men placed their paddles aside and climbed higher on the thwarts. We were again in the sun. Here the trees were tall and thick at the base. Their branches spread and hung like long fingers, touching the ground.

Bright Eyes had stopped drumming. The remaining paddlers lifted their paddles and the canoe drifted. The valley was silent and the air still, except for the distant sound of falling water. There was no wind. Beyond the gray and white beach lay the meadow. On the meadow I saw some fallen logs, white with age. The meadow was empty of life. We saw no deer, no smaller animals, nothing.

In the tallest tree, to the left, many ravens perched, silent, watching us.

"The Place People Were," Bright Eyes whispered.

We drifted toward the beach, watching, silent. Some insects buzzed in the canoe. The ravens rose as one and flew away, croaking, loud. An eagle flew down and perched atop another tree, watching us.

We came to the beach. Watcher and Fat Hair left the canoe and waded to shore, then climbed the beach to the meadow. They carried their throwers and darts. Together they wandered across the meadow and vanished in the trees.

The rest of us waited. The sun was bright and strong. To the right a stream emptied into the bay. At the end of the meadow, to the right, a deer poked its head from foliage and peered. Thrower slid from the side of the canoe and crept toward the deer, crouched below the slope of the beach. He moved quickly and quietly. The deer emerged from the trees, ears pricked, cautious.

Thrower rose and threw, all in a single smooth motion. The dart flew at the deer, striking just behind the front legs. The deer leapt once and fell, dead. Thrower retrieved his dart and carried the deer back to the canoe.

The deer was soon cleaned and hanging from the canoe's mast. When Watcher and Fat Hair returned, they trotted across the meadow and waved us in.

We jumped from the canoe, landing in the water, shin deep. We pulled the canoe to the beach, as far as we could, and unloaded everything. We pulled the canoe all the way to the meadow and rolled it on its side, braced.

While Anger, Long Braid and I gathered wood, Thin Hair started a fire. Weeps a Lot, Weeps a Lot More, Woman Too Soon and Watcher took the buckets and filled them in the stream and then sloshed out the interior of the canoe. This they did for a long time. The canoe was big and the canoe stank. Then three others and I took flat stones from the beach and scrubbed the inside of the canoe, spot by spot, then rinsed the canoe with water from the stream. We spent the rest of the afternoon doing this while the others built two lean-to shelters, one for the men, the other for the women. The shelters were not far apart. In ones and twos we went to the stream and washed in the cold water. We also washed our clothes. I could see everyone's ribs, even Anger's. We were all thin.

Once we'd lifted Bright Eyes from the canoe, she was able to stand. She took a few steps, leaning on Watcher's arm. Finally, she released his arm and limped further on her own.

"I now will be able to run free of your attention," she cried to Watcher, laughing.

"I will chase you."

"I hope you will." Bright Eyes practiced walking.

Watcher and Fat Hair had seen deer sign, small animal sign, but no sign of the big animals. They had found no heavy tracks, or piles of dung, or scratch marks against the trunks of trees, always a sure sign of big cats or the great bears. The forest was quiet and still. The sun finally dropped beneath the ridge where the bay turned. The sky turned pink. We posted two people on watch, each with a small fire of their own, closer to the trees, away from the canoe and our shelters.

We ate well. A long time had passed since we had eaten our fill. The deer was sweet.

"We will need more meat," Cold Eye was sitting beside Thin Hair.

"Tomorrow we will gather meat and smoke it." Thin Hair gazed across the water toward the rocks and the seals. Their barking started when the sun fell. They splashed into the water, seeking fish. "If we cannot gather deer, we will take seal."

That evening Thrower showed me how to hold a spear thrower.

That night, we women all stayed in our shelter. For those who were women their flow would begin as the moon came full the next night. Cold Eye was not yet a woman and I knew she wanted to be, and she waited in hopes her time had come. Long Braid and Bright Eyes were hoping this moon time to know for sure they were each carrying a journey child.

"Tell us of our new home," I said to Long Braid. "These people which we now are."

"This is a long and dangerous journey, this journey," Long Braid said. "When we take you at the headland you are not of the people, but you are people. You are our cousins, but you do not know that. By the time we return to our home you are of our people. This journey makes you so. You learn our way of talking, our ways of work and thought, our anger and humor. We come to know each of you as well, your good points, your weaknesses."

"Are there no other people where you live?"

"We have seen none, ever, not in our land, Strong Heart. Now and then one of our people cannot live among us and he or she is banished. Once, in distant memory, a small band left us, choosing to find a new home, and they crossed the flat barren plain and the great river south of us to the mountains beyond the razor stone. Perhaps they have made new homes somewhere, but never has anyone come and visited us. I think they have all died. The animals are many and terrible, everywhere."

"Including where we are going?"

"Everywhere, Strong Heart. We are careful. The animals avoid us when we are gathered, with fires."

"The animal that took Heavy did not avoid us."

"That animal would have never attacked me had I not thrown a brand against its fur." Bright Eyes was rubbing her calf. "The fire made it mad with terror. It was my fault Heavy died."

"Heavy was taken before you threw that brand," Anger said from the other end of the shelter.

Long Braid added a log to the fire. Not far away I heard the men laughing in their shelter. They were telling stories. "When we come to our home we will meet all together at the salmon time, welcome you, and then we choose one from among you to go into the mountains, to our special place, to greet the fall equal day. Mark your arrival in our Marking Place, where we keep our traditions and honor our world with ceremony and drawing. Once this has been done, then you will be fully with us. Just as Bright Eyes here and Anger are with us."

"When is your starving time?" asked Weeps a Lot. She was from the sea of grass and expected a starving time because on the sea of grass there was always a starving time. Tree Hide nodded, and that told me there was always a starving time in the forest and mountains also.

"We rarely have such a time," Long Braid said. All we future wives, from the sea of grass and the forest and mountains, were startled. "In our land we have salmon, and elk, and deer, and plants we can eat in the lowlands. Fruits and berries we gather in the summer up high. We have places that are open and filled with grasses where deer and elk graze. We rarely starve because we always have food from the sea, seals, walrus, sea lion, whale, fish, and shellfish. We do not understand how people survive away from the sea. This is a mystery to us." Long Braid paused, then asked, "Where you are from, your life is difficult, am I right?"

We nodded.

"That is true here, also. We have wolves, lions, cats, and bears. We have years without summer. We have mountains that throw their hearts into the sky. Great floods suddenly sweep to our south over the great river, the water deeper than many canoes are long. We have legends of times when the ocean runs away to hide, then rushes back and covers the earth. We have long dry summers and sometimes great and terrible fires, the sky black with smoke. These are all things that keep our numbers small, force us to travel far for wives and new blood. The oldest among us remember when we found no wives time after time and we dwindled to very few. Those were dark times."

Long Braid raised a hand, then lowered it.

"Our legends also say there were much darker times. There were others like us but not us. Some could sing, like the killer whale can sing. Others could hunt, plan, but remember little, like the bear. When these two joined as man and woman, in the dark time, their children were different. These new people became us. We could sing, and remember our stories with song, and this is what made us people. Even though we were very few, in that time, now before memory, it is said we traveled far, and some remained, becoming you." Long Braid stopped talking, took a breath. "When we became so few, we had to become like the salmon. Salmon grow in our rivers and then leave for the world, every year, and later return to our rivers to lay their eggs. Now we, like the salmon, must leave for the world to find wives."

We fed the fire and the coals glowed. The shelter was warm, the night clear. Stars filled the sky. I could see, over by the trees, the light from the two watcher fires, glowing against the underside of nearby branches. I saw the forms of

the watchers, crouched by the fire, heads turning, watching.
    I slept.

We stayed six days at The Place People Were. During this time we cleaned the canoe, again, then wiped the hull with seal oil. Watcher found a type of moss in the forest, which he brought back and mixed with seal fat. He rolled the moss into short ropes, which he then drove into the crack in the canoe where water had leaked. When wet, the moss and seal fat swelled and blocked the leak. At the same time Watcher went over the rest of the canoe and added moss in places damaged from striking ice.

We fixed our clothing. We washed and dried everything. Anger and Watcher fixed the broken paddles. We took sections of cedar bark from the trees and rewove the sail. Weeps a Lot, Weeps a Lot More and Cold Eye braided new ropes.

Thrower, Fat Hair and Thin Hair took several deer the first day. We cut the meat into strips and hung the strips over the fire.

We made many darts. We cut stone points from the razor stone we had not thrown from the canoe during the storm.

Always we watched the forest.

Thin Hair made a seaweed target and Thrower taught some of us to throw. Tree Hide and Rock Hide had done this before, using a different type of thrower, and they learned easily.

At first everyone laughed when I threw. I was smallest, but I soon learned that if I used a shorter dart the balance was right. I was determined and I practiced. I kept practicing when the others turned to doing other things. I would throw several darts, then walk to the target, find the darts, and retrieve them. At first I could not hit the target. Eventually I hit the target once in three times. By the second day, I was hitting the target every time.

Thrower gave one of his big smiles and walked me a few paces further away from the target. Once again I missed.

"Learn to place your hand behind you in the same place every time. Line up the point ahead of you the same way, too. Learn as you throw how this looks, and then adjust how you aim." Thrower was helpful and patient.

I practiced every day. I practiced alone.

My shoulder became sore. My throwing hand blistered. Thin Hair watched me. I would aim, and throw, five or six darts, again and again. By the third day I was walking several paces from the target. Still I could strike it.

Long Braid and Bright Eyes were now certain they carried journey children. Cold Eye became a woman. Only Cold Eye, Woman Too Soon and Anger remained in the woman shelter during the day. Along with the others who did not yet have their moon time, I worked in camp, drying meat, making rope, and cleaning and drying. Every afternoon, I threw.

Now Thin Hair, Fat Hair, and Watcher did not laugh at me. Pretty Face ridiculed my practice but he was alone. The others would look to see if I was still throwing, and I always was. They would shake their heads, and smile.

Thrower helped me, when I asked for help. By the fourth day I was many paces distant, using the longer darts, and still I could hit the target. The dart would streak ahead, whistling, wobbling, then strike, and pass all the way through the target.

On the fifth day Thin Hair called a contest, and all of us threw. Thrower as always defeated everyone. He was the most accurate, and most consistent. Thin Hair and Bright Eyes made Thrower do his best.

When we were many paces distant, Pretty Face hit the target four times out of six, but I hit the target all six throws. This made him very angry. When the others laughed at him I realized I should have let him win. But this was not my way, to let someone win, and now I was learning a lesson.

"You should have let Pretty Face win," Bright Eyes said to me that night in our shelter. "Some times you must let the other person best you, even if you can best him, because it does not matter to you but matters very much to him. Now you must be careful. Pretty Face is now your enemy."

On the sixth day we packed. I thanked Thrower for teaching me how to throw.

"I did little," he said. When Thrower smiled I forgot about his big ears.

Most of us spent that morning by the canoe. We gathered and folded the robes, packed the bone tools, finished weaving the cedar sail. Pretty Face was on watch to the left, furthest from us, and Thrower to the right.

"Take this to Pretty Face." Long Braid said to me. She had some dried meat, still warm from the smoke. "Offer this meat to him. This will ease the sting of his loss."

I took the meat and walked across the meadow. Pretty Face was leaning on a long staff, watching the forest. His thrower was on the ground, some distance away. I knew this was not what Thin Hair wanted but I knew enough not to say anything to Pretty Face.

"I bring this if you are hungry," I said, doing my best to smile and act friendly.

He would not turn to face me. He remained facing the forest. I walked around and stood in front of him, my back to the trees.

"I bring you some meat," I said again. I stood there,

holding the meat.

Pretty Face would not look me in the eye. He was looking beyond me. Then he saw something. High above me, an eagle cried, twice. At the same time I heard something behind me. It was not loud, and I might not have noticed among the many small sounds around us, but this sound was different, a quick slithering sliding sound. Out of the corner of my eye I saw Thrower move fast.

Pretty Face lunged for his thrower, but his thrower was on the ground and too far away. As he lunged for his weapon he dropped his staff, which I grabbed. A shadow fell across me. I heard a thump behind me.

Thrower screamed. "Cat." He had his thrower up and aimed as I spun to face huge yellow eyes and the dark, clotted fur of an enormous, approaching cat. I realized Pretty Face had seen this animal before he reacted and had not warned me. I also knew he was too far from his thrower. The cat crouched, legs outstretched, claws unsheathed. The mouth was open and the great teeth glistened.

I braced the end of the pole behind my feet to the left and thrust it forward with my right hand high on the staff. My left hand, by my waist, also braced the pole. The cat leapt. It only had to swing its paws together to crush my skull. From somewhere to my side I heard a swishing sound and I knew Thrower had thrown a dart. My right hand was high, holding the pole. Pretty Face was behind me, hopefully now with his thrower up and aimed, but I was between him and the cat.

Thrower's dart thudded into the cat's chest just behind the left shoulder, burying itself deep. The cat screamed. Before Thrower's dart struck, Pretty Face threw. His dart struck my right hand at the fourth finger, was deflected off the pole, and struck the cat's throat. I felt a pinch in the finger. At the same moment I dropped to the earth and rolled aside. I was certain that here I would die.

The cat struck the earth hard, limbs extended, one claw scraping my forehead in a great blow. Almost blind with blood, I saw Pretty Face's heels as he sprinted from the cat. The cat lay next to me on the ground, eyes open and blank. The huge cat was dead. I wiped the blood from my face. Thrower was standing by my side. The other people were all rushing our way. Pretty Face stood, confused.

I felt many things. I knew that now I had an enemy for life in Pretty Face. Besting him in a target game was one thing, but now he had revealed himself a coward before everyone. I felt pain in my hand and through the blood I saw that half my fourth finger was missing. If Pretty Face had not hit my hand and the pole, his dart would have missed the cat. I was surprised to see tears in Thrower's eyes as he observed me. My hand now started to hurt.

"That is a big cat, Strong Heart," Thin Hair said. "Thrower, that was a good throw."

"Pretty Face's throw is what saved her," Thrower said, speaking to Pretty Face.

"Yes," I said. "Thank you, Pretty Face."

"You are growing up," Long Braid said to me later, as she covered my finger with paste after sealing the wound with fire.

"I am still not a woman."

Long Braid's eyes crinkled. "You will become a woman, Strong Heart. Of this I have no doubt. When we reach home you will be the one who goes to the Marking Place. This I think."

My hand hurt. My head hurt. Anger and Watcher were skinning the cat and Weeps a Lot and Weeps a Lot More were staring at me.

The sun was bright but then the sun went away, as if a great cloud had come across the sky.

Then I knew nothing.

After four days they reached the trailhead and parking lot. The deciduous trees were bright with new leaf. William had lost so much weight his pants were falling off. Tom never mentioned the lost spear thrower the whole trip out. Nobody did. William knew Tom was very worried about Sarah's state of mind.

At Tom's, Sarah went to bed early. She was weak. They unpacked their gear, spread everything out in the sun, did laundry. They showered. Then they lingered on Tom's porch.

"You still have a job, Tom?" Myra asked. Tom had been on the phone for an hour.

"I'm not sure, Myra. We have a commission meeting tomorrow; the big push by Buckhorn for their pier lease."

"I'll be there," Myra said. "The Chair of the Fish Commission's going to attend, plus some fishermen. They want to show by their silent presence how important that pier is for our fleet."

"On my phone call, once Fletcher finished shaming me for losing my granddaughter, he made things clear: I toe the party line. It's going to be a long damn meeting."

William had planned to mow his tiny lawn the next day. Now he decided to go to the meeting himself as moral support for Tom.

"Will Sarah be all right?" asked Myra, looking back toward the house. "She believes what she told us really happened.

She had a head injury, maybe a concussion, and she lost a finger. Some small animal must have bitten her, badly, wherever she was, maybe after she fell. I'm worried."

"She has an amazing imagination." Tom leaned a hand on a porch post.

"Who'd believe her?" Myra asked. "Do we believe her? Exactly, Tom. The less said, the better, all around."

"I believe her," William said. "She had a great adventure." Myra was shaking her head. Tom studied William. "But I agree, the less said, the better."

With Sarah still asleep, Myra left for home.

Tom walked William to his car. "I think Roger and his goons took the tube, 'Eye. All I have left is that little sliver. At least we got up there to fix Bob-Bob's grave. And I guess in the end the words you spoke at his grave worked. Something worked. Sarah lived. But I don't think I'm done, not yet, not until I either get that tube back or confirm what I held and carried all these years. I want to date that spear thrower, just for my own information. Seems the least I can do if the thing's otherwise lost."

"So take the sliver over to the university."

"Are you kidding? This archeological community is damn small, especially because of this conference coming up. If I took that sliver to the university, word might get out they were dating something from the inner park. One hint, just a hint, that something very old came out of that valley, and Buckhorn's goons would be all over me. Not to mention all the gods in the archeological community, whose standings might be threatened by something that old being found that far in the park. Most of those experts believe the park was empty in ancient times. That sliver would just disappear like the atlatl did. I want your help on this one, if you agree. This is personal."

"Now I'm confused. I'm just a merchant sailor, Tom."

"You're the best naturalist I've ever known, 'Eye. Myra told me she thinks that atlatl was fossilized bone. She also confirmed that your friend over in Russia, the guy you mentioned at the start of this trip, does more than collect mammoth tusks."

"He has a lot of tusks, Tom."

"Myra said he's pretty well known."

"In Russia, sure. But he told me Russian ice age experts aren't very well respected over here."

"Exactly. He's not in the network. But he is an expert."

"Alec tells me his bear hunting stories. He's a hobbyist. His son is the expert."

Tom reached in his pants pocket, pulled out a two-inch by one-inch plastic case with a hard lid. "Here's the sliver. Will you ask your friend to identify what bone it is; date it?"

William opened the case. There, in smooth cloth packing, rested a dark sliver, like a slice from a thick wooden match. "Jesus, Tom. I could lose this."

"You never lose anything, 'Eye. Just take that with you, ask him to get an age, if he can. The end of this summer, I'll take the sliver back up in the park, place it near Bob-Bob. Then I'll have done all I can."

William held the sliver. It felt like a piece of old bone. "I'll see what I can do. You going to be okay with Sarah, Tom?"

"This won't be easy. She's subdued. Quiet. It's going to be day to day, with her."

"Long time each day, you working and her home."

"Myra said she'd keep Sarah busy over at the tribal offices. She said she needs help catching up. You've got a fine daughter, 'Eye."

"She was a big help, this trip."

"That was a stupid damn thing you suggested, 'Eye, taking Sarah up there. And I was a fool to agree. Unconscionable. Sarah could have died. Should have died."

"But she didn't."

"No, but she seems changed. Probably be scarred forever."

"Sarah is the most fearless human being I've ever known, Tom. I don't know what happened to her up there, none of us do. Of course she's not the same."

"We nearly killed her."

"Tom, you put your grandfather to rest. His great-great granddaughter was there and whatever else happens, her life from now on holds that memory. You took the spear thrower back up there, and that thrower may be there still. I didn't collapse. You weren't hurt. Sarah survived, well enough to come out under her own steam. Myra has the satisfaction of knowing she kept us old geezers going. Sarah experienced some extraordinary visions."

"Do you really believe her story, 'Eye, like you told Myra?"

"She believes it was true, Tom. I respect her belief."

"Still, 'Eye, that was irresponsible of me. Us."

"Tom, 45 years ago when you went up there and your grandfather died and you buried him, you were what, 21? Now your granddaughter went up there at age 13 with her grandfather. She went missing for eight days, alone, in the cold, the rain, the forest. It's no wonder she's subdued. Have a little faith, Tom. She has a strong heart. A strong heart."

"I hate it when you go all shaman on me, 'Eye." Tom was smiling.

"In my blood, Tom. In your blood, too, I now know. "

"Not as much, by a long shot."

"What do they call you down at the maintenance shop? Nuts 'n Bolts? That's a perfect name for you."

"When are you sailing again?"

"Friday. They won't recognize my new thin self when I come up the gangway."

"Get some new pants, those things are so loose it looks like you're wearing Depends beneath them."

The next day William attended the commission meeting to support Tom, but he arrived late. By the time he drove into the parking lot, Myra and her tribal delegation were outside, standing aimlessly.

The sun was out, the air balmy.

Myra walked over. "Tom was just fired, dad. Nastily and publicly. Lynch brought a motion which carried two to one. Tom's up in his office getting his stuff. Lynch wanted him gone. And now they're going to vote for the Buckhorn deal, the pier lease, close out the tribal fishermen, build Lynch's center."

William wasn't surprised. "Fletcher Lynch gets what he wants, Myra. Always has."

"More amazing, they went through all that and nobody seems to know yet this mining operation will be up in the park."

"I'll bet few people know Lynch is up to his elbows in this, either. He's Buckhorn's partner using Tom's family's old claim, Myra."

"Small town politics, dad. You know."

Tom emerged from a side door, carrying a box. Some of the people inside the commission meeting turned to look out the windows as Tom left. Beyond them, on the dais, William caught a glint from Lynch's glasses. He was watching Tom, too.

Tom approached Myra and William. "It was clear as soon as executive session started Lynch and the attorney had something cooked up."

"Tom," Myra said, "Fletcher Lynch is a vengeful, spiteful, small man. Most people in this town loathe him. He thinks that vote for Buckhorn will get him re-elected but what he just did to you, people won't like that. You're well respected here, Tom, no matter what Fletcher Lynch says. What an asshole." Myra gave Tom a hug.

Tom seemed fine. In fact he seemed relieved.

"Can they really fire you like that?" William asked.

"In that job, I'm an at-will employee, 'Eye. They can fire me as soon as two of the three commissioners vote." Tom turned away from the port offices. "I'll run down to the maintenance shop, say my goodbyes. Those are the guys I know, anyway. I think Ruth and Fletcher are going to try to take Sarah back, too; he made that clear to me. According to him and a lot of other people, I'm irresponsible, careless, and show serious lack of judgment."

"I'd take her, if she's willing," Myra said. "I like her. Maybe some of her orneriness will rub off on me."

Before Tom walked to his car he pressed William's shoulder. "Don't forget, 'Eye, that favor in Petropavlosk."

A day later, before returning to Seattle to rejoin the ship, William went to see Sarah. She was sitting on Tom's front porch, drinking lemonade. It was the first hot day of spring. She had a new brass pin in her nose.

"You doing all right, Sarah?"

"Hi, William. I read the paper. That's shitty, what my step-grandfather did."

"Yep. Are you going to go to school for the rest of the year?"

"I start next week."

"You don't seem too unhappy about it."

"Whatever."

"How's your finger? Your bruised head?"

"Better."

William sat in the chair next to Sarah. She had her feet up on the porch railing. "Sarah, I'm going to the ship. I'll be back in about two months, before the summer's over. You take care of your grandfather."

"Myra said I could stay with her, sometimes."

"Anything but Fletcher and Ruth, right?"

"I won't say anything, William, about the trip."

"Sarah, we know there's more you didn't tell us. Right?" Sarah's chin rose and fell. "I hope someday you do tell us, but for now, the less said to anyone – anyone – the better. You'll have trouble enough, fitting in here, without people hearing stories about your adventures."

Sarah handed William a manila folder from beneath her chair. Inside were copies of her sketches: Myra, the spider web, William, the bear, and the two sides of the atlatl. "Tom made copies. These are for you, on the ship."

"Thank you. These are a great gift, Sarah."

"William?" Sarah turned to William. She seemed 10 years old. "Am I crazy? What I told you guys?"

"I wish I could have a vision like that."

"It was real, William. It felt real."

"Do you feel crazy?" Sarah shook her head. "You sure don't look crazy to me, Sarah."

"I'll keep my mouth shut."

"Thanks, Sarah. Tom and Myra and I are considered irresponsible already. Your story gets out, we'll all of us be in real trouble."

"They'll lock me up, maybe."

"You'd escape."

"Easy."

"Take care, Sarah."

"William? One more thing, I didn't tell you."

"I know. Maybe someday we'll hear the rest of what happened, how you found your way to our camp. When you're ready."

"No, I mean something else." William had been rising to leave. He sat down. "I know where the spear thrower is, William. When I walked back to the camp from Bob-Bob's grave I was pissed at all of you. I grabbed the case. I had it when I fell. I don't remember having it with me, down there, but I know it's there. Somewhere down there. I think I could find it again." Sarah's gaze was direct, unblinking. William realized she was perfectly capable of returning to the place where she had been trapped.

Where did this girl find such courage?

William drove to Seattle, via the Edmonds ferry, and joined the ship, *Seattle Express*.

They had a busy trip. They were carrying a lot of stuff north, containers on deck, machinery, frozen food, supplies, lumber for St. Paul and the NOAA weather base, plus fish for Petropavlosk. When they got to Petro, William was able to get off the ship for a few hours to see Alec. He had the sliver and planned to ask Alec for help dating it.

He'd emailed Alec from the ship's system to tell him he was coming. When he got through the port gate, he was surprised to see Alec's son, Sergei, standing there, not Alec.

"Sergei. Nice to see you. Where's Alec?"

Sergei was as tall as William, but thin, built like the cross-country skier he had been as a youth. He was not smiling. William threw his bag in the car.

"He will tell you," Sergei said, starting the car. "He had things to do at the museum today. We will meet him when we get there."

Petro lies at 53 degrees north latitude, same as Haida Gwaii. That June, just before the summer solstice, the days were long, the twilight evenings endless. Alec lived 30 miles south of Petro near a hot spring, on a knoll surrounded by birches and spruce. His daughter was away, studying for a nursing degree somewhere. William had thought Sergei lived in Magadan, south by the Chinese border, a big city. He knew Sergei held

➤

a doctorate as a genetic scientist. He'd studied in California. They'd met once or twice when William had visited earlier. Alec was proud of him.

William knew something was wrong as soon as Alec walked from his front door to meet him. William had lost weight during the hike, but Alec had lost more. When he'd seen Alec the last time he'd been almost as big as William, covered with a winter pelt, as he would say, robust, ruddy. He now was drawn, pale. His eyes still blazed and he'd lost none of his bushy eyebrows.

"Come," he said. "Sergei will drive."

They went to the hot spring, as always. This was a former camp for party officials, close to Alec's home and museum. The springs themselves were a deep pool and several smaller pools, lined with rough concrete, reached via steep stairs, surrounded by bare lights strung on poles. The water was sulphuric and hot. After two weeks on the ship it was heaven to sink into the brine, lean back, look at the sky above. Across lounged a couple, all over each other. They were both large. Three younger women were in the smaller pools, laughing.

When Sergei walked from the dressing room to the pool, the three women noticed. He was thin, but thin the way an elite athlete is thin. His father, standing beside him, was thin the way a man with a terminal illness is thin, bones jutting, skin pale, loose and hanging. Alec needed help descending the three steps to sit in the pool. William wondered what was wrong, how much time he had.

"You have lost much weight, William. What is your secret?"

"Alec, I went on a two-week hiking trip. The trip was difficult. I lost weight."

"You look very well. Better than I have ever seen you. I should take such a hiking trip myself, but as you can see, my winter coat has left, deserted me."

"What is it, Alec?"

Alec sighed. "This battle is one I will not win, William. Seven bears, three years in Afghanistan, two times, shot. All those, I survived. This lymphoma, I will not. I laugh because otherwise I cry."

Sergei was staring into the water, jaw tight.

"You cannot come to the conference, can you?"

"I will be with my ancestors, William. Sergei will deliver my paper, and his." Alec seemed small next to his son. "We were to have a battle, he and I, at that conference. My paper argues that humans lived in Berengia many years ago, and may have travelled to North America long, long ago. His paper argues that genetic data shows that humans came to North America at most 15 thousand years ago." Wincing, Alec shifted his body. "I was to be the token other point of view, there. The one paper arguing for an older arrival. Me, a hobbyist."

"You are not a token, father. But you are wrong."

Alec's booming laugh had left him. Now he sounded reedy. "At least we still argue. We agree, Sergei and I, that modern man arose 70 to 100 thousand years ago. Something happened then, because while brain size did not change, behavior did. Burials, art, painting appeared. We also agree that the Toba eruption, 75 thousand years ago, created a decades-long dark period, due to the ash in the air. Humans dwindled to a few hundred, maybe a few dozen. From this small group, all modern humanity arose." Sergei was nodding. Then he smiled, rueful, and started shaking his head as Alec continued. "I speculate that moderns may have arisen in Berengia, scattered over the earth from there. Arisen when Neanderthal joined with Erectus, or Denisovian, and the mixture made us modern."

"Too cold, that far north, father. Ridiculous. Absurd. And convenient, to argue this occurred on a land mass now beneath the sea. Too convenient."

William felt the hot water soothe his legs. Sergei was still shaking his head. William realized this was an argument Sergei and his father had had many times. He saw how much Sergei would miss this battle when Alec died.

"I was looking forward to sailing with you on the ship, Alec."

"I, too, William." Alec gently tapped his son on the shoulder. "I am trying to convince Sergei to take my place on that ship. He needs to go to California for a few days before the conference and I am hoping he will travel with you on the ship first. Perhaps you will show him this park you speak so highly of. Like you, Sergei is a fisherman, but he fishes for the delight, not for the money."

"We have some great trout fishing, Sergei."

"I should remain here, with you, father."

"No. William, my revenge on my son is he must deliver my paper. He will have to argue against himself."

Sergei frowned. The women across the way stared at him.

"A romantic," Sergei said. "My father here has romantic notions about ancient history. I use data."

Alec snorted. "Pah. Every year there is a new theory after every new find. And you speak of romantic notions, Sergei. You are 37, yet never a wife. You had a future wife in Vera but she broke your heart 10 years ago. Now you have girlfriends. Many girlfriends. I was hoping for grandchildren. Don't you have a daughter, William?"

William pictured Myra with Sergei. Myra had nothing but contempt for scoundrels and players. But a scoundrel and player with a doctorate in genetic biology? William started to laugh. "Myra has a mind of her own, Alec." Then he settled back deeper into the wonderful brine. He knew Alec would miss his son, but he knew Sergei would miss his father more.

"Well," William said, "I have a story for both of you. One I think you will both find interesting."

Alec coughed, racking. Sergei fetched him some water.

They sat in that hot pool for hours while the afternoon sun crossed the sky. The couple across from them left, the three women left. Alec and Sergei listened as William told his tale of the journey, Sarah's sighting, her disappearance, and her return. At one point he rose from the pool, retrieved his pack, and showed them the copies of Sarah's sketches. Then he told them Sarah's tale, just as she had told it to Tom, Myra and him.

Back at Alec's house, Alec asked if William would leave the atlatl sketches with him, and he did. It was time to return to the ship. William reached in his pocket and removed the case holding the sliver.

"Tom took this years ago, to have the atlatl dated, but he never got around to it. As I told you, the atlatl's missing, lost somewhere up where Sarah disappeared. Can you date this sliver?"

Alec removed the sliver from the case. "This is bone. Yes, I think I can date this. I must invent a small story for the university here. A month, perhaps."

"The less said the better, Alec."

"Nobody listens to me these days, William. I have been humored these past few years, invited to conferences as a gesture only, welcomed as a hobbyist. My theories of the past are not mainstream."

"He is lying, as always," Sergei said. "His theories are junk, but many experts pay attention to him. Even I pay attention, despite my training. The atlatl and sliver interest me, very much. I will help with this."

"William you must return to that valley. You must retrieve that atlatl. You must." Alec was weak but intent. "If she took it and can find it again, then you will be able to answer many questions. Many."

William said goodbye to Alec. They shook hands. Alec had

been a good friend and William was not someone who had many friends. He held the picture of Alec standing stooped before his door, holding the copies of the atlatl drawings, watching them leave. William knew he would never see Alec again.

They drove back to Petropavlosk. The waning moon hovered over the gravel road. When they reached the port gate, William had to wake the sole customs agent on duty. The summer solstice, even near midnight, kept the sky light.

"After hearing your story, William, I will come on this ship in August to visit you, see this park. This is my father's wish. Now this is my wish, too. Your story was most interesting. Most interesting."

William took the ship back to St. Paul, then Dutch Harbor, then Seattle. In Dutch, he went ashore, went online, and learned from Sergei that Alec had died three days after he visited.

The rest of his trip across the Gulf of Alaska was easy. They docked in Seattle, but because they had to do some emergency repairs on one of the hatches, he was unable to get off the ship. He did manage to telephone Tom.

"What did you learn, 'Eye? How old is that splinter?"

"I won't know for another trip, Tom. I just left it with Alec and Sergei. Alec was very ill when I got there and he passed away just after I left. I'm pretty sure Sergei is following up on the sliver. How's Sarah?"

"Ruth and Fletcher got Sarah back, 'Eye. They went to child services and then contacted Sarah's stepfather in Europe. I fought them, but the stepfather supported Ruth and Fletcher after he learned where we'd taken her. They put her in school to finish the year. Some Sol Duc members at that school told Myra Sarah seemed like a zombie. She never talked, sat in class quiet, and went home alone on the bus."

"You haven't seen her at all?"

"Talked to her on the phone twice, that's all. That bastard Lynch won't let me over there. But she's not the same, 'Eye. Ruth doesn't know what to do; she's even called me. Says Sarah stays at home. Disappears out in the back yard. Plays with sticks. They took her to Seattle, had her checked out. The doctors said Sarah's had a great shock. The dehydration, exhaustion, the lost finger, the head injury, may take months to recover. Most disturbing to me, she does whatever Ruth and Fletcher ask. Ruth thinks it's because she and Fletcher provide a better home environment. I'm damn worried."

"Did Sarah say anything to you about the atlatl, Tom? The spear thrower?"

"The atlatl? No, nothing."

"She told me she took the thrower, not the surveyors. Says she knows where it is. I think she wants to go back and find it."

"I was too rough on her about seeing that bear, wasn't I, 'Eye?"

"You were honest, Tom. Being honest with a child is a gift. I think she accepts you as her grandfather and the reason she's so angry at you is because what you think matters to her."

"I'd sure like to hear the rest of her tale, 'Eye. I don't think she knows that, though. She knew I wanted her to stay with me after we came out. I fought to keep her from Lynch's, but Ruth is her blood, too."

"I know."

"So she took my atlatl."

"I think she thought Myra was going to talk you into bringing it out, for use as an artifact, and Sarah wanted to help you honor your wish that the thrower remain in there."

"Now even I'd like to find that thing to stop Buckhorn and Lynch, 'Eye."

"Ruth and Fletcher have any idea about all this?"

"Not a clue, unless Sarah said something. Hell, it's bad enough, her over there, if they found out what she's been saying they'd put her away somewhere."

"Well, Tom, stand by. I'll be back in a month."

In Petropavlosk, two weeks later, Sergei came aboard after passing through the tiny customs shack at the port. His visa was in proper order. He had two enormous bags, so large that in the end they used the stores crane to bring them to the deck. William brought him up to his cabin. Sergei met Captain Steve, who, desiring a chess opponent, was on his best behavior.

When they left the harbor the captain set the course and remained on the bridge. William made fresh coffee. He seated himself in the secured chair near the wheel and Sergei braced on his stool, leaning an elbow on the railing that extended beneath the windows facing forward. He kept looking around, nodding.

"Alec went fast," William said. "Was it difficult?"

"He was in pain, of course. But he died at peace, still defending his ridiculous theories. I am donating his museum contents to the state museum in Petropavlosk. My sister came back from school and we arranged the funeral." Sergei reached in his pocket, pulled out the plastic case. "Your friend will have little remaining to take into the park, William. The dating process consumes material."

William opened the case. Little remained of the sliver. "What did you learn?"

"I have good news and bad news." Sergei pointed at the case. "This is mammoth. Unmistakable. I knew as soon as I first saw it, but tested it nevertheless. This would be the first atlatl ever found made of mammoth. This makes it an amazing find, if you could recover it. This is the good news. Unfortunately the dating process failed. This is the bad news."

"It didn't work?"

"Many times this happens, if the material was in acidic water, if the way it is fossilized brings in other chemicals with different signatures, if it is older than carbon dating can register. We need to find that piece, William. There are other dating methods, but we need more material. I took a small piece of the splinter, had its DNA checked also, but the results were confusing. Very confusing." Sergei paused, pursed his lips. William expected him to add something else, but he did not. Then he went on, "William, think of it. You may have seen and handled an artifact created and used by the first people who came to your land. Such a find would be dramatic. We must convince Sarah to return to the park. "

"Even if found, Sergei, even if Sarah goes back up there and finds wherever she dropped it, there is no proof it was originally found or placed where Tom first saw it. For all Tom knows, it could have been given to his grandfather, or his great-great grandfather, by someone else after discovering it in, say, South America. Or New York."

"But if we can recover it, then it can be properly dated, analyzed. Imagine. A spear thrower carried by the first people who ever visited the western hemisphere. Now that would be the paper to deliver at that conference. Sensational. I would go to the podium, everyone expecting a dull discussion about genetic clades and DNA, and instead I would raise the spear thrower, really tell a story. With your permission, of course." Sergei's eyes burned, looking forward, imagining.

The ship began to work easily in a gentle southeast swell. The roll was slow, steady, back and forth. Sergei braced on his stool. The bow rose, then fell. The ship drove ahead. Twilight was descending. The water ahead darkened as it met the sky, seamless, merging at the eastern horizon, beyond which lay, far to the east, past the Aleutians, past southeast Alaska, past British Columbia, the silent peaks of the Olympics awaiting the next dawn. On the bridge, fans hissed, the deck vibrated, and steel creaked. Steve connected his iPod to a small speaker mounted by the chart table, began playing blues. Lights glowed on the electronic console, the radar screen. Here in the dark throbbing wheelhouse they were secure, comfortable, and well underway.

"So we are sailing over the land bridge, the route taken by the first people, then?" Sergei waved an arm toward the water outside, the Bering Sea.

"We're not far away, Sergei."

"I am pleased to think I am following the ancient route. This is one reason I wanted to ride this ship."

"You'd think there'd be legends, memories, of such a journey." Steve had been working on the chart table.

"That time was at least 12 thousand years ago, sir." Sergei got off the stool and stood, bracing as the ship slowly rolled. "At 30 years a generation, 400 generations have lived and died. Memory is short. The eyewitnesses to history die. Those who hear the eyewitnesses die. Stories become second, third, fourth hand. Who among us knows what our great grandparents did? Do you?" Steve shook his head. "I am not surprised there is no memory of those times of ice, of the big mammals. All we have, today, are random discoveries, debris, ancient garbage, fossilized shit, occasional bones and tools, and now genetic sequences. Theories. Many theories. To think my ancestors may have been the first to reach your land. To think you might be my cousin, William."

"We have always been there, Sergei. This means you may be my cousin." This was an argument William had had had with Alec many times.

"I am glad I chose to make this trip, William." Sergei stretched. "I feel I am walking an ancient path."

They stopped in St. Paul on the way to Dutch Harbor

and there they discharged some empty containers. The weather was clear when they arrived and they could see the high headland rising above tiny St. Paul harbor from well offshore. William and Sergei went ashore and hiked as high as they could. From that high the view was far. They could see hundreds of square miles of ocean.

They arrived in Seattle at the end of the third week in August. The skies were clear, the sun hot. Riding the ferry across to the peninsula, they had to wait an hour because the Friday weekend traffic had backed up even before noontime. On the ferry, tourists took pictures from the rail and children ran screaming across the upper decks. Just off the ferry landing, they saw dozens of skiffs, fishermen with rod and reel seeking salmon. Mt. Rainier loomed to the south, huge and white. To the north, Mt. Baker gleamed even whiter than Rainier. The Olympics stood like a wall to the west, sharp against the sky, peaks still with patches of snow.

As they drove through Port Angeles, William saw signs in lawns. No Mining. We Want Jobs. Use Our Pier. No Buckhorn. Yes, We Need Buckhorn.

The battle was on, it seemed.

They stopped in town for groceries.

At William's place, they unloaded his car. His lawn was brown. He showed Sergei the spare bedroom. They returned outside to get their bags.

William was about to call Tom when Tom drove in and parked behind William's dusty car. "Saw you in the store but you were just leaving, William. Is this Sergei?" Tom and Sergei shook hands. "Sorry to hear about your father, Sergei. William here really liked him. Spoke of him often. Is that a fishing rod in your pack?"

William pulled the plastic box holding the sliver from his pocket. "Here's what's left of the sliver, Tom."

Tom opened the box and poked the tiny sliver. "What's it made of?" Tom pointed into the box.

"Mammoth bone. We know that," said Sergei.

"How old?"

"At least 12 thousand years, perhaps more." Tom whistled. "We tried the carbon dating method, and could not get a reading. Often, this happens. But this is mammoth, and that itself makes this an astounding find. This could have come from a spear thrower fashioned by the first people who visited this land."

"'Eye, we'll have to go get that atlatl."

"Only if we can get permission to take Sarah back in the park," William said. "How is she, by the way?"

"Not good, 'Eye. Ruth called me again last week. You know what that must have cost her. Says Sarah won't leave the property. Says all she's been doing is playing with willows and branches in the back yard. I'm worried."

A jeep stopped out front. Myra got out from the passenger side. Myra was with Pete, one of the surveyors who had helped them find Sarah the previous spring. Pete got out, too. Tom put the sliver back in the small case and placed the case in a pocket.

Myra was in shorts and a short-sleeved shirt. Her long braids hung beneath a hat. She was dusty and her hands were dirty. Pete was dusty too. They seemed at ease together as they walked across the small front lawn.

"Dad. Tom." Myra did not look happy. "We have a problem."

Pete stood uncomfortably behind Myra. Myra was focused only on Tom.

William stepped forward. "Sergei, this is, er, Pete, Myra's friend, and this is my daughter, Myra. Myra, this is Sergei,

Alec's son. He came across on the ship with me. He'll be with me here for a few weeks. He wants to see the park."

Pete shook Sergei's hand. Next to Sergei, Pete was short.

"Tom." Myra sounded urgent. "Have you heard from Ruth?"

"Not since last week. Why?"

"Sarah's been with me since last night. She showed up about seven o'clock. I hadn't seen her for weeks." Myra tugged Tom and William away from Sergei and Pete. "Pete's been helping me rebuild my kitchen. We're putting in a new sink. Now Sarah's helping us, too."

"Have you phoned Ruth and told her where Sarah is?"

"No, Tom. Sarah said Lynch pulled a Mitch on her. She was upset."

"Pulled a Mitch?"

"Don't you remember, Tom? On our trip she said her stepfather's son, Mitch Junior, came after her. Whatever he tried to do, Sarah says Fletcher Lynch tried to do."

Tom went pale. "Do you believe her, Myra?"

"She believes it, Tom. She knows the consequences of running away. She'll be sent away, to foster care, or juvie, until her stepfather calls for her. She knows that, and she'll do anything to avoid that. Yet she still ran anyway."

"Who knows she's at your place?" Tom asked.

"Well, me, Pete, now you guys."

"Will Pete tell Lynch? Doesn't he work for Buckhorn?" William asked.

"I think he can be trusted, dad."

William watched Pete. He was trying to talk to Sergei. Sergei was half listening, while watching them. "No call from Ruth, Tom?" William asked. It was mid-afternoon. Sarah had been away for nearly a day.

"Nothing, 'Eye. No visits, either, to see if Sarah was with me. Jesus." Tom kicked the ground. "Her word against Lynch's, unless there's physical evidence."

"He didn't rape her, Tom," said Myra. "Sarah was clear about that. She said she nailed him, that's the word she used, nailed him, when he came at her."

"Hit him? Was she bruised herself?"

"No. She said she gave him a good one with a dart, right across the kisser."

"Dart? You mean, like from a spear thrower?" Tom asked.

"I think so, Tom. She hurt Lynch, somehow. Now she's afraid, and alone."

"And if she's found she'll be returned to the Lynch's. Or placed in a youth home somewhere while they investigate her allegations. My God." Tom paused, thinking. William felt Tom quivering beside him. Tom was pissed. "That son of a bitch Lynch abused my daughter all those years ago and she ran away, at 15, and now he's done it again, to my granddaughter. And Ruth must know what's going on and is afraid to confirm it. Maybe she fears him." Tom looked back at Sergei and Pete, who had wandered to Pete's jeep, where Pete was showing Sergei a box of fishing lures. "They won't place her with me, not after last spring. Lynch accused me of lack of judgment. Carelessness. Possible dementia. Damn."

"How much does Sergei know?" Myra asked, her eye on Sergei and Pete.

"I told him and his father Sarah's tale when I saw them in July. Thought that was the least I could do, after they agreed to test the sliver. Sergei wants to see where all this happened, because his father was planning to go there himself, before he got sick. Sergei wants to go back in there, get the thrower, and date it properly."

Myra observed Sergei. She seemed suspicious. "Dad, if we go back in there with Sarah to find the atlatl, we can't let anyone know what we're doing. She has to disappear, and so must we." Myra shook her head. "Yet if she stays here, she'll be placed somewhere, and no place is safe."

"At some point, Lynch and Ruth will have to sound the alarm if she's missing," said Tom. "And if we took her back in there we'll all be kidnappers, again, and irresponsible, again."

"What choice do we have?" Myra scuffed her toe in the grass. "If Sarah stays with me they'll figure out where she is eventually, with me on the res, and come for her. If we return her, it's back to Lynch's abuse, Ruth's silence. Or she enters the foster system and maybe even worse. She deserves better than that."

"If we take her, we just hold off the inevitable. When we come out she'll be taken then, Myra." William spoke quietly. Pete and Sergei were still occupied with fishing lures. William imagined Sarah hauled away by the authorities, branded as a half-crazy, out-of-control, problem child. Then he pictured her returning from the park days from now with an ancient atlatl. Wouldn't this give her some credibility to stand up to Lynch? "If we take her back into the park at least she'll have some distance from the event with Lynch, and maybe we'll find the atlatl. If we return with that, and Sarah found it, that might help."

"If we're going to go, we need to leave today, 'Eye," Tom said. "I can't believe we're even talking about this. Myra, what about Pete?"

"I don't know. He's paid by Buckhorn and he knows I hate them. That's a whole place we never talk about, his beliefs in the value of this mining and my objections. He'll figure out where we've gone fast, though. He's damn smart."

"Will he remain quiet?"

"I don't know, Tom. We're not dating, really. He's a decent guy. He'll give me a ride back to my place now. I'll tell him I'm going to wait there for someone to come for Sarah. He's got to leave, anyway, he's going to the Mariners game tonight with some friends. He wanted me to go too but then Sarah showed up."

After Myra and Pete left, William explained to Sergei what had happened.

"Now? Today?"

"You wanted to go into the park, Sergei."

"Yes, William, but like this? This feels like escaping into the park. Your daughter does not like me, I can see that. I don't want my presence to make this impossible."

"Sergei, we need to take that girl out of here, otherwise she will be forced to go back with the Lynches."

"But surely, William, Tom could take her to live with him?"

"I'd like to think so, but Tom and Myra and I are the ones who took her away from school last spring without permission, into the park, and then lost her for eight days. Tom's been fired. Lynch has been telling stories that Tom has dementia and that Myra and I are just a couple of natives. I don't think the state foster system will let Tom have her."

From William's shabby front lawn, the ridge of the Olympics towered. Mt. Angeles and Hurricane Hill shone brightly in the sun. Sergei studied the view and started to smile. "I am your captive, it seems. Like you, I very much would like to retrieve that spear thrower. How can I help?"

William and Sergei quickly packed. Sarah was at Myra's, also packing. After seeing his granddaughter, Tom returned home, packed his own gear, and then came over to William's place. On the way, he stopped at the park offices to pick up a small radio to receive weather reports. They knew if they left their vehicles at the trailhead, they would show everyone where they had all gone. Myra arranged for two friends, tribal members, to drive them to the trailhead, then return their vehicles to their homes.

"'Eye, now I need you to come with me, as my witness, before we leave. I need to have a heart to heart with Fletcher Lynch."

Tom had talked with Sarah, who told him what had happened. Tom was very angry.

William rode with Tom over to Port Angeles. They drove into Fletcher and Ruth Lynch's drive. Tom knocked on the door. William stood behind him. Ruth opened the door. She was stiff, rigid. William didn't think she was surprised to see Tom.

"I need to talk to Fletcher. And you." Tom was unflinching. "I know he's here."

Ruth saw William, looming behind Tom. "Why is he here?"

"Witness," Tom said, just as Fletcher Lynch appeared in the hall. A large bandage ran from below his nose to his chin. Whatever Sarah used had been sharp.

"Ruth, call the police, please." Fletcher spoke well enough.

➤

"I know Sarah is not here." Tom stepped into the doorway. Ruth could not close the door on him. "I know where she is. I just talked to her. I know what happened."

Ruth's brow furrowed. She seemed confused. She turned to Fletcher.

Lynch stepped forward and pulled Ruth back from the door. "That girl went crazy, tried to kill me. Now it seems she's sending her grandfather to our home to threaten us."

Tom ignored Lynch. He spoke to Ruth. "I always believed when Becky ran away there was more to her leaving than a drug problem and immaturity." Ruth was confused, but Tom pressed on anyway. "I didn't know Fletcher Lynch had a problem with little girls, not then. First, my daughter. Your daughter too, Ruth." Lynch tried to pull his wife away from the door. Ruth resisted. William could see, in her face, dawning awareness. "Fletcher, yesterday you tried to abuse my granddaughter, a 13 year old girl. You tried to get her to play with you, and then threatened to send her away to foster care unless she cooperated." Tom stood straight, bearing down on Lynch. Ruth, face gone pale, pulled her arm from Lynch's grasp. "Sarah is a fugitive and needs protection," said Tom, "protection from you, the abuser."

"This is just a story, a fantasy," Lynch turned to Ruth. "Honey, this is ridiculous."

Ruth, William could see, did not think this ridiculous at all. She held the wall for support, mouth partly open, staring at her husband.

Lynch turned back to Tom. "Leave. You are not welcome here."

"I know that's why you didn't call me today, Ruth, or why Fletcher here didn't come over to see where Sarah was. I think you knew what might have happened, and you didn't want to know. I'm sorry, but you have to know, because that young girl is having a rough time and she's your blood. Our blood. Ruth, I'm sorry."

When the door closed, Ruth's cry echoed through the walls. They started away from the house,

"They won't call out the posse for a while, 'Eye. Jesus. Ruth always pissed me off, but Jesus. She's been blinding herself, all this time. Let's grab Sarah, Myra and Sergei and get out of here. This trip, I don't think Sarah will be complaining, given her alternative back here."

"She didn't complain last trip, Tom."

"She complained about me."

"Well, maybe she had her reasons. This time, out there, don't give her any reasons."

Myra's two friends drove them to the trailhead. Once dropped off, they arranged their gear and mounted their packs. Sergei loaded his pack some distance away. William helped Sarah put on her pack. He was surprised to see his aluminum fishing rod case on Sarah's pack, four feet long, three inches in diameter. "You're going to try fishing? That's an awkward thing to carry when we go off trail. It'll catch branches."

"Not fishing, William." Sarah followed Tom onto the trail. Sergei followed Sarah. Myra and William were alone in the parking lot. The sun would set within two hours.

"Myra, what about your job?"

"I talked to my boss, Marcie. Fortunately, she hadn't left for the day. I explained that Sarah was fleeing a bad situation and I needed to take some unpaid time to work with her."

"Tom might have some claim to Sarah, Myra. He's Sarah's grandfather. But you and me? We aren't family. "

"Sarah thinks we're family."

His pack was big and heavy, as always. He didn't weigh as much as he did at the start of the last trip but the pack still hurt.

"Dad, are you worried you aren't up to this?"

"We're going to have to move fast, Myra."

"Look, dad, you were fine by the end of the last trip. You'll be fine this time too. Just be careful."

They started in. Once the trail entered the trees the light

➤

grew dim. The sun, to the right, barely lay above the ridges. The light was long, yellow, slanting.

A half-mile in, Sergei was already sitting beside the trail, pack off, tending to his feet. He waved them on. He and Myra had not spoken to each other. Just beyond, Tom and Sarah had stopped. As soon as William and Myra appeared, they headed off.

William caught up with Sarah. She shrugged ahead, her small form leaning forward, pack rising above her shoulders and head. He could see the top of her knit hat, bobbing. The rod holder stuck up high. She had grabbed a branch from alongside the trail for a walking stick. The stick plunked on the ground as she walked.

Tom was further ahead, setting a fast pace. They wanted to camp near the stream where Sarah had fallen in the previous trip.

"Why are you bringing my fishing holder if you aren't going to be fishing?" The battered rod holder had travelled with William for many miles. It was strange to see it on someone else's pack.

"My experiment," she said. "We get up there, I'll show you."

Their voices echoed through the dark trees.

"Experiment?"

"There was nothing to do there." Sarah was referring to the Lynches. "Nothing. Their television had rules and they had nothing to read. Fletcher followed me around. Only place I felt safe was out back, so I went out there."

William remembered Tom mentioning Ruth's comments about Sarah working with willows and twigs in the back yard. "You made a spear thrower. Then you made darts. You practiced."

"Shit."

"Am I right? How'd you know how to make darts and a thrower?"

Sarah stopped and turned, faced him as if he was an idiot. "How about, I went on the Internet one day and saw some videos?"

"What did you use for points?"

"I raided Fletcher's collection and used them. He hadn't noticed by the time I left. Asshole."

"So you have darts in that holder, not my rod. And the thrower you made, is it in your pack? What, you fought off Fletcher Lynch with one of your darts?"

"Cut him with his own point. What else could I do?"

"At least you didn't throw a dart into him. Wiry person like you, it would have gone right through him."

"I wish it had."

Sarah swung forward and started off. William watched her march away. Myra caught up with him.

"What's so funny?"

"Myra, Fletcher Lynch doesn't know how lucky he is."

It was nearly dark by the time they reached the cabin and campsite. The stream, which in May had been flowing, was now, in August, a trickle. They pitched the tents and gathered water. Sergei, Sarah and Tom went for wood.

"I don't like Sergei." Myra could see Sergei and Tom down on the meadow gathering wood.

"Give him a chance, Myra. He and I spent time together on the ship. He's a serious scientist. Like you, he defends his beliefs. Try thinking of him as someone who can help carry me out if I collapse."

"I think I'd leave him in here, if he collapses."

"Ah. You like him."

"I do not. He's arrogant."

"He's half Koryak. A cousin."

"Not my cousin."

They started a small fire. There were some mosquitoes.

Down on the meadows by the river, fireflies danced. Tom made tea.

"Looks to me as if nobody moved any of our backrests since we were here last spring," said Myra, leaning exactly where she had leaned months before. Sarah was next to her, and Tom and William were across the fire. Sergei was off to the side. He had said almost nothing. He'd pitched his tent some distance away, beneath trees.

"So did you date that thing?" Sarah asked Sergei. "That sliver?" Sergei had been gazing at the fire, sad. William believed he was still mourning his father.

Sergei spoke quietly. "If the authorities find out where young, er, Sarah is, will we be arrested?"

"That's what you think about," said Myra, "being arrested? You're probably afraid you'll be deported before you can deliver your precious paper at that conference."

"I am Russian, Myra. My nature is to worry about such things. Our history, even our country today, makes me think this way." Sergei leaned forward and spoke just to Sarah.
"My father and I tried to date the sliver, but we were unable to. We did, however, confirm that the bone is mammoth. We tried genetic testing, but those results were confusing."

"We don't know how old it is?" Sarah sounded disappointed.

"At least 12 thousand years, Sarah. That is when mammoths disappeared. The bone is at least that old. The carbon dating test did not produce a result, I am sorry to say." Sergei grinned at Sarah. His face lit up. "I think it is wonderful that you have decided to retrieve the spear thrower, Sarah. We need the piece to properly date it, using another method."

"We?" Myra asked. "You're speaking at that damn conference sponsored by Buckhorn. The whole premise of the conference, even the center they want to build, is that people came here within the last 12 to 15 thousand years. That theory absolutely conflicts with our legends, which say we have always been here."

Sergei leaned back. "Surely that long ago is the same as always? That was a time before writing, agriculture, and memory."

"That argument supports the view that we native people in North America are somehow junior to humans from Asia, Europe or Africa because we came from them. It is an insult."

"Well, if that's so, then we Koryaks should be nearly equally insulted, as the same argument holds for us. Our area produced the people who came to North America, and our area is almost as far from Africa and the Middle East as here."

"What does your genetic work say?" Myra was leaning forward aggressively. "Isn't your paper going to support this argument?"

Sergei was becoming angry. "You don't know what my paper is going to say. You are making assumptions. You are making judgments, also."

"I am making judgments? You, someone who has never been here, accuse me of making judgments, about a place where my ancestors and I were raised?"

Tom watched them talk at each other, back and forth. Sarah's eyes went from one to the other. The angrier Sergei became, the more pronounced his accent. It was very pronounced now. "I would suggest you read my paper when we return and you can decide for yourself about my thesis. I am a scientist, and trained as such. In my field, we use data and evidence to confirm or deny theories. I do not, as do so many these days, confuse strength of belief with fact."

"You think I am confusing belief with fact?" Myra was amazed. "Oral traditions, legends, and memory are as useful for understanding the past as fossilized pieces of bone. You scientists discount that because our legends don't fit with your theories about European and Asian people being older, and therefore more important, than we are. You say we came over here from you, and therefore, we are like your children, inferior to you."

Myra was leaning forward, speaking past Sarah, as if Sarah was not there. Sarah, catching William's eye, rolled hers. Tom coughed uncomfortably. Sergei took a breath, and waited. Minutes passed. The fire crackled. Myra remained leaning forward, as if waiting to challenge whatever Sergei might say. Sergei's face was all planes and shadows, eyes dark. Everyone was silent. Finally he spoke.

"I did not say you are confusing belief with fact, Myra. Only you know that. In America these past few years, many people now do confuse belief with fact. They feel something is true only if they strongly believe it is so, as if utter faith equals truth. Such attitudes lead to zealotry, whether religious or scientific. But data is data. Data is not political. My paper reports on what current genetic data says about populations, how DNA is passed down and altered, and what this may mean for history and origins. We know little. There are many theories." Sergei spoke slowly, like a good teacher. He was clear, and he took pauses between thoughts. "This is even harder when global paradigms prevent new thinking. For centuries, anyone who suggested the earth was not flat was burned at the stake."

"We have always been here." Myra was unflinching.

"Perhaps you are right, Myra. The current paradigm is that humans did not arrive on this continent until 14 thousand years ago, perhaps slightly earlier. Of course, a century ago theory held that humans arrived here three thousand years ago. Then evidence was found for older visits. It took years for this evidence to be accepted. Many scholars today believe, as you do, that humans have been here longer. But to date the evidence proving that has not been accepted."

"That is because the standards keep getting tighter."

"Perhaps. All I can do is work with the data I have, Myra. As the data changes, so do theories. I wish my father were here instead of me. He and I argued all the time and he, like you, disliked my data and evidence. He, like you, wanted to believe people arrived in North America earlier." Sergei paused and frowned. "We had so many arguments that, in the two years before he became sick, we hardly talked. I thought he was a romantic hobbyist. He thought I was an ambitious new scientist, breaking into a new field. We were both right. I had hoped this conference, where we were to each give a paper, could mend our breach." Myra was silent. Sergei continued to speak, his voice quiet. "Now he has died. I will deliver his paper. I am here because he asked me to come in his place, to see this park, for him and his spirit. I did not want to come, but then I heard Sarah's story from William, or at least that part of her story she told, and then I wanted to come, very much. Sarah's story raises questions, questions that require data, perhaps not yet available. This atlatl she says she can find, this will be data." Sergei dusted off his pants, straightened his back. He gestured across the fire. "William, your father, invited me into this park. I am his guest, not yours. You are here with your father, and I envy you, because your father lives still, and mine does not. I had hoped you would respect my reasons for coming but I now think you will not. I will leave in the morning." Sergei rose and went to his tent.

There was a long silence.

"Nice going, Myra." Sarah had watched Sergei disappear in the dark to his tent. "He and his dad didn't have to date that sliver, you know. Now he's leaving. Nice. Going."

Myra moved away from Sarah. "What do you know, Sarah? You're just 13."

Tom chuckled. "Out of the mouths of babes, Myra."

"Shit." Myra folded her arms and faced the fire.

Later, next to William in their tent, Tom adjusted his sleeping bag. "Think they'll kill each other, if he stays?"

"He'll stay, Tom. He really, I mean really, wants to see that spear thrower. He stands up to Myra. She's not used to that."

Sarah and Myra were talking in their tent. William could hear their voices, back and forth, mumbling. They were still talking when he went to sleep.

I n the morning, the air was cool. They shook heavy dew off the tents, then rolled them. They'd be heavier wet, but if they waited for the sun to reach their site they'd not be on the trail until mid-morning. Tom made breakfast. Sergei packed up his gear and came to the fire ring. Sarah watched him and nudged Myra. She nudged Myra again. Sergei, William saw, was preparing to leave, and not with them. Before Sergei could open his mouth Myra handed him a cup of tea.

"I hope you come with us," Myra said. Watching Sarah, William knew what the discussion the night before in their tent had been about. "Sarah wants you to come. She says we will need your strength." Sarah nudged Myra again. "I also would like you to come with us."

"You are afraid I will depart the park and inform the authorities where Sarah and you are." Sergei was making a statement, not asking a question.

"Yes, that had crossed my mind. But I think they know anyway. Pete is smart and he can put two and two together." All Sergei had to do was turn and start down the trail. "They'll figure something else out, too, I think." Myra glanced at Sarah. "Sarah is sure two of the Buckhorn surveyors overheard us when we were talking about the atlatl up there in May, and know when we came out with Sarah we didn't have it. Their leader, Roger, isn't stupid, and neither are the Buckhorn people. They'll wonder, did we leave it up there, and are we going now to retrieve it? They know that if we find that spear thrower, the Bear Valley would become an archeological site, and that would cause them all sorts of problems. Sarah thinks they may follow us and try to get it back."

Sergei's eyes opened wide. "You are surely part Russian, then, Sarah. That is Russian conspiracy thinking at the maximum. William? Could this be correct?"

William nodded. Sarah's theory made sense.

Sarah poked Myra again.

"Come with us. Please. Sarah wants to listen to us argue."

Sergei spoke to Sarah. "This will be dangerous, Sarah. Myra will be a difficult opponent."

"I will defeat you, easily." Myra hoisted her pack. "You will come with us, then?"

"If this company sends their police after us, you will need my help. What is the American expression? In for a penny, in for a loaf?"

"Pound. In for a pound."

"Thank you, Myra. I stand corrected."

"The first of many times." Myra started for the trail. Sarah beamed at Sergei, then fell in behind Myra.

"This could be dangerous." Tom watched them walk off. "If they come after that spear thrower, they won't mess around."

"Then we better move fast and be smart." William lifted his pack.

"I hope to hear the rest of Sarah's story," Sergei said.

"You're enjoying this, 'Eye. Both of you are."

"Beats mowing my lawn, Tom. Doesn't this beat fiddling around in your workshop?"

They were on the trail by the time the sun broke above the ridges. Sarah charged ahead, setting the pace. William was the person who held everyone up, as he had feared. His back ached, he sweated, his pack dug into his hips, his feet became sore. By the time they reached the Lillian River crossing, he was firmly convinced he had made a great mistake.

Sergei chose to remain with William, silently walking behind, never pressing, never coming close, just allowing him to move at his own pace. William stopped when he had to, continued as he chose. The others were well ahead by the time they reached the dark bridge, and he rested there for some minutes.

"This is beautiful country, William. But drier than I expected."

A shaft of sunlight reached down into the deep gorge, striking the end of the bridge. In the light, motes swarmed. The Lillian River, fed by glaciers on Mt. Lillian and McCartney Peak, chattered and sang.

"Wait until we get up into Bear Valley, Sergei. That's closer to the high country. The high country is totally different, and in its way, even more beautiful. It's dry because this time of year there's actually a drought." William stretched. "Thanks for staying with us, Sergei. We can use another strong set of legs."

"I do not think your daughter would agree with you."

"She's just not used to someone standing up to her. Might do her some good, actually."

They left the bridge and climbed. William fell into a rhythm, a steady slow pace that carried on and on. At noontime they were still on the high bench over Elwha canyon, but starting their descent back to the river. They could hear the river far below. Somewhat later, they found Myra, Sarah and Tom resting on a level spot among the thin trees. Tom was heating some food with the stove. William dropped his pack and sat.

"You don't look good, dad."

"I never look good." His heart was thudding. Sweat rolled down his chest.

Sergei stood, easy and relaxed. William was happy to see two lines of sweat running from his hair to his chin. Sarah had her sketchpad open, drawing Myra. Tom crouched by the stove, tending the pot. Myra was stretched out beneath some sunlight falling between trees, using her pack as a pillow. William straightened his legs and felt the pull behind his knees.

Sarah, spoke, still drawing. "I'll find the atlatl. I'm sure. We brought that rope so you could lower me down into the hole. I'll find it."

"Why'd you take it, anyway?" Tom was stirring the lunch.

"I was pissed. I didn't want you to have it. Better it stay up there than be taken out of the park, taken away from Bob-Bob."

"Maybe it is better that you took it, Sarah," said Tom. He finished heating the soup. They had their cups and spoons out. "If you hadn't taken the atlatl when you disappeared, I'm sure Roger and his gang would have grabbed it. They were looking for it, I know that."

Myra removed her hat and sat up. "There's a lot of money riding on this thing. A lot. People get nasty when the stakes are high."

After they ate, they descended off the high traverse to the river. The Elwha here was 50 feet wide, fast, and waist deep. They washed their bowls and spoons and filtered fresh water. William pictured a big bear swimming, silent. When Sarah saw whatever she saw, it was spring, not August, and the river was faster and deeper, the snowmelt high.

Sergei dropped his pack, walked to the river and squatted. "Salmon?" He waved at the river. William joined him along the bank.

Myra was crouched, washing her hands. She glanced up at Sergei, squinting in the sun. "There used to be. Once huge salmon runs used this whole watershed, the 50-mile river, all its tributaries. The biggest king salmon in the world lived here, 100 pounds apiece. Then they built two hydro dams to power the logging mills, blocking this run about eight miles from the strait. That was 100 years ago. Now the dams have been removed. Maybe the salmon will come back."

"Good trout fishing, though, in the upper river." Tom had joined them. "Right, 'Eye?"

"You'll see, Sergei," William said. "Tonight, wherever we camp, you can try fishing. Find out if your Russian flies work here, on this side of the Pacific."

They lingered in the sun. The sun felt nice. William was happy to stay here as long as anyone wanted to. His feet hurt. His legs hurt.

Sarah was drawing their packs, which lay on the ground. Sergei could see over her bent shoulders.

"You can draw."

"I'm ok."

"No. You are an artist. William here showed me and my father copies of the drawings you did last trip. Myra, William, the spider web, the bear. You also copied the inscriptions on the atlatl handle."

"Maybe that's all we'll have, if I can't find it. That and the tiny sliver."

"William left a copy of the atlatl inscriptions with my father, and he and I together did some work with them."

"What do you mean?" Sarah closed her pad and waited.

Sergei began to smile, sad. "My father and I had an enormous argument, right after William left us. My poor father was very weak, sick, but his spirit was as strong as ever. He had this idea, seeing those designs you drew. I thought his idea was foolish, but that was because in order to test his idea it would have to be me, in the lab, stealing computer time at the branch station in Petropavlosk. Oh, we argued, but, weak as he was, he still had that terrible cold shout which made me a three year old boy again." Sergei looked out at the river, then up at the slopes. He leaned over, tapped William's knee. "This is why I was on the bridge when we came in to St. Paul on the ship, William. I wanted to see the outline of the headland there, as soon as we could see it."

"What are you talking about?" Myra asked.

"My father saw those inscriptions and immediately was reminded of another carving he had in his collection, a shoulder blade inscribed with what appeared to be the outline of a range in Kamchatka and the sun rising between two peaks, possibly at the summer solstice. My father believed that ancient people knew the sun, the stars and seasons better than we think, and greatly depended on the solstices, the equinoxes." Myra seemed confused, Tom blank. Sarah listened, waiting. "My father thought the inscriptions Sarah copied from the atlatl might have been drawings of horizon outlines, the sun."

"That's what I thought," said Sarah. "Exactly."

"Computer time?"

"Tom, my father thought the outline on that shaft might be a headland, something one would see from a distance at sea, or over a plain. That morning when we came to St. Paul there was a moment when the lines on that copy I had from Sarah exactly matched the slopes and angles of the St. Paul headland, including the two small peaks. "

"There must be a million headlands all over the world that look similar," said Myra. "It all depends on the angle of approach, the time of day, a million things."

"True. I felt that, as well." Sergei paused. "But, with that terrible voice of his, my father sent me to the computer and demanded I make as many runs as I could. The goal was to plot where the sun rises between those mountains on St. Paul on that date." Sergei reached in his pack and pulled out the copy of the atlatl drawings William had given him in Russia. "I did this for my father, but then for myself. I stole many hours from that computer. My father died just after you left, William, but I kept on." Sarah opened her sketchpad to the original atlatl shaft drawings. "That St. Paul headland looks very like the outline on one side of that atlatl. My computer work showed that during the summer solstice, on June 21st, the sun rises directly between those peaks on that headland along a line that anyone coming east along the Berengia coast would have followed."

"Are you serious?"

"Myra, a group travelling to that headland would know they needed to be there by the solstice in order to have time to return, whether east or west, before the season turned and the ice came."

"This is from Sarah's story?"

"Her story is data, Myra."

"Yes." Sarah pumped her small fist.

Myra was staring at Sergei as if he had grown wings. "A fantasy, Sergei."

"Didn't you say, Myra, this is a land of magic, history and legend?"

"Who told you I said that? I didn't say fantasy, Sergei."

"It was the long day moon we had to get there by," Sarah said.

"What I want to know, Sarah, is where did you eventually go? After The Place People Were?" Sergei refolded his copies of the sketches.

Myra grabbed William's arm. "He's crazy."

"Why," Sergei asked, "do you support young Sarah's vision of the short face bear, but refuse to even consider that what she copied from that ancient atlatl might actually refer to a real place? "

"Now you're defending Sarah?" said Myra.

"Sergei may have a point," William said.

"I think this is a big mistake, coming in here." William was sure Myra meant it was a mistake to bring Sergei.

"I thought it was a drawing of mountains, the sun." Sarah was pleased with herself.

The trail followed the river. They passed nobody else. They reached the meadow and shelter where they had camped in May. Now the empty shelter lay dusty and tired in the sun. Brown grass filled the meadow.

"I saw that bear just up ahead, around that bend," Sarah said to Sergei, pointing. They had been walking since the stop by the river. William was glad to rest. It was the middle of the afternoon.

They dropped their packs. Sarah led them further up the trail, past the meadow, to a smaller meadow beyond. "Right here, this is the stump I was sitting on." Sarah patted the big stump. "And the bear swam the river, right there, and stood there." She pointed. The distance between the stump and the trees where she pointed was less than 100 feet. "Then it went up that slope there. It stopped and peered back at me."

"That's damn close," William said.

"Good distance to draw."

"You say the bear swam the river?"

"Right there, Sergei. Didn't make a sound."

The small meadow was empty. Dragonflies hovered and then darted to hover again. They returned to the large meadow.

"How you doing, 'Eye?" Tom asked.

"I'll survive." William wasn't really sure he would survive, but he had his pride.

"If we camp here, I'll have time to fish," said Sergei, eagerly examining the river.

"We'll have time to fish up ahead, another mile or two." Tom wanted to get far in as fast as he could. "Can you do that, 'Eye?'"

As William nodded, Myra reached out and tapped Tom's pack. "Here. We'll stop here, Tom. If anyone's coming after us, they'll catch us anyway. But why would they? They'll just wait until we get the piece and hike back out." Myra dropped her pack.

"Maybe Sarah's bear will reappear." William was hopeful.

"I hope so. Maybe this time I'll see it." Tom smiled at Sarah.

"You wish." Sarah scowled.

They set up camp, pitching their tents a distance from the shelter. They collected firewood. The sun was bright and hot. A thick cloud, billowing, white, approached from the west, distant still. The top of the cloud stood high, like an anvil.

"Thunderheads."

"It's that time of year, Myra," William was unlacing his boots. "If we're lucky it won't rain here. And if it does, it'll pass soon."

Sergei sat on a log, preparing his fishing rod. Myra stacked firewood. Sarah fiddled with her pack.

"I wanted to support my father and his ideas," Sergei said. He was threading a leader through the eye of a fly. "I told him, 'We scientists, if we are honest with ourselves, live to destroy our theories. The bad scientist is one who stands in the way of new findings, protecting his thesis.'"

"What is your thesis, then?" asked Myra.

"Uh oh," said Sarah.

Sergei considered Myra. "All right, Myra. Genetic data to date tells us the first modern people came from Africa or the Middle East, that we Siberians are descended from clades formed earlier. It also says that Native Americans are descended from Siberians."

"Your data tells you that people came here after first coming to your home in Russia, then? "

"Just as we Koryaks came from people who lived north of India, China, and Mongolia."

"What about legend?"

"What evidence are legends?"

"What evidence are a few bones, taken over the years? From just these you build whole cities of thought."

Sergei threaded his fly, then tied it. He pulled the knot tight with his teeth. Myra was standing straight, facing him. "This is human, Myra, to create patterns from scraps of evidence. We do it always. We are born this way. You say you have always been here. How long is always?"

"Always is always, Sergei."

"We don't even remember anything that happened two or three centuries ago. Whole civilizations in the last five thousand years have risen and fallen and we have remembered none of them. Now imagine twice that time, or three times that time. You think legends last from that long ago?"

"I think it's possible, yes. Why else would the flood legend be universal among humans?"

"Perhaps." Sergei hooked the tied fly into the bamboo handle at the base of his rod, over the reel. He rummaged in his plastic case for another fly. "What does the data say? The oldest human fossils are from Africa. Other hominid fossils have been found in Europe, Asia, and Indonesia. Hundreds of Neanderthal and Cro-Magnon skeletons have been found, but only in Europe and Asia. Compared to these, what has been found in the Americas? The oldest skeletal remains found to date are 10 to 13 thousand years old. No ancient hominids, no Neanderthals, no Homo Erectus. Nothing."

Myra started to interrupt, but Sergei kept talking. "Human

sites and camps have been found in Africa, Asia and Europe, which are tens of thousands, hundreds of thousands of years old. The oldest verified sites found in the Americas, Myra, are less than 14 thousand years old." Myra started to interrupt again. Sergei was speaking loudly. "Yes, Louis Leakey, who discovered the fossils of ancient hominids in Africa, came to this continent. He said he thought there were ancient stone tools in California, but by then he was ill and not thinking properly. Yes, there was that site in Mexico that supposedly was dated to a quarter million years, but the data was never accepted and careers were ruined. Supposedly they found a carved mammoth on a bone too old to date, but the carving vanished, and the site's age has never been verified." Sergei stood, holding a fly. The approaching thunderheads rolled over the meadow, blocking the sun. "No skeletons. No sites. No tools. Clear DNA links to European and Asian populations. That is what the data shows, Myra. With that data, no wonder the Clovis theory, that the Americas were first populated no more than 15 thousand years ago, is considered the correct theory."

"Are you finished?" Myra was shorter than Sergei, but she faced him eye to eye. Sarah opened the fishing rod holder that had been tied to her pack. She was listening to Myra and Sergei but keeping her distance. Tom and William were keeping their distance too.

"I am finished unless and until new data appears that forces me to change my thinking. Belief will not change my thinking."

"Well, here's some data, Sergei. I'm not a PhD like you, and I'm not a genetic expert, but I am an anthropologist with a minor in archeology." Myra stepped closer to Sergei. He backed up, still holding his fishing rod and the fly. "Based on language groups and number of separate languages, the Americas are the most diverse and complex systems of languages anywhere in the world, except possibly New Guinea. Linguists believe that people needed to be here in the Americas at least 40 thousand years to develop such diversity."

"You tell him, girl." Sarah squatted on her heels, watching.

"The route to the Americas across that land bridge and along the coast was in existence many times during the last two million years. It was present from about 70 to 12 thousand years ago, and again from 160 to 130 thousand years ago. Mammoths and other mammals crossed to the Americas, but they also crossed from the Americas to Siberia. The mammoth that went extinct in Asia 12 thousand years ago was a version of a North American mammoth that travelled west, replacing the local Siberian mammoths at least 50 thousand years ago. If mammals could make that trek, so could people. Coming this way, or going that way."

Sergei leaned forward. He had been nodding as Myra spoke, and now he seemed excited. "As a matter of fact, Myra..."

Myra had the floor and she wasn't going to let it go. "No. You listen, please. I don't want to hear another of your points, so smugly smashing down my ideas. Not now, maybe not ever." Sergei closed his mouth. William suspected if they had been closer to the trailhead he'd have risen and left. "Homo Erectus, the ancestor of all humans, including us natives here, travelled as far as Asia over a million and a half years ago. Why not to the New World? Maybe Leaky wasn't losing it. Maybe what he saw in California were ancient stone tools. That place in Mexico, Hueyetalco, yes, I know about it, maybe that was a quarter million years old. Of course we'll never know now because they made a reservoir and flooded the site. Convenient. Jesus."

"Myra, you may be right. The more we study genetic admixture among peoples the less clear the history. It seemed simple 20 years ago—everyone on earth descended from a common mother in Africa, 200 thousand years ago. Then we thought other ancient people, Neanderthals, Denisovian, Homo Erectus, were separate species that died out. Now we know we all carry Neanderthal and Denisovian genes. Surely we carry Erectus genes as well. We know ancient people bred together, often. This is human nature, it seems." Sarah smothered a smile. Sergei opened his hands. "Someone in America sent the same genetic sample to three separate companies, all promising to list the ancestry. Those three companies, using the same samples, gave three totally different answers. Nevertheless, what data we do have supports what I was saying."

"The absence of data doesn't mean there is no data, Sergei. Maybe the data hasn't been found, yet."

"I hope data is found, and then I will change my theories, Myra. For me, now, the evidence in favor of an African and Asian origin is still overwhelming."

"That's typical, coming from someone raised in Asia."

"I'm going fishing." Sergei turned and marched across the meadow to the river. The cloud overhead passed and the sun re-emerged. More thunderheads could be seen approaching from the distance.

"That was fun." Tom eyed the small pile of wood by the fire ring. "I'm going to get some more wood."

"I'll help you. Jesus. What an arrogant jerk." Myra glared after Sergei. He was now standing barefoot, calf deep in the cold river, casting. Sergei's back was to Myra.

People appeared, coming up the trail. William recognized Roger, the head surveyor, at once. He wore his trademark sunglasses. Sarah's group was off the trail, near the shelter and trees, but William suspected Roger saw them, even though he didn't even look their way.

In all, six people, walking 40 yards apart, passed. Tom, Myra and Sarah all watched them stride along the trail through the meadow. William paid close attention to their packs. They were heavy, tools swinging, coils of rope hanging. Their packs were carrying empty canvas sacks, surveyor tape tied to straps, small tools, mirrors and radios.

They marched by, packs creaking. Raymond and Bernie followed Roger, then two men William had never seen before. Pete brought up the rear. When he saw their tents, he veered off trail and approached. Myra watched with cold eyes.

"Myra. William."

"What, Pete, you told Buckhorn where we went?"

"Myra, no. We've been in here four times, last time two weeks ago. This was long planned."

"Survey?" Tom asked.

"We're not here to bring Sarah back, if that's what you're thinking." Pete hesitated. "Roger's under a lot of pressure. We all are. I'd stay away from him, from all of us, if you can."

"This isn't Buckhorn's park. That isn't Buckhorn's Bear Valley. We're going up there." Myra's voice was icy. "Tom's

➤

grandfather is buried there and Sarah left something. We have the right."

Sarah froze, watching Myra. Tom shifted. Pete squinted, confused.

William spoke up. "We're just getting away for a few days, to let things cool down for Sarah." He wasn't sure whether or not Pete had picked up what Myra had foolishly told him. If it had been Roger or Raymond, they'd have known in a second.

Pete adjusted his pack. "I better get going. Anyway, keep an eye out, all right? I think Roger's planning to camp by Godkin Creek, like before."

Pete headed for the trail. They all watched him walk across the meadow and disappear in the trees.

"Myra, you've got a big mouth." Sarah was standing before Myra. "Now they know we're looking for something."

"Maybe not, Sarah." Myra was defensive.

"Yes," Sarah said. "They'll know exactly."

"Only if Pete says something."

"You think Roger won't figure it out?" Sarah shook her head.

"Firewood." Tom said, looking at the sky. Sergei kept fishing in the river. "Come on, Myra, let's get some before the rain starts."

William leaned against the log where Sergei had been selecting flies. Tom and Myra headed down the trail. There was wood on the flat benches by the river a few hundred yards beyond.

Sarah found a rotten piece of wood, an old stump, which she rolled slowly across the meadow to rest against a broken tree at the base of the slope to the east. Then she returned to her pack.

"I think Myra likes him."

"Who? Sergei? I'd say the opposite, Sarah."

"What do you know? You're just her father."

"What are you doing, anyway?"

"My experiment."

Sarah pulled six sections of straight thin branch from the fishing rod case. They were darts. On one end were feathers, on the other, stone points, lashed to the willow shafts.

"Can I see one of those?" Sarah handed William a dart. The shaft was straight, firm, and clean. The feathers had been wedged in notches cut into the shaft. The sharp stone points were lashed with thin cord, wrapped many times around the head of the shaft. "You made these?"

"What else was there to do there?"

William lifted one of the darts. It was three and a half feet long, light and balanced, well made. Sarah came and stood by him while he examined the dart. She held a wooden thrower that resembled the atlatl Tom found under Bob-Bob's hat. This one was wood, not bone, and had no carved raven. William wondered which of these darts was the one Sarah had used against Lynch.

Sarah took the darts and walked across the meadow. She turned and faced the stump section she had rolled against the broken tree. She stood about 20 feet away, well off the trail and away from the shelter.

"Don't watch. I'm not that good."

"Be careful, Sarah. That's a dangerous weapon."

Sarah took a dart, fitted it, and threw. William wasn't sure what he expected, but he didn't expect the first dart to whistle through the air and strike the rotten stump in the center. There was a solid thunk.

She threw again. This time the dart missed the stump, but only by inches, striking within a hand span of the first. Her third throw hit the stump, as did her fourth. The fifth hit the tree, the sixth the stump. Every throw the darts wavered and whistled.

She had to work to remove the darts from the wood, even though the wood was soft. William was surprised to see how hard the darts struck. Sarah was a small girl, not 100 pounds, yet the darts flew like missiles.

The next time she started to throw she was another five paces distant. Now she was 35 feet from the stump. The stump was about a foot and a half in diameter.

William had searched for spear throwers on the Internet when he had returned from their trip in May. He watched some videos of people throwing darts, a shooting contest. He thought, when watching the videos, if people had wanted to hunt with these weapons, they better learn to throw with a lot more accuracy than they did on YouTube. Once they were more than 40 feet away, most of them were lucky to hit the target anywhere.

Yet Sarah, who had been practicing behind her grandmother's house for only a few weeks, demonstrated a deadly aim. Even 80 feet from the stump, she struck the target five times out of six.

Tom and Myra came back with armloads of wood. After watching Sarah throw, they went for more. Sergei, now well down the river, also watched.

Sarah kept moving farther from the target. She went across the trail and threw darts all the way across the meadow to the broken tree. Still she hit the stump, or at least the tree. Finally she gathered the darts and returned to the fire, holding the darts and the thrower. She was sweating.

"That's fun." She packed the darts in the rod case and stowed the thrower.

"You're my choice, Sarah, we get stranded up here. Deer wouldn't have a chance."

"I'm no good, not really." Sarah plopped down next to William. "You should see someone who's good."

"I saw some YouTube contests. Nobody was very good, not that I saw."

"Well, people can get very good at it if they have to."

"Fletcher Lynch is going to be pissed off when he sees some of his stone points missing."

"Well, I just took the dart points. I left the arrowheads."

Sergei reappeared carrying four good-sized trout on a branch, already cleaned. Tom rubbed his hands together, then rummaged for the small frying pan and some oil. Thunderheads kept rolling by, but it never rained. They could hear thunder faintly to the south, perhaps over the Bear Valley. It became cooler. Wind blew high on the ridges. Myra and Sergei said nothing to each other. Myra was seated at one end of the log and Sergei the other.

"There have been a few ice ages, right?" Sarah was speaking to Myra.

"So you listened to me."

"Jeez, Myra, we all listened to you." Myra colored. Sergei was silent, replacing his flies. Sarah sat, elbows across her knees, chin on elbows. "So maybe there were people here, lots of people, before this last ice age. Then when the ice came, it crushed and ground up all the evidence of them." Sarah seemed to be directing the comment to Sergei.

Sergei was braced on the log, long legs straight out. "If there were people here, they'd have moved south when the ice came. But there's no evidence of them to the south."

"Isn't Mexico south, Sergei?"

Sergei blinked. "Are you planning to become a scientist, Sarah?"

"Are you kidding? What, so I can argue all the time?"

"Good. Because if you did become one, the rest of us would have our work cut out for us. You're smart."

"At least we agree on one thing," Myra said.

"What did Tom say, yesterday?" Sergei had his fly case open. "Out of the mouths of babes?"

"I am not a babe."

"You will be, Sarah." Sergei grinned.

"Asshole."

"Told you she was ornery," Tom said, passing around the cooked fish. The fish was delicious.

"You may have a point, Sarah," Sergei said. "The ice covered much of the good habitat for living, and south was desert and dust. South of the desert, the environment is tropical and acidic and nothing lasts in those conditions. One place that hasn't been examined much is the high country, the alpine areas, in the mountains. It seems people went high very early, and it can be dry up there. Evidence may be up there." Sergei waved toward the high ridges over the river. "You see, Myra, Sarah has me thinking, now."

"But no data, right?"

"Not yet, Myra."

"Of course not." Myra leaned back.

"That was some nice throwing," Sergei said. "I watched you from the river. Did you make that weapon yourself?"

"I did."

"So you learned much during your journey."

"I practiced at Ruth's this summer."

"Still, you knew what to do."

"Yes."

"I don't get it." Myra wouldn't look at Sergei. "On the one hand we have a scientist who only uses data, and yet on the other we have a man who apparently thinks Sarah learned how to throw during a dream."

"Data, Myra. Sarah made the darts and thrower. Maybe she learned how to do that on the Internet. You can learn much from the Internet. She may have used YouTube and practice to become accurate, as well. But I know a little about ancient lashings and ties from my father's hobby. Sarah's workmanship is hard to credit to a YouTube video alone. Her ability to hit something a foot in diameter from well over 100 feet away is more than impressive. Perhaps there is more to learn about skill development, learning, and the power of dreams."

"You're not making sense."

"I'm Russian, Myra. Why would I make sense?"

"Aren't you Koryak?"

"That, too." Sergei pocketed his flies, stretched his legs. "I know, Myra, because of your history, the broken treaties, the disease, the abuse, even today the hatred of native people by whites, you think the debt to be paid is unpayable. But in my land, we native people have no reservations, have no government support, have no treaty fishing rights, have few cultural traditions left. They were all torn from us generations ago. Perhaps I envy you."

Myra stared into the fire. Sergei settled back.

"We get a good day, tomorrow," said Tom, "we might be able to get all the way to Bear Valley. 'Eye, think you can make it?" Tom had been watching William massage his legs.

"I can try."

Evening was approaching. William took the bowls, spoons and pot and washed them in the river. When he came back to the fire, Sarah was sketching Sergei. Sergei was retying some flies. He wore glasses, perched on his nose, and bent his head close to his work.

Sarah closed her sketchpad. William could see a scar on her forehead, a long thin line remaining from her cuts the previous spring.

"You know, we could leave the thrower up there." Sarah was hesitant. "That's what you wanted, Tom-Tom, isn't it? Take it in there to be with Bob-Bob?"

"I'm Tom-Tom, am I?"

"Grandpa makes you sound too old. We could leave it up there. They'll never find it. They don't want to find it. I mean, I'd like to get the thrower. Try it out, even, but I don't want to be attacked."

"If we left it, then you wouldn't get the chance to try, Sarah."

"I know, Myra, but we'd be alive. That Pete was warning us. If they think we have that thing who knows what they'll do."

"I think Sarah makes sense." Sergei continued his fly tying. "One of those Buckhorn people was carrying a gun."

"Come on, Sergei," said Myra. "We aren't in Russia, here. They aren't going to attack us. Sarah, you retrieve that thrower, and when we get back out, you'll have something that will give you and us cover, show that you aren't crazy, and neither are

➤

we. Maybe then you can stay with Tom, because people will stop thinking we're all demented and dreaming."

"And, more important," said Sergei, "the mining enterprise will be stopped. Above all, stop the mining."

"You think I only care about the mining."

"You don't know what I think, Myra. But, yes, in this case I think you want that thrower both for Sarah's sake but even more because that artifact is what you need to stop Buckhorn."

"It's important that we stop Buckhorn."

William had never been able to get Myra's mother to come down off her indignant high horse once she started to ride. Over the years he'd had better success with Myra. He tried now. "Just as it's important to Buckhorn to bring in this material. Just as it's important for those surveyors to do their job. Everyone has a motive, here, Myra. Sarah is only asking that we be sure we want to go on, tomorrow, because once we get there and she finds the piece, things could become difficult. I'm happy to stop here, turn around, and not just because my legs hurt and my feet are sore. I think there is some danger, to Sarah and all of us, if we persist. But I think it's unlikely they will try to permanently silence five of us over an old bone thrower that cannot really be confirmed as from this area."

"I want to get that thrower and put it with Bob-Bob, and maybe first use it once or twice."

"That's what I wanted to do last spring, Sarah. Leave it up there." Tom watched Sarah. "But I now see a good reason to bring the piece out and date it. I agree with Myra. We should go on."

"I would like to see this atlatl after all I have heard about it, and especially after trying to date and test the sliver." Sergei placed the retied fly in his case.

"I will go on, if the rest of you go on." William shifted his legs, wincing.

"See, Myra, we all agree with you." Sergei bowed to Myra, opening his hands. Sarah reopened her sketchpad and pulled out her pencil. William watched the fire, felt heat against his lower legs and feet. Tom pulled out a small camera, took a picture of Sarah drawing.

"I didn't know you brought a camera," Myra said.

Tom aimed his camera at Sarah. "I brought this because I wanted to be able to take pictures of the Bear Valley site, and the atlatl once Sarah retrieves it. I regretted not having a camera last spring."

Sergei reached into a pocket and pulled out his own camera. Sarah almost smiled when he took a picture. "Sarah, William here told me your story." Sergei aimed and shot.

"I was wondering when one of you was going to ask about that."

"We all agreed, Sarah, last May, not to bother you," said Tom, leaning back. "You had your injuries to deal with and we knew it wouldn't help to pester you then. And then of course the Lynches took you. Sergei, we all agreed we'd not ask Sarah anything unless she said something first."

"I never agreed. I wasn't here." Sergei added a branch to the fire.

"Well, you should honor what we agreed to."

"Why is that, Myra?"

"I think none of you asked me anything because you didn't believe me," Sarah said, while shading her drawing. "Just like you didn't believe me about seeing the bear." Sarah put her pencil down and handed her sketchpad to Sergei.

Sergei's eyebrows rose. "I have a large nose."

"You do."

"You could earn a living today drawing portraits in Russia." Sergei handed William the pad. Sarah had drawn Sergei working on his flies, head bent, glasses halfway down his nose, black hair parted in the middle and falling over his ears, lips pursed. The likeness was perfect. William handed the pad on to Tom, who chuckled. He passed the pad to Myra.

"Why look at a drawing when I can see that big nose right here?"

"Before you two kill each other, Sergei, what did you want to know?" asked Sarah.

Myra turned the page in the sketchpad to a drawing Sarah had done of her. She handed it to Tom. William could see over Tom's shoulder. In the sketch, Myra was laughing, eyes alight, head back. William handed the drawing to Sergei. He held it for some time.

"You are a beautiful woman when you look happy."

Myra colored. "Are you saying I am not happy?"

"I am. Certainly not around me."

"That's easy. You are impossible."

"Of course. I am Russian and Koryak." Sergei placed his hand across his chest as he said this. Sergei handed the sketchpad to Sarah. "Sarah, when you awoke in that place, at that headland, in your dream, did you remember who you were? Did you know you were Sarah?"

"No. Yes. No. I didn't think about it. I was just there."

"Did you wonder?"

"I had lost my memory. My head hurt. I only wondered what I had forgotten about life on the sea of grass." As she spoke, her voice changed, slowed down, and her look seemed distant.

"And now, Sarah, three months later, do you remember everything as well as you did in May?"

"Everything. It was real."

"And making the darts and thrower at your grandmother's? Lashing the stolen stone points? Knowing which of the stone points was a dart point and which an arrowhead? Some of that knowledge, was it from your time wherever you were? Your dream?" Sarah's head moved, twice. "This is interesting," Sergei said to the rest of them. "I have heard there are stories of people dreaming and then, upon awakening, knowing how to perform a skill they had dreamed of. Perhaps those stories are true." Sergei observed Sarah for a long minute. "There was more, wasn't there. To your story?"

"Yes."

"Will you tell us?"

"Maybe."

"I look forward to that time, Sarah." Sergei settled back. He did not ask Sarah any more questions; he did not persist in getting further information. Sarah had told them, on the walk out in May, that maybe she could and would tell them the rest of her tale, and William now saw that Sergei was content to leave it at that.

That night, shortly after they turned in, the wind began
to blow. Thunder growled, closer and closer. Rain fell
for an hour, starting at 10. North, south, and then over them,
they heard heavy thunder. Lightning flashed outside their
tents. Yet, by the time the sun rose, the sky was mostly clear.

Tom wanted to push on this day all the way to Bear Valley.
It would be a long day, over 13 miles.

Tom tried his little radio to see if it picked up any signal.
Here, by the Elkhorn camp, deep beneath two high ridges,
the scratchy forecast could be heard. The radio mentioned
reports of several fires caused by lightning from the storms of
the night before.

They packed rapidly and were on the trail before eight.
Three times, approaching Hayes River, they had to work
around trees that had fallen across the trail. At the Hayes
River junction, the ranger's tent was tied shut, the ranger
somewhere on patrol. Clouds passed by overhead. A strong
wind blew from the south.

Tom listened to his weather radio again. It reported two
fires started by lightning, one back toward Whiskey Bend,
not far from the Lillian River crossing, and the other up on
Dodger Point. When they came to the Hayes River bridge,
they looked back north to Dodger Point ridge and saw some
smoke halfway up the slope.

They took a break at Camp Wilder for lunch. William's

feet hurt, but his back hurt more. He could see Tom was not having much fun either. Tom's stride had developed a slight hitch. They were both happy to sit and rest.

Because they'd made the same trip the previous spring, they knew where to go when they left the trail. Sarah had some difficulty with her fishing rod holder catching branches. She stopped, removed the aluminum tube, and carried it in one hand.

When they reached the slide area below the Godkin Valley, the slope was dry and the rocks hot. Broken trees and stumps, bleached from the sun, littered the rockslide area. They picked their way across the slide toward Godkin Creek. They followed the creek upstream.

As before, the Buckhorn group had chosen a sandbar on the Godkin for their camp. The gravel bar was wide and open, close to water and firewood. There were three tents on the sand bar, but nobody in sight. Next to the tents were two bulging canvas containers, stacked. William wondered if the sacks were erbium samples.

They moved through cedars and spruce to the small headwall leading to Bear Valley. They climbed the headwall and crossed the wide slide area to find the north bench leading to the overhang. The snow here was gone, long melted away, leaving only thick piles of trees, limbs, and stumps tangled together.

They reached the overhang late in the afternoon. Tom and William brought up the rear. William's feet felt like fire. His heart slammed in his chest and he groaned from the pain in his back. Tom's left knee had apparently stiffened; he walked straight-legged, swinging his stiff leg awkwardly in a half-circle as he moved.

Sergei, still wearing his pack, reappeared from ahead. He took William's pack and hoisted it atop the pack on his back.

Then he took Tom's pack and swung it over his head so that it rested atop William's pack. Then, carrying three packs, he walked ahead toward camp.

"Jesus." Tom was breathing hard. "Look at that."

Sergei disappeared, walking effortlessly.

"Depressing, Tom." Sergei was carrying over 150 pounds, easily. William felt 100 years old.

"Maybe he'll carry our packs on the way out." Tom swung his leg, lurching along.

"You going to be all right, Tom?"

"It'll get better. I hope. Besides, I know I look better than you."

"You do not."

Myra appeared, followed by Sarah. Tom and William were tired, sweating, flushed, and in pain.

"Long day, dad. You guys did well."

So they arrived. They set up camp not under the overhang, but out where they had first camped last May, where Tom and his grandfather Bob-Bob had camped many years before. Myra and Sarah walked downstream a distance to wash. Tom, Sergei and William heard them laughing. Then the men washed. William's feet burned in the cold water. The water felt great, but afterward, both Tom and William stiffened up badly.

When they returned from their wash in the creek, they saw Myra and Sarah with Roger and Pete. Roger was without sunglasses and his eyes seemed pale and empty. Pete stood slightly behind his boss, awkward. Roger was waving a piece of paper. He turned to face Tom.

"Anything found in the ground here is ours. We have the claim. Maybe once this was in your family, gramps, but it's ours now. You can camp up here, but when you leave we'll be checking to make sure you aren't taking anything on your way out."

Myra spoke. "This is a national park. We have a total right to be here."

"That's what I just said, princess, just don't remove anything."

Myra spoke past Roger to Pete. "Pete, this is ridiculous."

"I don't disagree," Pete said. Roger turned on him.

"This isn't your fight, Pete. Back off."

"What's the problem?" Tom moved next to Myra.

"No problem. You heard me."

Tom stood before Roger. One set of pale eyes faced another.

"Thanks for your concern." Tom turned his back and walked away. Roger realized he'd been dismissed. He gave Sergei and William a hard look, shook his head, and put on his sunglasses. He and Pete headed toward the headwall and their camp, disappearing among the trees.

Tom took a pullover from his tent. The afternoon had grown cooler. He tugged it over his head.

"They don't have the right to check us, or inspect us, when we leave," Myra said.

"They think they do. He kept waving that paper." Tom rubbed his sore leg.

"Tom," William said, "the way I see this, there are six of them and five of us. Their six are all big, strong, and on a mission. At least one is armed." William had not liked the look in Roger's eyes.

"Well, aren't we on a mission too?"

"We are, Sarah," William said. "But wasn't it you who suggested yesterday we just leave the atlatl here, for exactly the reasons we now see?"

"I'm not a quitter."

That evening Myra cooked dinner with Sarah's help. Sergei went down to the creek to seek fish. After dinner Sergei and Myra took the bowls and spoons to the creek and washed them. They crouched together, backs to the fire, bent over, washing.

"Wow. Think they're talking to each other?" Tom was grinning.

Sarah was drawing again. "She's probably telling him how to clean the right way."

"Or he's telling her," William said.

They were laughing when Myra and Sergei returned, bowls and spoons clean.

The sun had dropped below the ridges. The sky glowed red to the west, clouds under lit. Above, behind them, the cliff face rose to stars. They were warm, fed, and comfortable. Tom was recovering his color.

They heard very faint shouts and laughter. The breeze from the west was carrying up the noise from the Buckhorn camp.

"Wish they weren't here," Tom said.

"First thing tomorrow, we'll go look for the thrower," said Sarah. She had removed the coiled line from Tom's pack and was checking its condition. "I should find it if the water hasn't carried it somewhere. I should be able to get it right away. You guys will lower me down and then use the line to help me climb back up."

"You're sure about this, Sarah?" Myra watched Sarah prepare the rope.

"I got out once, didn't I?"

"Yes, you did. At the cost of a possible concussion, torn hands, and a lost finger."

"That's not how I lost my finger, Myra."

Myra opened her mouth, then said nothing.

"Tomorrow, we find that thing. And then what? Pack up and skedaddle?" Tom rummaged for tea bags.

"Any way we can avoid passing their camp?" asked Sergei.

"Not really," William said. "We have to follow Godkin to get out of here." There were no trails out of this valley. Climbing to the top of the ridge at the head of the valley only led them into further backcountry, filled with cliffs and snowfields.

"I don't think we'll be stopped." Myra sounded hopeful. "We're a lot of witnesses, five of us, if they take things from us."

Sarah poked the coals with a stick. "If they take the thrower and our cameras, no matter what we say, they'll put their word against ours."

"Well, maybe we're wrong." Tom sounded as hopeful as Myra. William could tell Sergei didn't think Roger was bluffing.

The next day, they rose early. A hint of frost rimed leaves and branches. They cooked oatmeal, had tea, cleaned up. The morning sky was blue, with occasional passing clouds.

"OK, Sarah." Tom took hold of the rope. "Lead the way."

Sarah stood at the fire ring and paused, looking back toward the cliff, then up toward the head of the valley, as if she was orienting herself. They watched her. William was reminded of the night up here the previous May when she'd reappeared in the middle of the thunderstorm. He and Tom had had no idea, really, where she'd come from. She'd just appeared, then collapsed.

William tried to imagine what this must be like for her, to willingly go back to that place where she had been trapped for eight days, alone and surely terrified, thinking she would die and never be found. Then he caught himself. To her, there was light, the bear, and then she was in a great canoe.

She lined up her angle based on the fire ring. Sarah mimed picking up the atlatl case and started forward, angling to the right of the cliff, in the direction of the head of the valley, She worked around the jumbled boulders. William expected her to pause at one of the many voids, but she continued, past the boulders. She walked 100 yards, all the way to the base of the slope.

The base of the bare cliff face, 120 feet wide, was to the left, jumbled with vegetation and fallen trees. William remembered searching here for Sarah back in May. Sarah came to a rise in the slope, then stepped forward to climb to a higher, smaller shelf on which trees grew. She worked herself behind the trees.

She disappeared.

"Sarah?" Tom held the coiled line. They all stood there. They could see nothing, hear nothing. She had been 10 feet away, and now she was gone.

"Here." Sarah's face appeared, to the right of the trees. "It's here."

They scrambled up onto the small ledge. Behind the trees, on a small ledge, a broken rock covered a void. One had to be on the ledge itself, standing behind the trees, to see this rock, and beneath it, the narrow opening.

"How did you come to this spot, that day?"

"I was pissed, Tom-Tom. I was looking for a good secret place to hide the thrower. Maybe to hide myself, too. Figured I'd let you guys panic trying to find me."

"Well, we did panic trying to find you, Sarah." Myra was not amused.

"I saw this rock and the space below." Sarah gestured toward the void. "Be careful. I wasn't. Give me the rope. The headlamp."

Tom pulled a headlamp from his pocket, then handed Sarah the rope. William stepped forward.

"Let's get you properly tied in, Sarah." He ran the rope around her waist, and then made a sling called a bosun's chair. He measured the loops around her narrow legs and tied the bowline. She stepped into the chair. He adjusted the rope. "Stay upright if you can, Sarah. With this chair we can lower you, then help lift you out. You'll have your hands free to brace yourself."

The hole was just a narrow gullet dropping straight down

eight feet and then twisting to the left. William could see how she might have been crawling over leaves and branches covering the hole and simply fallen through, tumbling down headfirst.

Sarah put on the headlamp. She wore a long-sleeved shirt and long pants.

Sergei came forward and took the rope from William. "I will hold her." He straddled the gullet with his long legs, holding the rope directly above the narrow opening.

Sarah turned on the headlamp.

"I'm not sure about this," Myra said.

"Well, I am, Myra." Sarah adjusted the lamp on her forehead.

Sergei let out some line. "Sarah, when you need to be lifted up, three pulls on the rope. Three, all right?"

Sarah sat on the leaning rock and lowered her legs into the void. As she went down, Sergei took up tension on the rope. Sarah started descending.

"Jesus." Myra had her fist to her mouth.

Sarah disappeared. Sergei fed the rope through his hands.

Sarah spoke as she dropped. "More. Hold it. Now, more. OK. Wait. OK." The light grew dimmer. She started twisting, following the void as it turned. "More, More. Wait."

Her voice grew fainter and she disappeared. They heard nothing. The rope moved inch by inch through Sergei's hands. Myra, Tom and William were on their stomachs, looking down into the hole. Sergei continued to stand, immovable, feeding line.

Suddenly the line went slack. From below, unbelievably faint, William heard Sarah's voice.

"OK. OK. Wait."

Then, nothing. Sergei continued to hold the rope. He was sweating. Long minutes passed. The rope stayed motionless.

"What's she doing?" Myra backed away from the opening.

"This is crazy." Tom peered into the void. "We're nuts. I'm not sure any of us could fit down that chute to follow her, if we had to. It's too tight."

Sergei continued to hold the rope, hands loose, waiting.

The rope remained motionless. Time slowed, then stopped. William watched sweat drop from his forehead into the void. Myra had moved off and stood facing the trees. Tom lay on the ground, his head hanging over the opening.

The rope remained slack, still. Time passed.

William's watch said Sarah had been below for 40 minutes.

The rope jerked three times.

Sergei started to pull on the rope. It came too easily. He lowered it again. The rope jerked again, harder.

"She wants you to pull something up." Tom spoke into the void.

Sergei pulled the rope, to which something was tied. It snagged down around the twisted turn, but then came free. The atlatl case hung on the end of the rope, dripping and streaked with mud. Sarah had tied the rope around the case above the bosun's chair. William grabbed the case, then untied the rope and handed it back to Sergei.

Sergei lowered the rope back into the void. The bosun's chair hung up near the turn, but by wiggling the rope and hauling it up once or twice it passed the obstruction and continued down.

The rope went slack and then, five minutes later, jerked three times. The way Sergei pulled, William was certain Sarah must be in the bosun's chair below them. Every once in a while, the rope went slightly slack as Sarah repositioned herself.

Sergei's hands were red with effort, his forearms corded and thick. Finally they could hear Sarah.

"Lift. Wait. OK. Lift."

The top of her head came over the edge of the hole, headlamp shining. They pulled her free. Sarah collapsed on the ledge, breathing hard. She was scratched and streaked with mud. Somehow she had cut her ear. Her long-sleeve shirt and pants were wet and muddy, the pants torn.

"You OK?" Myra asked, as she helped Sarah stand up. They moved from the narrow shelf to the base of the ledge below. Sergei coiled the wet, muddy line.

Sarah sat in the sun, handing the headlamp to Tom. She held the atlatl case in her lap.

"I knew I'd never be able to climb out that way," she said.

"What?" Myra asked. "Isn't that how you got out last spring?"

"No. The bear showed me another way."

Myra said nothing. Sergei observed Sarah. Sarah brushed off some mud.

"Was the case where you thought it would be?" asked Myra.

"No. I got down there, took off the sling, had to go looking."

"Jesus, Sarah, you agreed not to take off the sling."

"Myra, I had to."

"You don't take direction well, do you?"

"Not when you give stupid direction. The case had been washed a ways. We were lucky. It caught in a crack right before another long drop. I was able to reach that far, but not easy." William imagined Sarah untying herself from the lifeline and heading off into the dark, probably on her knees, to search for the atlatl. "I was OK." Sarah stood up.

Sergei watched Sarah, fascinated. Now his face broke into the widest smile William had ever seen.

"Thrower smiled like that," Sarah said, and then, taking the case, she started toward camp. Sergei blinked. Myra watched Sarah walk off.

"We're all crazy," Myra whispered.

Tom took the coiled line from Sergei. "Let's go look at this spear thrower. Take photos, have Sarah make a drawing, too. She went to some trouble to retrieve it."

"That she did," William said.

It was not yet 10 a.m. when they returned to their camp. Tom cleaned off the case, then pulled out the atlatl. The atlatl had remained dry during all that time underground. Myra bandaged Sarah's ear. Sarah was shivering. Tom and Sergei both took photographs. William kept watching for Buckhorn's people, but the woods were silent. Sarah, warming up, took the atlatl and held the piece as if throwing, looking back at her outstretched arm.

"I gotta try this a couple times." She gestured over toward the cliff where she had stacked her thrower and darts the evening before.

"Sarah, that's an ancient artifact. It could be damaged if you use it." Myra was frowning. Sarah started drawing the thrower.

Myra, Tom, Sergei and William struck camp. They emptied their tents, rolled up the sleeping bags, packed their gear. The forest seemed empty. William had concluded the Buckhorn people would simply wait for them to leave the valley and intercept them down by Godkin Creek. The fine day had deteriorated. Thunderheads were rising in the sky and the wind began to blow. They'd have rain by nightfall.

By the time Sarah had completed her sketch of the atlatl, they had broken camp. The fire was nearly out. They gathered together by the fire, avoiding the blowing smoke. Sergei took the atlatl and examined the raven's carved beak, the marks showing the wings. He spent long minutes tracing the lines and marks on both sides of the shaft with his fingers. He was almost reverent. "This is very old, William."

"I know." When William had touched the atlatl last May, he felt the same thing.

"Very old," Sergei said again. He handed the piece to Tom, who wrapped the atlatl in the cloth and then placed it carefully in the case. They were ready to leave. Sergei straightened and opened his hands. "There's something I need to say. Myra, you said earlier you didn't want to hear my points, and I did not persist then, because you did not want to listen. You offended me, actually. But now that we have retrieved this atlatl, I have something I need to say."

"Wait, Sergei." Sarah turned and trotted toward the cliff. She disappeared behind some brush below the overhang.

Just then the Buckhorn survey crew emerged from some trees beyond those that had been felled by lightning the spring before. They had crept up under the sound of the wind. They were suddenly right there, close.

Tom held the case containing the atlatl. Myra stepped in front of him. Sergei and William were to the side, beside their packs.

Roger approached, closely followed by the others. He was carrying a pistol. His eyes were on the atlatl case.

"Good morning." Roger's voice grated. William regretted that Sarah hadn't carried the atlatl case back to the cliff with her; she might have been able to hide it. But it was in Tom's hands, now in plain sight.

Roger stood just ahead of the felled tree, flanked by Raymond and Bernie. Pete stood next to Bernie. He would not meet William's gaze. The other two stood by Raymond. Roger pointed the pistol toward Tom's feet. "We need to see anything you might be taking from this site. Where's the girl?"

"She went to the latrine." William said the first thing that came to his mind.

"She isn't missing again, is she? You didn't lose her again, did you? Add wood to that campfire, Pete." Pete was confused. He threw some branches on the coals. They burst into flame. "Make it good and big, Pete."

Pete built up the fire.

"You don't need that gun." Tom said. "Last thing we all need here, a bad accident."

"I know how to handle a gun, gramps."

Tom said nothing. He continued to hold the atlatl case.

Sarah was somewhere behind them. William prayed she would remain out of sight until these men were done.

"Cameras, Raymond. Cell phones. iPods."

Raymond approached and held out his hand. Tom shifted the case to his left hand and, with his right hand, pulled his small camera from a pocket, handing it to Raymond. He had no cell phone. Sergei was absolutely still next to William. Raymond approached him.

"Camera, please," said Roger, raising the gun until it was pointed at Sergei's knees.

Sergei said something in Russian and handed over his camera.

"Cell phone?"

Sergei took a cell phone from his pocket.

"You, too, Tonto." Roger was talking to William.

"I don't have a camera. Or cell phone."

"You as well, Pocahontas."

"Kiss off."

Roger's face twisted. He stepped close to Myra and pointed the gun at her belly.

"Do you have a camera?"

"No."

"Search her, Raymond. The rest of you guys, check

their packs."

Raymond started patting Myra down. Roger held the gun to her belly. The others each grabbed a pack. Gear began to fly onto the ground - clothing, bowls, sleeping bags.

Raymond took his time with Myra. He checked everywhere, lingering in her pants pockets. Myra shuddered. William could probably kill Raymond with one good blow, but by then Roger would have blown a hole in his daughter.

Raymond found no camera on Myra. Roger removed the gun from her belly. He took the atlatl case from Tom with his left hand. Bernie placed the two cameras and the cell phone on a wide, flat rock by the fire and stomped on them. Then he kicked the broken pieces into the flames. William watched the plastic melt, dark smoke rise.

"Does the girl have a camera?" asked Roger. William didn't like the look in Roger's eye, and he liked the look in Raymond's even less. Pete was standing to the side, ashen.

"Where's the latrine?" Roger asked.

William pointed toward Bob-Bob's grave. He was certain Sarah had not gone that way. "We use the woods that way, back 100 yards or more."

"Mark. Clarence. Go look." Roger gestured to two of his men. The two men standing by Raymond headed off, leaving Roger, Raymond, Pete and Bernie. The packs lay on the ground, gear scattered. Roger handed the gun to Raymond.

Roger unscrewed the top of the case and pulled out the cloth-wrapped atlatl. He pulled the cloth away. The bone gleamed in the sun. He stood directly in front of the broken blasted tree. At his feet lay several rocks. "I can see this is it, from your expressions."

Pete stood off to the side. Raymond stood right beside Roger, in front of the blasted tree. He aimed the gun toward Tom, then Myra, then William, finally Sergei.

Roger held the atlatl carelessly, swinging it by his side. "I have no idea what this thing is, but I know it's old. We heard you last spring, knew this thing might have come from here."

"Maybe not." Myra spoke fast. "There's no evidence, really, that it was here. Tom found it because his grandfather had it with him, but Bob-Bob might have found it anywhere."

"Nice try, princess. This thing is a bona fide artifact, that's art-ee-fact. This thing is your wet dream, to stop the mining."

"Just as it's your worst nightmare, if it gets out." Tom ignored Raymond's gun.

"Not any more, gramps. As of now, you have no cameras, no photos, and no evidence."

"What, you're going to take that atlatl and hide it?"

"That's what you call it, princess? At-lat-ell? Hide it? Here, watch me hide it."

Roger took the atlatl and placed it on a rock. Then he picked up another rock and lifted it over his head. Myra yelled as Roger slammed the rock onto the thrower. He struck again and again. Pieces and powder flew. Sergei shifted, as if preparing to charge, but William held his arm. Raymond was looking their way, almost begging them to try. Roger took the shattered pieces of the thrower and threw them into the fire. The bone flared as it landed in the hot coals. Myra was weeping.

Pete had been watching, shocked. Now he roared and leapt for Roger. Raymond fired the gun. Pete grabbed his knee and fell.

William heard the fire crackling. Bernie stared in shock at Pete. Raymond, now giggling, swung the gun. Roger's eyes were eager, watching Raymond.

He and Raymond were standing shoulder to shoulder on the root knees of the broken tree. They were standing somewhat higher than the forest floor. Raymond held the gun. Roger dusted his hands, picked up the remaining shards of the destroyed atlatl, and threw them into the fire. Raymond was swinging the gun toward them. Roger said nothing as Raymond took aim. William was certain Raymond was about to shoot.

William heard a fluttering whisper. A dart shaft suddenly pierced the bicep of Raymond's right arm, which held the pistol, and struck the large tree behind, quivering. Raymond recoiled from his arm as the gun fell from his hand. Sergei lunged forward and grabbed the pistol before Roger, beside Raymond, could move.

William heard the fluttering again. A second shaft struck Roger's left arm, just beneath the shoulder, and, like the other dart, passed through into the tree. Roger shouted. Raymond was shrieking. Bernie ran. Mark and Clarence, returning from looking for Sarah, broke and ran when they saw Sergei with the gun and their two companions pinned to the tree. Sarah approached from the cliff, thrower in position, a third dart aimed, totally focused.

Sergei checked the chambers of the pistol, then put it on safety. Blood dripped down the sleeves of the two trapped men.

Sarah walked forward, lowering the thrower and taking the dart in her left hand. She hardly glanced at Roger and Raymond. "I didn't think he was going to smash it. I should have shot sooner." She started to cry.

"Jesus, Sarah." Tom stared at his granddaughter. "You could have killed them."

Sarah went over and stood before Roger and Raymond. "If I'd wanted to kill them they'd be dead, Tom-Tom."

Roger was hissing with pain.

Raymond was crying. "You crucified us."

"You asked for it."

"We'll die here."

"Then die, asshole."

"You won't die." Tom peered at the darts. "These went through your muscle. Unless they hit an artery, you won't bleed to death. It's gonna hurt, cutting them off and pulling them out. Be better for professionals to do it. You have a radio?"

"You little shit." Raymond spat at Sarah. "This is attempted murder. You're going to be locked up. You need to be."

Roger, grimacing, eyed Sarah. "That was some shooting, girl."

Myra gently pulled Sarah away. "You should be happy, Roger. You win. No pictures, no thrower. No evidence." Myra crouched by Pete. He was in a lot of pain. "Thanks, Pete, You didn't have to do that."

Pete gritted his teeth. "Yes I did."

Tom radioed for help. When he got through, he said they needed medical help immediately. Three people were hurt badly, one with a gunshot wound. He said to bring stretchers. Two of the hurt people were impaled against a tree. When asked how two people could be pinned to a tree, Tom didn't bother to explain.

Myra and Sergei managed to straighten Pete's leg and bind the wound. He was in shock.

Roger and Raymond had to keep standing. If they started to slide down, the shafts pinning them to the tree quickly stopped them.

The other Buckhorn people, who had fled, heard Tom's shouts and returned to the camp and the injured men. With Sergei holding the pistol, watching them always, the Buckhorn people helped Roger and Raymond remain on their feet.

While waiting for the helicopter, Tom, Myra and William repacked their gear. William wasn't sure whether police would emerge from the helicopter or medical people. At this point he didn't care. The atlatl was gone. They had no evidence aside from Sarah's sketches. Sarah was certainly going to face some difficult legal issues when she came out of the park. Tom, Sergei, Myra and William were going to have questions to answer as well.

It took 90 minutes for the helicopter to arrive. It landed, rotors thudding, at the lip of the headwall dropping from Bear Valley to Godkin Creek. Tall thunderheads approached from the west.

A medevac team with drugs and stretchers and one ranger arrived. They were astonished to see Roger and Raymond fastened to the broken tree. The medevac team cut off the darts near the tree. Roger and Raymond were carried to the helicopter, a length of shaft still sticking through each of their arms, by the other Buckhorn people and the medevac team. Sergei, Tom, Sarah, Myra and William carried Pete.

The ranger who had come with the medical crew gathered

them together as the unhurt Buckhorn people started back to their camp on the Godkin.

"I don't know what happened here, but we can't take statements from the injured parties and I'm not equipped, really, to take yours. When you get out, we'll take your statements then. Are you heading out now? The helicopter's full and we need to leave to beat the weather."

"We're leaving." Tom was definite.

"There's a fire down by Lillian River, also another on Dodger Point. Be careful, they may close the trail. Then you'll have to exit via Hayden Pass or Low Divide." The ranger kneeled eye to eye with Sarah. "You're the girl who went missing last spring, right?" Sarah nodded. The ranger stood. "You people come in here in May and this girl here disappears, and now you come back and one man is shot and two others seem to have been attacked by a strange kind of bow and arrow?"

"Spear thrower. It was a spear thrower." Sarah was looking at the ground.

"What the hell happened here? Just tell me you'll check in at the ranger station when you come out. We can take your statements then. And for God's sake, be careful. And you, little lady, you might want to be more careful about who you allow to take you into the park. These people here seem to draw trouble."

Sarah said nothing. Myra and William started to laugh.

The ranger was at least a foot taller than Sarah. She stood next to William, back straight, staring up at him. The ranger almost smiled. "I won't ask who threw those things."

The helicopter left. The thumping rotors could be heard for a long time. They were suddenly alone. The points of the two darts, shafts cut clean just at the level of the bark, remained in the broken tree.

"Sarah, you could have killed someone." Myra was standing

before Sarah. "You could have killed Roger or Raymond. You could have killed any of us, too."

"Raymond was getting ready to shoot you, Myra. Roger wasn't stopping him. I did the only thing I could."

"Well I, for one, thank you." Sergei knelt down, took Sarah's hand. "When I killed my first bear, I was 15, and I was terrified even though my father was by my side. When the bear died, I cried, a little. It had been such a magnificent animal."

"Those two aren't magnificent, Sergei."

"No, that they are not. You did not kill them, either."

Sarah went over to the now-smoldering fire. No evidence remained of the thrower. "What will happen when we get out?"

"Let's hope none of those three dies." Tom checked the straps of his pack. "They came to our camp, attacked us, destroyed our things, shot their own colleague, and were about to shoot us, all to destroy any evidence this might be an ancient site."

"They succeeded." Myra hoisted her pack.

"I'm sure Fletcher Lynch will try to use this as another excuse to keep Sarah from living with me." Tom lengthened a strap. "If she can't stay with me I'm not sure where they'll send her."

"I will testify for you, Tom. Even though I am a Russian and someone with no authority in this land."

"Now they'll claim I'm violent in addition to being crazy," Sarah said.

"They may try, Sarah, but you have us four to say you were acting in self defense."

They all hoisted their packs. Far off William heard the low rumble of distant thunder. They'd lose the sun in three hours.

"Let's see how far we get before we have to stop," Tom said. "Everyone ready?"

William brought up the rear, Sarah ahead of him. When they

reached the lip of the low headwall, she stopped, looking over the Godkin Valley. The others were in front, working their way down the slope. William could see, beyond the trees, the opening at the creek where the Buckhorn camp lay. Smoke rose, lazy.

"This is messed up, William."

"Why do you say that, Sarah?"

Sarah was standing on the lip of the headwall. "We lost the thrower. Worse, it's destroyed. Tom-Tom didn't get anything like what he wanted. Now the thrower's gone. The photos are gone."

"We have your sketches, Sarah. We remember what we saw."

"But it's our word against theirs. Now there's no evidence. Tom-Tom didn't even get to use the thrower to stop the mining. Myra doesn't have anything to help her in fighting Buckhorn. I just proved I'm violent and dangerous. There's no way they'll let me stay with Tom-Tom, or anyone. And you, Myra, and Tom-Tom look bad, like irresponsible grownups, because you took me back in here again, secretly. They'll say I've been kidnapped, and now I'm a criminal and you're all accomplices, and we have nothing to show for this. Nothing." Sarah stood facing the sun. A tear rolled down her thin cheek. West, clouds approached. Beneath, dark ropy whirls twisted. Lightning flickered. "This is gonna be a long sad walk out, William."

They worked their way to the creek, passing the Buckhorn camp. Bernie, Mark and Clarence were sitting on their camp chairs. Behind the chairs were two large canvas sacks, with green trim, streaked, discolored, half covered with a poncho. Bernie saw William looking and said something to the others, and Mark pulled the poncho over the sacks. William wondered how the three of them were going to be able to pack everything out.

They followed the elk track for one hour to the Elwha Trail. As they moved, clouds rolled over the Elwha Valley and it began to rain. By the time they reached Hayes River, they had their rain gear on and thunder rolled across the mountains. Some lightning struck close by. Ahead, still distant, smoke rose from Dodger Point. The ranger tent at Hayes River was empty. A handwritten sign was posted by the tent.

"Listen to weather radio for fire and trail conditions."

Tom tried his radio. He could get nothing.

They continued. They saw nobody. With fires closer to Whiskey Bend, few people would be coming into the park. The brown meadows in the Press Valley lay flattened by the rain. Leaves on the trail caught raindrops. As they left the Press Valley William turned back the way they had come. He saw smoke. Lightning striking close to Hayes River, probably just after they left, had started a fire.

A half-mile further, light fading, they decided to camp. They found a place beneath some trees, on level ground, where their tents would be sheltered. They gathered wood and rigged a ground cloth as a shelter to sit beneath while the rain tapered off. They could hear thunder growling for hours. They were physically tired, emotionally exhausted, and numb from the loss of the thrower and their cameras. They sat, watching the fire.

That night Sarah finished her story.

was beneath robes in the bottom of the canoe, the same place Bright Eyes lay after the bear tore her calf. My head hurt. Most of one finger was missing. I feared the hot flesh Bright Eyes had feared. I did not want the dark lines under my skin reaching for my heart. We were at sea. I heard water sounds and the singing wind, the thunk of paddles against the side, the "Hut-hut-hut" of the paddlers. The sky was blue. Watcher stood with the steering oar. The sail spread above us. Weeps a Lot and Weeps a Lot More, Cold Eye, Tree Hide and Rock Hide sat under the tent with me. They worked on fixing ropes, robes, and clothing.

"She is awake." Weeps a Lot saw my eyes were open. "Strong Heart is here."

Cold Eye sniffed. "Strong Heart is a trouble maker. She brings bad spirits. The bear took Heavy. She called the cat to The Place People Were. She is not of the people."

Tree Hide overheard Cold Eye. "None of those things does she carry." Tree Hide was taller than Cold Eye, almost the same age, and strong. She was not afraid of Cold Eye like the weepers were. "You bring poison with your words. You think because you have Thin Hair's favor you are now his wife. You are not yet his wife."

I did not know how much time had passed since the cat had attacked me. I had no memory of being taken to the canoe or the canoe pushing off.

Weeps a Lot whispered to me. "You have slept more than three days, Strong Heart. You have been here on these robes all this time and all this time you have been breathing but not here. You did not eat, or drink, but you were alive."

"Do you remember the cat?" Rock Hide was sewing a robe.

"I remember the cat leaping and Pretty Face dropping the pole. I remember trying to brace the pole to stop the cat. Pretty Face shot the cat."

"Thrower first shot the cat in the heart. It was his throw that saved you, Strong Heart." Rock Hide whispered even lower. "Pretty Face ran. Everyone saw. He turned and ran. You did not."

"She was falling." Cold Eye was being cold in her speech. "She was cowering before the cat."

"We have been in the canoe three days?"

"No, Strong Heart. Yesterday we came to an island and camped. A small island, with no animals, but with water and wood. We brought you ashore."

The fresh air smelled good. The canoe smelled good. It must have been cleaned when we stopped.

Later, Watcher gave a shout and the paddlers changed. Those who had been under the tent, except for Weeps a Lot and Weeps a Lot More, replaced those at the thwarts.

Now with me under the tent were Bright Eyes, Fat Hair, Pretty Face and Woman Too Soon. Pretty Face did not look at me. Woman Too Soon was happy to see me awake. Pretty Face, Fat Hair, and Bright Eyes stretched out and slept on slats and robes near the stern, in the open air. I then understood we would be paddling the entire night.

Woman Too Soon whispered. "You have an enemy in Pretty Face. Now he is my enemy, too, because I will not share his robe."

"Cannot he choose his wife?"

"With these people the woman chooses. Did you not know that? Cold Eye chose Thin Hair. I chose Pretty Face and now I have not chosen him." I saw Woman Too Soon gaze at Thrower. Thrower was still paddling, forward with Anger. "Cold Eye will stay with Thin Hair. I think Pretty Face will want Tree Hide, but I do not think Tree Hide wants him."

Woman Too Soon stopped talking. I lay my head back. Surely Woman Too Soon had not been right, that we chose. Then I found myself angry with Woman Too Soon, for she was a woman and now she was seeking Thrower. If she shared Thrower's robe, then perhaps Thrower would no longer teach me how to throw. I enjoyed throwing.

We travelled for many days, stopping at small islands, for water and seal. During this time we had to wait on land three days more because of strong winds. Everyone was impatient and sick of the journey. People argued. Much of the way ice was everywhere on the shore, many times into the ocean. All this time, Pretty Face measured me with his eyes.

When we came again to land and beached the canoe, we were in some kind of inlet, a deep, well-sheltered place. Thin Hair climbed with Fat Hair and Watcher to the top of the rise beyond the beach and faced south. The wind blew steadily from the north. The sun was out. All except me pulled the canoe ashore and braced it. Here we found driftwood, trees, and fresh water. Anger and Long Braid reported some sign of bear inland, deep scratches against trees.

Now we had both a bear robe and a cat robe. These were the largest robes we had. At night we needed these robes. It was growing cold when the sun went down.

Thrower and Long Braid took a seal along the shore. Others turned and cleaned the canoe, then leaned it as a shelter. That evening, as we all huddled under the canoe, Thin Hair sat at one end and Fat Hair the other, far apart.

When Thin Hair and Fat Hair talked, they spoke across the rest of us.

"The wind is fair." Thin Hair planned to depart the next morning.

"You are too impatient. This is a long coast we must traverse. It will take us two days. We need to wait."

"Wait for what? Days to become shorter? The bears to find us?"

"This north wind will not last, Thin Hair."

"You wish to travel the inner channels around these ranges. There the water is shallow, at times exposed by the tides. Many animals are there."

"It is safer. Had we taken that way going to the headland we would have been there sooner and started back earlier. This is your fault."

"We chose not to take that route because even you were uncertain, last spring. Now you are changing the past." Thin Hair spoke forcefully. Before, Fat Hair had become quiet when Thin Hair spoke this way but now, sitting with the others, emboldened, he said more.

"I am the finder," Fat Hair said.

"I have been on this route more often than you. I too know the route. The season is late. We will leave tomorrow, and we will take the north wind along this coast."

Fat Hair rose. "I will take Pretty Face's place on watch now." He gathered his thrower and darts and left.

Thin Hair settled back.

Anger, next to me, whispered. "Because Thin Hair killed the people who brought you to the headland, Fat Hair believes Thin Hair's father will lose authority when we return. If this happens, Fat Hair's clan would lead. Pretty Face will side with Fat Hair. The two of them may try to remove Thin Hair as our leader during this journey home, and to do that they may try to remove Watcher who is now on watch, to reduce Thin Hair's allies. I will replace Watcher on watch now. "

Anger rose and followed Fat Hair.

Now it was Thrower on my other side who whispered to me. "You and the other journey wives will need to choose. In the canoe all of us must work, but in camp on shore, this is where trouble can happen."

When Pretty Face came to the canoe, he was followed by Watcher.

This was a long night.

The next morning, we left the cove under a clear sky. Something had happened beneath the canoe that night as Fat Hair and Thin Hair spoke, and now everyone was watchful. Long Braid, though married to Fat Hair, did all she could to find peace between Thin Hair and Fat Hair. As his woman, she could say things to Fat Hair that nobody else could say. Long Braid might have been more successful, but Cold Eye, defending Thin Hair, could not remain silent and said things that made Long Braid angry. After this Long Braid stopped trying to make peace.

I knew that whatever might happen, in the eyes of Pretty Face I was an enemy and would be considered part of Thin Hair's group. Fat Hair did not care, because I had seen that in his mind I was not much of a woman, now or in the future. Long Braid seemed to like me. She spoke to me often, and was kind, taking the time to tell me legends and stories. But she was Fat Hair's wife. With the two of them bringing home a journey child, her concern for me was tiny compared to her concern for the child growing within her.

I felt alone. This was a familiar feeling.

We paddled day and night. The wind continued. We used the sail. Large waves came from the west, marching, like hills, and the smaller waves driven by the north wind crossed these seas and created a steep rough cross-sea, but the canoe rode well.

My cut finger was sore but did not become hot and deadly. By the second day Thin Hair told me to start paddling with the others. I was able to paddle on the left side, curling my good hand around the shaft and the hand with the cut finger over the top of the paddle and holding steady. The finger hurt but did not start bleeding. We chanted "Hut-hut-hut." First we saw the high peaks to the left, the snow, and then nothing but water, seas around us, lost in a field of blue. Birds followed, crying out, and Tiny Whales swam with us, playing under the bow, blowing near.

The fourth day, we pulled behind a long, low, tree-covered barrier island, behind which lay calm water. We stopped where a small stream drained the rise running down the center of the island. Anger and Thrower went ashore looking for animal sign and returned to report no animals. The distance from this island to the main shore was not far, and the water was calm. An animal could swim to the island easily. The sun was dropping to the west. To the east, beyond the close water, I saw a plain, and high ice further on. A crescent moon rose.

Thin Hair looked across the water to the mainland, where a river drained into the sea. "It is time for salmon, and the bears will be gathered for the fish. If the fish have come, the bears will be fat and lazy. If the fish have not yet come, the bears will be hungry and there will be many."

Thin Hair instructed us to beach the canoe. We left the canoe near the water, held by an anchor stone, in case we had to depart quickly. We built a lean-to on the beach and a fire pit. We started a fire. We filled the stomach bags with water. On the highest points nearby, Pretty Face and Thrower were posted to watch the mainland, the water, and the rest of our island. The sun fell toward the sea and the sky turned red.

"Our journey is nearly done." Thin Hair finished chewing smoked seal meat. "There is one more place we can stop before crossing the last ice wall. Perhaps we will find seals there. We need food." Thin Hair peered at the moon. "We may reach our home for the same time moon. I have chosen one among you to travel to the Marking Place and record our coming." He nodded at me as he said this.

"Only if the weather holds," said Fat Hair. "You have waited too late, Thin Hair."

"You are the finder, Fat Hair. As finder you chose the way to the headland. If we are late home because we were late making it to the headland, this is not my fault."

"If the weather turns, we will not arrive."

"We will arrive."

At Fat Hair's end of the lean-to, Long Braid stared at the needlework in her hands. Fat Hair observed Thin Hair with disgust. I was grateful he and Pretty Face were only two against Thin Hair, Thrower, Anger, Watcher, and Bright Eyes.

"If we are late," said Thin Hair, "when we arrive on our land's north shore some of us can reach the Marking Place from the north before the equal time moon. This has been done before."

"Not in our lifetime, Thin Hair." Fat Hair laughed.

"It can be done. Two or three can travel from there on foot, the rest of us bringing the canoe to our west shore. It is not a long way and we can do it with fewer people."

Anger spoke to me quietly. "Thin Hair will land on the north shore. He, Thrower, and perhaps I will travel with you to the Marking Place where we will honor the equal time moon. From there, we will go home through the mountains. This way it will be Fat Hair returning in triumph with wives and journey children, but it will be Thin Hair and his son who have taken one of the new wives to the Marking Place. This will mean that while Fat Hair's return will be a great thing, Thin Hair's action will be even greater."

"I am to go to the Marking Place? I am furthest from being a woman of anyone. I am damaged, now missing a finger."

"It will be you, Strong Heart." Anger chuckled. "Thin Hair has chosen you to go to the Marking Place. He said so after the cat attacked, when you slept."

I could now see Thin Hair watching me. He saw me looking and he nodded to me. Thrower was out on watch.

"You choose Thrower. This is what he wants. This is what Thin Hair sees."

"I am not ready to choose anyone, Anger."

"Thrower will be patient."

"His ears are much too big."

Anger watched me. I could feel my face grow hot.

"Animals. Two."

Thrower's call was clear. He had been on watch to the south, a short distance away. I could see his outline against the purple sky. Now he was pointing with his thrower. He was pointing toward the shore. From the other position, we heard Pretty Face.

"In the water. Swimming."

"Quick." Thin Hair was already moving.

I saw two patterns in the water, like geese flying, patterns made by small waves. At the point of these waves, I could see bobbing dark heads, each head facing us, one head larger than the other. The smaller head was in front. It was 10 canoe lengths distant, and the other head one canoe length beyond that.

Thrower and Pretty Face ran from their spots back to the lean-to. Long Braid and Anger gathered robes, gesturing to the rest of us to move fast and quickly to load the canoe.

Thin Hair watched the bobbing heads approaching. "A yearling. This young bear is curious and coming to see us. He is hungry and stupid. Behind him is his mother, following.

She will be even hungrier, but she will not be stupid. She will die to protect him. Before she dies, many of us will die, too, unless we can paddle clear." The two bobbing heads approached, trailing whiskers of wake. I could hear the bears breathing. "Hurry."

We threw everything into the canoe, the robes, the ropes, the food, and the baskets. Thin Hair and Watcher took burning brands from the fire and scattered them along the edge of the water where the bears might land, hoping the smoke and embers might slow them down. Everyone else pushed the canoe into the water after untying the anchor stone.

"Wait. Wait." Fat Hair turned back to the fire. "The bone pieces."

He and Long Braid returned to the fire and gathered the bone pieces, including some half-carved throwers. Now they rushed back to the canoe with the tools in their arms. Long Braid tripped, scattering her tools, crying out.

The heads were so close we could see the eyes of the two bears. Once their paws touched the shore, they could set their hind legs and run.

We were out of time.

"The fire," called Thin Hair. We ran for the fire, in hopes the flames would frighten the bears. Those of us who could use throwers grabbed our darts and prepared to die. Even I found a thrower, one carved of bone.

The animals reached the beach, leaping over the coals and smoking brands, coming our way, the young one running clumsily but fast, the mother coming faster, overtaking.

Long Braid lay on the ground, holding her ankle. Cold Eye and the weepers cowered inside the canoe. Woman Too Soon, Tree Hide, and Rock Hide all grabbed burning torches from the fire, scattering sparks and smoke. Tree Hide and Rock Hide ran fearlessly toward the approaching animals.

The young bear, almost as large as its mother, and almost as fast, veered away from the approaching fire and headed along the beach toward the canoe. The mother did not avoid the fire, but instead came roaring, fur flying, eyes alight, directly at the people holding brands. I threw my dart. We all threw at the bear charging Tree Hide and Rock Hide.

I saw three darts plunge deep into the torso of the animal, and my dart struck the bear's throat. Yet another entered its open mouth. But she did not falter or slow down. It was as if the darts had been a breath of wind, ruffling the animal's fur. The bear swept a massive paw through Rock Hide's burning brand and struck her across the head so hard her head was ripped from her body. Her headless trunk, still on its feet, spouted blood, while the head flew through the air, spinning, then hitting the water.

Tree Hide screamed. The bear now faced her, standing just before the fire. Tree Hide thrust her brand into the bear's face. The burning brand singed its hair. It shook its head and bellowed, then seemed to become aware of the darts in its torso, throat and mouth. We threw again. Several darts hit the torso, and one passed through the bear's eye. The bear stood high on its back legs, towering over Tree Hide, towering even over the brand Tree Hide held aloft over her head. Then the bear erupted blood and collapsed.

Just as the mother fell we heard screams from the water. The young bear had leapt inside the canoe as if it was something to play in.

We raced toward the canoe, Thin Hair leading, a dart ready in his thrower. The bear, when leaping into the canoe, had driven it back toward the water. Now the canoe was floating, no longer secured. The canoe rocked and bobbed as the bear grunted and attacked. From inside the canoe, we heard cries. The bear flailed one way, then another. Pretty Face stood behind Thin Hair, thrower ready. Fat Hair and Watcher leapt into the water and somehow grabbed the canoe before it drifted beyond reach. With the canoe floating in the water, the sides were too high for us to throw down at the bear inside.

Weeps a Lot, bloody, suddenly appeared on a thwart. Thin Hair waded close, trying to reach the canoe so he could throw a dart at the bear. Weeps a Lot jumped out of the canoe and landed on Thin Hair's shoulder, destroying his aim, just as the bear rose. It stood looking at Thin Hair. I expected Pretty Face, who had an easy shot, to throw, but he did not. The bear raised an arm and swung, striking its paw against Thin Hair's shoulder. I heard bones snap. Thin Hair tumbled sideways into the water. He tried to rise, but could not because his shoulder was crushed. Weeps a Lot fell against him, driving him deeper into the water. Finally Pretty Face threw, striking the bear just before it dropped to all fours to resume feeding in the canoe. Cold Eye stood silently in the stern, the end of the canoe furthest from the land, while the bear ate and grunted in the bow.

The bear paused in its feeding and rose again. A dart stuck out from under its throat. It saw Watcher and Fat Hair close by, at the bow, holding the canoe. The bear roared, its face covered with blood. We threw again. Although now hit by many darts, the bear continued to move, rocking the canoe. Watcher, holding the bow, made the canoe rock even more. The bear lost its balance and tumbled into the water. It splashed for long minutes before dying. Watcher and Fat Hair tugged the canoe back to the shore.

The mother bear lay dead. Long Braid keened as she lay on the ground, her ankle twisted. Tree Hide sang the loss song for Rock Hide, whose headless body sprawled on the beach. Thin Hair, now dead, bobbed in the water. Thrower began his loss song. Weeps a Lot had staggered ashore, bleeding. Cold Eye, still in the stern of the canoe, had not moved. She was pointing toward the middle of the canoe, trying to speak.

We pulled the canoe to the beach. Watcher and Fat Hair gently pulled Thin Hair's body onto the land. Inside the canoe was blood, pieces of flesh, a torso, legs and arms--the remains of Weeps a Lot More. Anger began to throw the partly eaten body parts out of the canoe. Pretty Face stood alone, watching me. He knew I had seen him delay his throw. Now Thin Hair was dead, as Pretty Face and Fat Hair had wished.

Fat Hair stood on the beach looking toward the mainland across the water. Judging by the sky, very little time had passed since the bears swam to us, but it felt as if days had gone by.

Fat Hair pointed at some new geese-shaped ripples in the water. "The salmon have not come yet. The bears are hungry and coming for us." Three more were swimming for the island. They were already halfway across. "Quick. We must leave now."

Watcher, Anger, Fat Hair and Thrower carried Long Braid into the canoe, placing her on robes.

Thrower stood by his father's body. "We must burn Thin Hair, Rock Hide, and Weeps a Lot More to free their spirits."

"We have no time. We must leave," said Fat Hair. Anger, Watcher, Thrower and I carried Thin Hair and Rock Hide to the fire. We threw their bodies on the flames and piled as much wood as we could. Then we ran back to the canoe and pushed off.

We began to paddle. We paddled as fast as we could.

We had many losses. Three people were dead. Weeps a Lot had been badly gashed by the bear. Long Braid's foot lay at a strange angle. Fat Hair was now our leader.

Watcher steered as we paddled. The three bears, still swimming, followed, now falling behind. We struggled south between the barrier island and the shore, hoping we could find safety. We had little water, virtually no food, and a long distance yet to travel. Long Braid lay in the bottom of the canoe, eyes blank. Weeps a Lot continued bleeding. We wrapped a robe around her cut, but we did not have time for paste and herbs. Long Braid, the person who best knew the healing arts, was herself unable to move. Thrower continued to hum his loss song, not talking. His father was dead.

The fire behind us blazed. The red glow lingered against the darkening sky until the shore curved and we passed around a gentle point.

The barrier island was long and we were able to stay in calm waters until the sun rose. We picked our way south, watching the shore, always watching, even though now we were leaving behind the river where the bears were gathered. When the sun broke above the ice to the east, we stopped near the south end of the island and Anger and Fat Hair went ashore and checked for animals. Here the island was narrow, with a tall tree-covered ridge in the middle. A tiny stream fed a small pool. We found no animals where we landed, no scratched bark, no footprints.

We pulled the canoe ashore and gently removed Long Braid and placed her on boughs. Bright Eyes started a fire. Tree Hide and Cold Eye filled the stomach bags with water. I helped Woman Too Soon bind and secure Long Braid's foot. It was very swollen. She gasped as we straightened and lashed the foot between stout sticks, making it rigid.

Thrower and Pretty Face went seeking seal, but found none. They took two raccoons. These we butchered and cooked, hanging the meat over the flames. Weeps a Lot was not eating. We ate all the meat. The meat was bitter.

We did not wash the canoe. We loaded the water, placed some boughs in the bottom, and pushed off.

➤

Other narrow islands lay far ahead. The shore, east, rose to high mountains and ice. The ice reached the sea in many places. Ice chunks floated in the water. We paddled for six hand spans, away from land, until the mountains and the ice were distant. Out here the water was deep blue and Tiny Whales were everywhere. We raised the sail and began moving south.

Now there was no singing, no "Hut-hut-hut," no drum. We all were silent, working, not thinking. The only people who spoke were Pretty Face and Fat Hair. They talked excitedly about how far we would go this day, when we would reach the next camp before the ice bear, how we would share the food and water. They talked all the time, back and forth. Long Braid, on the bottom of the canoe, listened and said nothing. The rest of us said nothing. Thrower paddled in the bow, alone, facing forward. I paddled opposite Thrower.

After a long time paddling, Thrower and I rested under the tent while others took over.

Long Braid slept while Weeps a Lot stared at the sky, awake but not seeing. The sail sounds and water sounds and the chatter of Fat Hair and Pretty Face meant Thrower and I could whisper without others hearing.

"Did you see what Pretty Face did?" Thrower leaned close to me. We were retying ropes.

"I thought only I saw."

"So you saw."

"Fat Hair saw, too, I think."

"This was murder, Strong Heart. I will have revenge."

"First we must reach your home. Fat Hair and Pretty Face need all of us alive and healthy to get there."

"It will be most dangerous when our home is in sight."

I heard Pretty Face laugh and Fat Hair join in. Thrower twisted a section of rope in his hands.

"Pretty Face is clever. If we tell my grandfather what Pretty

Face did, Pretty Face will say that he did not delay throwing to allow the bear to kill my father. Instead, he will say he needed to wait for the proper time, because my father was between him and the bear, and his aim is not that good. He will remind everyone that he removed your finger with a throw, and then he will remind us how he placed a dart high in that tree because of another wild throw."

"Pretty Face was trying to shoot me when I lost my finger. And your father was not between Pretty Face and the bear."

"He was close enough. Fat Hair will support his story."

"Yes, it will be the word of Fat Hair and Pretty Face against Thin Hair's son, you, and me, a young stranger, who some say is a bad spirit. That is how they will argue."

"My grandfather is wise, Strong Heart."

"Then we must live until we can stand before him."

We continued. The day passed. Late in the afternoon, the north wind died. By sunset, the water lay smooth, like fresh ice, stretching away, except this ice moved as the big marching animals beneath the surface strode toward land. We paddled and the canoe left a slight trail behind, but from hand span to hand span we could not tell if we were moving at all. To the east the high mountains and the white ice shone brightly, with black jagged lines where the rocks broke through. Even this far away, we could see the thick rise of spray when a section of ice fell into the sea, but we were so distant the waves from such falls arrived weak and small.

Thrower and I were again paddling.

Thrower turned to me and his teeth were bright in a wide smile. "You will force me to have a much stronger right arm. Your hand forces me to always paddle this side."

"Just as I am forced to strengthen only my left arm."

My left hand and arm always ached with a dull pain from pulling the paddle. When we rested, I had trouble relaxing my fingers after gripping the shaft of the paddle for so long. The damaged finger on my right hand slowly healed. The stump closed with a fresh scab and thin new skin. "If your right arm is made stronger, Thrower, then I will have helped you become an ever better and longer thrower because you throw right-handed."

"I will need this help if you keep throwing, Strong Heart. You will one day be the best thrower of our people."

"This is a day even further away than the distant time I become a woman."

"That time is not so distant."

"You know nothing."

The sun fell to the edge of the sea. The surface lay like a vast still puddle. With no wind, the sail hung slack. Six of us paddled, yet the canoe seemed motionless. Still, when I took my position again at the thwart, I saw that the tallest mountain to the east, once well ahead, was now behind us, and further ahead were more mountains, higher still, heavy with ice.

We drank water, only water. We had no food.

Stars rose in the east and then the moon, growing fatter, growing to her fullness. Long Braid woke and we made her comfortable. Thrower held the cup for her so she could drink.

"This has become a steep price for wives." Long Braid drank. "Thin Hair was our shaman and now we have no shaman. Thrower, you are not yet ready, even though you have taken your mystery time." Long Braid reached out and took my hand. "You are the one chosen to go to the Marking Place, Strong Heart. This is also the place our shamans go for their mystery time. This place is a mystery for the people, a sacred place."

I did not know what Long Braid was talking about. "What is this Marking Place?"

"This is the place where one from the new wives goes and

marks arrival. A place where we honor the animals that rule our land. Some of us can paint these animals on stone, using herbs and animal oil to make paint. Many cannot. This is something we also ask you wives to try, when you come, to see if you have the gift to make animals with paint. We hold our stories and history through these markings. Now I am tired. I will sleep." Long Braid closed her eyes. She was very weak.

"Where is this place?" I asked Thrower.

"The location cannot be told, but I have been there twice, with my father. I can tell you it lies with the eagles and the sun, and takes four days to reach from our home to the west."

Fat Hair called out. Thrower and I moved forward and took our positions on the first thwart. I felt air against my face. East, the ice gleamed beneath the moon and stars. The sky seemed to hold more stars than all the people who had ever lived or thought to live.

We paddled the entire night. In the morning, we faced a head wind. Clouds rose in the sky. The wind ahead was gentle but steady. Fat Hair directed Watcher to steer the canoe toward land, which had grown distant.

My belly was hollow. We were almost out of water. Far ahead, we saw the ice bear, white in the morning sun.

"There." Fat Hair pointed. "There, where the land ends, and the ice can be seen beyond, there we must stop and find food."

The wind blew against my face as I paddled. The canoe shuddered as it pierced the steep, small waves. Birds circled above, following us.

Later that morning, when Thrower and I went to the tent from our time paddling, Long Braid, on the wet robes, lay in pain, her eyes dull. Her strapped foot had swollen so much the flesh wrapped around one of the branches holding her ankle, and the skin had become cracked.

Weeps a Lot was gray. Her deep cut was not healing; it seeped blood.

The canoe lurched. Spray flew into our faces. Water sloshed across the bottom, against the robes and our feet. It was foul in the bottom of the canoe. We were down to our last water, and we still had far to go.

Anger, now forward paddling, worked as she always did, tireless, heavy bones moving as she pulled. Her long, misshapen head turned this way and that. She had become thinner. Her bones showed. Tree Hide had also grown thin. She spoke seldom, and moved with weariness. We all had drawn faces and hollow eyes. We were beginning to starve.

Fat Hair urged us to continue, faster, for the day was passing, the shore distant, and still we had to find the place to land.

The wind strengthened. The clouds approaching from the southwest began to arc over our heads. The day fell pale and dark.

"We must all paddle now," Fat Hair said.

Thrower and I joined the others. We had lost several good paddles in the bear attack, and when all of us paddled I had to use one which had been broken off at the top. I had no level handle on which to rest my right hand. I had to grip the shaft and try to guide the paddle while pulling with the other hand. This was difficult.

We could now see the shore. Ahead, it curved and seemed to end, and I knew Fat Hair wanted to bring us around this point to more sheltered waters beyond. Past the point, the great ice wall loomed, teeth deep in the sea, gnawing, stretching south, eating the sea.

We let loose the sail. Our speed increased.

We surged forward and leaned to one side as the wind pressed on the sail. We reached the point and then moved past. We slid by a rocky beach against which the deep seas from the west rose and thundered. Finally, we turned back north, and with the wind now behind us, we sailed into a sheltered beach.

In the protected cove, I saw a fire pit on the beach, and I knew this was the place Fat Hair had aimed for. He was a good finder.

We brought the canoe ashore. Ahead, I saw driftwood and a raven in a tree. Further down the beach, a group of seals, seeing us, scurried into the water.

Anger found an anchor stone. We pulled the canoe onto

shore and secured it. We made a lean-to near the fire pit, facing north, the direction from which animals might come. Watcher and Thrower disappeared inland, looking for sign of animals. Fat Hair, Tree Hide and Cold Eye took stomach bags and sought water. We left Long Braid and Weeps a Lot in the canoe, on the robes, because they could not move. After helping finish the shelter, I did my best to clean the area in the canoe around Weeps a Lot and Long Braid.

Long Braid's eyes opened. She saw me and she reached out, taking my arm. "Strong Heart, I have not yet taught you all you need to know."

"You have taught me much. You should not talk, Long Braid."

Long Braid was dying. Her eyes had dropped deep into her skull. Her jaw was sharp. Veins stuck out on her neck. Her foot was blue, swollen, the cracked skin now oozing thick, yellow fluid. She had the hot flesh. I was surprised she was able to see me, to speak at all.

"There is so much yet for you to learn."

"Hush, Long Braid." I did not know what to say. Weeps a Lot, now awake, lay next to Long Braid.

Long Braid struggled to speak. I had to lean close to listen. "My journey child will sleep before he wakes. Where is Fat Hair?"

"He has gone for water, Long Braid."

Long Braid coughed, a weak hollow rasp. She coughed again. Then, with her hand still on my arm, she died.

Watcher and Thrower returned to say there was animal sign and we would need watcher fires. Fat Hair returned with water and began his loss song. Anger and Tree Hide took throwers and went down the beach looking for seals or any food they could find. They moved slowly. We moved Weeps a Lot from the canoe to the fire, for warmth.

We were weak. We had trouble gathering wood for our main fire and then we had to gather more for the watcher fires. We needed enough wood to keep the fires blazing brightly through the night. We had to gather even more wood to build a pyre for Long Braid.

"People died because we did not set Thin Hair's and Rock Hide's spirits free on a proper pyre when the bears attacked us," muttered Anger, as she gathered wood next to me. "We are now building a pyre for Long Braid, but this will not balance our failure to set the others free."

The sun began to set. The clouds grew thick and we felt rain in the air.

We made another fire, north of the canoe and the fire pit, so the smoke would blow north, away from our camp. As evening fell, we carried Long Braid from the canoe and placed her on the pyre. Long Braid burned while Fat Hair sang his loss song. The pyre burned for a long time, throwing sparks high and sending smoke north in waves. The flames took Long Braid's body, freeing her spirit to return to her home.

Fat Hair had lost his wife and his journey child. He sat by the fire in silence. Pretty Face told us what to do when Fat Hair stopped talking.

We placed people at the watcher fires. With so few left, I had to stand guard by a watcher fire for several spans of the moon. I was comforted because the person at the other fire was Watcher. He could see better than anyone. I held a thrower and I hoped to see the red flash of eyes approaching.

It began to rain. I kept a long branch in the fire with a flaming end, which I could use to frighten or slow down any animal that might attack.

Watcher's fire was to my right, many paces distant.

"Ahead." Watcher's call was sharp. "Your side."

Between Watcher and me, but much closer to my fire, I saw

the red flash of eyes, glowing, low to the ground, approaching, and circling. These were not bears.

Watcher called out. "Wolves. Kill one now and they may flee."

Watcher ran toward me. I could see his torch swinging from the corner of my eye. Instead of picking up my torch, I took my thrower and darts and ran toward the wolves. I could see their eyes in the light cast by Watcher's torch. I stopped, placed a dart in the thrower, and waited. It was dark and I could only see their eyes.

The eyes backed away from Watcher's approaching torch, moving toward my fire and me. I now saw their bodies as well as their eyes. These were the great wolf, with fangs the length of my fingers. From behind me, I heard feet, people from our camp coming to help.

The wolf leader, tall and long, hesitated and turned. For a moment, he was outlined against the dark forest. I threw. I heard the whistling sound of other darts. The big wolf went down. My dart had struck just behind the left shoulder, passing through its heart, almost through its body. A second dart had struck a glancing blow near its rear legs.

Pretty Face strode to the wolf and pulled out the killing dart. He turned to me. The large animal lay on the ground, blood flowing from its mouth. "Your shot would have crippled this wolf had mine not killed it, Strong Heart."

The others were not close enough to hear us. Watcher and some of the others were chasing down another wolf.

"I killed this wolf." I spoke as I watched Pretty Face holding the dart I had thrown.

"No. This is my dart. This one here, it is yours." Pretty Face handed me the dart that had struck the hind legs. It was not my dart. As the others now approached, he said, "My shooting is better." His smile was large, and triumphant. He was one of those people who are good at lying because, in the moment they lie, they completely believe whatever they are saying. He acted just like a man who had killed this animal.

"You saved Strong Heart again." Cold Eye was behind Pretty Face.

"This is food we can now eat," Pretty Face took the dart I had thrown and held it as if it was his.

Watcher came up to us, bearing a torch. "We took no other wolves."

"We can eat." Woman Too Soon was already working with Bright Eyes on the dead wolf.

Fat Hair appeared, holding a thrower and darts. "You have fed us, Pretty Face."

I said nothing.

Pretty Face pointed. "Strong Heart hit the wolf also. I saw her throw. If my dart had not killed the wolf, she had crippled it and we would have taken it. This is partly her wolf." Pretty Face smiled at me and I saw in his eyes that he intended to kill me, but he would be patient.

If I took credit now for killing the wolf, it would look like I was trying to boast, and for this the others would ridicule me. By giving me some praise, Pretty Face had cleverly silenced me. He had already allowed Thin Hair to be killed, which opened a path for him. Now, with Fat Hair grieving for Long Braid, Pretty Face was taking all credit for killing this wolf and saving us from starvation. He was establishing himself as someone who helped others, someone who deserved leadership.

Pretty Face continued to smile. I said nothing. We ate. We were so hungry we found the sour flesh delicious. After we had eaten our fill, Watcher and I walked back to the small fires.

"I know you threw that dart, Strong Heart. I saw the throw. Pretty Face's throw was not the killing throw."

"He plans to kill me."

"You frighten him because you are not frightened of him.

You frighten him also because you know what he did with Thin Hair. He is afraid you will speak of this."

"It seems I do not need to speak of it if you already know."

"Strong Heart, Thin Hair named you well."

"My heart almost froze when those wolves came, Watcher. I was cold with fear."

"I also was cold with fear, Strong Heart. Fear keeps us alive."

It rained most of the night. No other animals came. In the morning, the rain had blown past and the wind shifted to the west, then the northwest. The sea churned with whitecaps and steep waves. Even when the sun rose above the mountains to the east, it was too rough to leave. We gathered more wood and smoked the rest of the wolf meat. We filled all the stomach bags and Watcher and Bright Eyes repaired two paddles. Cold Eye scraped and rolled the wolf pelt.

The wind continued as the skies cleared. The sun felt warm. The waters south of our camp were tossed and filled with scattered whitecaps, but our canoe had survived waters rougher than these.

"We must now try to sail," Fat Hair said.

Bright Eyes tended to Weeps a Lot's cut, which continued to seep blood. Weeps a Lot had become pale, and was empty in her eyes.

"If we place her in the canoe she will die," said Bright Eyes.

"If we do not place her in the canoe she will die." Pretty Face watched Cold Eye trim the wolf pelt. He had already claimed it for his own.

We loaded the canoe with our robes, weapons and bags of water. At the beach the water was calm, lapping the stones, but when we pushed off and turned south we would come to large waves.

"Place the boards," Watcher said. We carefully placed and

➤

secured the boards that raised the sides of the canoe.

Weeps a Lot still lay by the fire. She watched us, but she was not really watching. Her eyes moved from one thing to another without aim. The robe around her cut was red with new blood.

Fat Hair killed Weeps a Lot with a large rock, crushing her skull. He killed her quickly, coming up behind so she was unaware of his approach. It seemed she was unaware of anything, and now her spirit was trapped in the body lying by the fire.

Anger watched Fat Hair as he strode back to the canoe from the killing. "We have wood for her death pyre."

"She has not yet been accepted into the people and we need not send her spirit," Pretty Face said, handing in the last of the water bags.

"Thin Hair said we were all of the people, Pretty Face."

"I do not remember that, Strong Heart. You also are not yet of the people and you talk too much."

"We must leave now." Fat Hair started to push the canoe off the beach. The rest of us were in the canoe except Watcher and Anger and Fat Hair.

"You invite trouble." Anger waved at the motionless dead form of Weeps a Lot. "We always send the spirit of the people."

"Did we send the spirit when Thin Hair and Rock Hide were killed? We did not have time then. We do not have time now." Fat Hair pushed the canoe.

Anger left her position at the canoe and strode back to the shelter. She threw all the remaining wood onto the coals, then lifted Weeps a Lot and threw her onto the wood. Weeps a Lot lay on her back, her head loose.

Anger, Fat Hair and Pretty Face pushed us off, then hoisted themselves aboard.

"We will sail," Fat Hair said, not looking back at this place when we departed. Here his wife had died, and his journey child, yet he faced south and focused on being the finder, because more than anything now, we needed a good finder. We had to stay well away from the dangerous teeth of the ice bear.

I watched our camp as we left, looking at the body as it smoked on top of the flaming driftwood. Weeps a Lot lay upside down. The eyes in her smashed head followed us. I felt a cold breath in my soul. It was not the terror of facing an animal, but the deeper fear of an unknown spirit watching and judging before taking revenge.

We passed to open water. Ahead all we could see was water. If the people's home lay ahead, it was not yet in sight.

Now we were four new wives, not seven. Rock Hide, Weeps a Lot More, and Weeps a Lot were dead. Cold Eye lived, and was now under Pretty Face's robe. Tree Hide and Woman Too Soon were both gaunt, like women who had reached the end of their lives, not women barely starting. I had been small when I had been taken, and I was smaller now, this I knew. My hipbones jutted like spears, and my ribs were just beneath my skin.

Fat Hair was no longer soft like a woman. His small eyes were pinched and sad. Watcher had been thin and all vein and muscle when I first saw him and he remained so. Bright Eyes, like the rest of us, was all bones, yet she was carrying a journey child. When the sun rose she was ill. Then she paddled.

Pretty Face was not so pretty. His thin face, once flush with smooth skin and life, now held lines. His chin was sharp and cruel. His beautiful limbs and muscles were scarred and, like me, his hipbones stuck out. Thrower's big ears seemed bigger yet. He had become thin and bony, his eyes huge. Since we had left the headland he had grown half a hand span. He was now as tall as Bright Eyes. Anger remained broad, with huge bones, a long head, but she too was worn. Her breasts were gone, and she had a rash on her skin made worse by the salt water. Each day her skin was more and more scabbed. She would scratch until she bled.

The canoe leaked. We had to bail.

I could feel Pretty Face's eyes on me as I paddled. I knew he feared I would speak of his treachery to the others. I knew as the days passed his uncertainty about me would grow.

As the sun crossed the sky the wind continued. Gulls flew around us, crying. We saw several big whales, leaping from the water and landing on their sides, throwing water the way the ice bear's teeth threw water.

All of us paddled. Fat Hair would call out if he wanted someone to bail, and then that person would untie his or her paddle and take a bucket and empty the canoe.

We paddled through the night. Nobody slept. The sky was clear, the moon high and only days from being full. Spirits streaked across the sky, our ancestors calling our names.

The sun rose. We were out of food. The canoe was foul. Still, we had to keep on, always on.

Cold Eye slowly bailed. I could hear her behind me, throwing water, and the throws were far apart. When she finished, I did not hear her retake her place at the second thwart behind me to paddle. Instead she squatted on the robes under the tent.

"I will rest." She lay back on the robes.

Woman Too Soon, who had been on the second thwart paddling opposite Cold Eye, brought in her paddle and loosed the strap around her paddling wrist. She said nothing and joined Cold Eye on the robes. Now instead of nine of us paddling, we were seven.

"Return to paddle." Fat Hair, paddling opposite Pretty Face in the rear of the canoe, spoke with force. "We are losing our race with the teeth of the bear."

We had been blown toward the ice bear. Off to the left, I saw large pieces of ice, barely rising above the waves.

"I cannot." Cold Eye remained on the robes.

Fat Hair came forward, passing Tree Hide. The canoe lurched. Watcher struggled to brace himself as he fought with the steering oar.

Fat Hair took hold of Woman Too Soon and struck her with his fist. He hit her on the shoulder, but not too hard. She cried out. He struck her again. She stumbled out of his grasp and climbed forward of the second thwart and took her paddle. She was nearly asleep, even while standing.

Cold Eye did not move, even after Fat Hair struck Woman Too Soon. She lay on the robes, first looking at Fat Hair and then toward Pretty Face. Fat Hair struck her just as he had struck Woman Too Soon. Cold Eye cried out and seized her shoulder. She behaved as if Fat Hair had broken her arm. Cold Eye was acting, trying to make Fat Hair appear cruel in hopes Pretty Face would come to her aid.

Pretty Face did not move, but then Fat Hair struck Cold Eye again, on the other shoulder. Pretty Face threw off his paddle and rushed at Fat Hair. Watcher, standing above in the steering position, reached down and grabbed Pretty Face's long hair. Holding the steering oar in a grip between his right arm and his side, tight, Watcher pulled Pretty Face's head up by the hair with his left hand, hard.

Fat Hair had his hand raised to strike Cold Eye a third time. Watcher held Pretty Face by the hair. For a moment everyone stood so, as the canoe lurched and swung and some spray came aboard. Then Cold Eye, cowering, came fully to her feet and took her paddle. Fat Hair said nothing. He returned to his thwart. Watcher continued to hold Pretty Face, whose eyes were wild.

Fat Hair ignored Pretty Face and retook his paddle. Now Watcher let Pretty Face go. Pretty Face nearly fell when Watcher let go. He was dark with rage. Cold Eye paddled, her face purple with shame and anger. Pretty Face returned to his position and took his paddle. He was across the canoe from Fat Hair. Between him and Fat Hair, Watcher steered.

"Paddle." Watcher spoke clearly.

The high, jagged ice to the east rose to a distant, domed crest that seemed to stretch across all the sky north and south. South, I now saw mountains. These must be the mountains spoken of by these people, blocking the ice to the east, leaving open land to the west for the people's home. Watching Thrower, I could see how much it meant, seeing his home rise before him.

As we sailed, I saw a distant mountain ahead, with two black points like ears, great wide ice between, rise before me. The two points rose somewhat higher than the mountains around. These mountains blocked the great ice.

Watcher cried out, pointing east, and I saw, beyond the distant crest of the ice bear, a perfectly shaped mountain, smoking. "We are home. There lies our mountain that smokes."

I heard Watcher, Fat Hair, Anger and Bright Eyes all talking. I heard joy and relief as they spoke, but in Fat Hair's voice I only heard a deep sadness. He was returning with wives, but not his wife. He was returning with a journey child, but not his journey child. I did not hear Pretty Face.

East, the ice bear came closer, the face rounded like a great snout into the ocean, pushing west, eating. The sun was bright, the wind strong. We could see, ahead, mountains, thick green forest, and the long slope of the lands west of the mountains, with no ice, there for use by the people. I could now even see, ahead, the shore we were approaching, distant but clear. I saw the flat sheen of a river, and beyond, the river's deep valley, extending back into the mountains, leaving a deep shadowed wedge extending south and away. I wondered what my life would now be like, here, in this land.

Watcher began to sing the return home song and Anger joined in. Bright Eyes sang with them. They sang to the twin-eared mountain ahead standing guard over their land.

Pretty Face struck.

I heard a great crash. Someone screamed. The canoe swung left, across the waves, and nearly turned over, leaning to the right. I was tossed against Thrower, who in turn nearly fell into the water as we rolled. Behind me, past the swinging sail, Fat Hair and Watcher tumbled toward the lowered side of the canoe. Pretty Face stood behind, knife in his hand. A great gash stretched across Fat Hair's throat, and Watcher had a long gash in his leg. Fat Hair fell. Watcher fell against the lower rail of the canoe, held only by the ties around his waist to keep him on the thwart. Pretty Face cut those ties and Watcher fell out of the canoe into the water, bleeding. Bright Eyes, thrown to the bottom of the canoe, now rose with a razor stone knife in her hand. She threw it in one motion at Pretty Face. The knife struck his left eye, point first, and entered his brain. In an instant, he went rigid and collapsed, dead.

"Come." Anger leapt for the steering oar. Bright Eyes kept her eyes on Watcher, who was trying to swim in the steep seas. His flailing arms rose and then he was seen no more. Bright Eyes began her loss song.

Thrower helped Anger grab the steering oar. The others struggled to pull down the sail, because the canoe had turned and the wind in the sail pushed the canoe on its side. We lowered the sail just as Anger and Thrower got control of the steering oar. Thrower tied himself in and began steering the canoe.

We managed to turn the canoe downwind. Tree Hide and Bright Eyes reset the sail. We surged ahead toward the shore, the mouth of the river now close. Chunks of ice filled the water, which we struck, again and again.

Watcher was gone. Fat Hair lay dead, his throat cut open and bloody. Pretty Face lay on his back, the handle of the razor stone knife sticking from his eye. His other eye faced the sky. The smell of blood and death filled the canoe.

Long Braid had been correct—life is difficult. Now, facing the beautiful mountains, hearing the calls of the gulls above me, seeing rainbows in the sea spray, I knew life was also beautiful.

The shore approached. The waves grew steeper. Thrower struggled to keep the canoe straight. Then we slewed to the left as the waves from the sea fought against the outgoing river current. In the water below me I saw many huge salmon heading toward land, seeking their home just as we were seeking ours. Then I stumbled and fell.

I awoke to feel cold water splashing on me, yet my hand was in hot water. Across the water, I saw the eyes of a bear. I was in the dark but for the light cast by those eyes. I lay there for a long time, until I understood I was no longer in the canoe.

The eyes watched me. They blinked, and I knew it was time to leave. I followed the bear as it led the way. The path was difficult and frightening, leading down, then climbing up. The bear patiently led me. My head hurt and my hands hurt. At times I felt as if I was back in that canoe. I saw us swamping in the surf, then, half-filled, coming to shore, my small form lying in the bottom, in the water. But this was like a dream, not real. Being in the dark and trapped under the rock, this was real.

We climbed. It was not far, this rocky passage, and then I saw light. I had to crawl beneath low rock, on my belly. My hands were torn and slick with blood. I crawled out into heavy rain and thunder. My eyes hurt. Lightning flashed close by. Thunder roared. I smelled smoke, and in the lightning flashes, ahead, I saw two people behind a sheet of falling water. I felt weak. I could barely walk. I fell.

When I woke, I was dry and clean. I seemed in another dream, another place. Everything I had been through, all those days, all those memories, became as a dream. All during that time on that journey, I had not given a thought to this time and people, nor the way people spoke. I slept again.

When I next awoke, I knew this language and I knew these people, the big ugly Haida who could be Watcher, his Sol Duc daughter who had captured me and carried me, and the man who was my grandfather, the man who had come to love me. I did not know why I was here, but these people, I knew.

"Smoke, Tom."

It was still dark. William had risen and put on his boots. The sky was clear, with no wind. He had smelled smoke, but not campfire smoke. This smoke was acrid and sharp, the smoke from burning trees. Myra emerged from her tent, and Tom poked his head from their tent. Sergei rose from his tent, pulling on a long sleeved shirt.

"Probably smoke from that Dodger Point fire," William said, but he was doubtful. That fire was high on Dodger Point ridge, west. The fire was a long way above them. It wasn't a threat to them here.

"Maybe." Myra laced her boots. "It could be whatever started last night behind us, too. I'm going to take a look."

"I'll go with you," William said. "Tom, Sarah, Sergei – we'll be right back. Start packing up. Tom, try your radio, see if you get anything."

Myra and William mounted headlamps, turned them on, and started quickly up the trail. Without the lamps they would have been much slower, for here by the river the trail was beneath trees, rocky, and twisting, covered with branches and roots.

They walked half a mile. The smell of smoke was strong but it was not hard to breathe.

"I don't know what to think, any more." Myra led the way. "How could Sarah tell a story like that?"

➤

"I've heard elders describe their visions, Myra. So have you."

"But a months-long journey? Like that? Do you believe it?"

"I always know the bear's behind me in the sweat lodge, but I've never had an experience like Sarah's. I don't know what to think. I envy her."

"When she claimed to see that bear, near here, last spring, I envied her then, dad. I still do. I think Sergei, of the three of us, may believe Sarah the most. Did you see him, last night, listening to her? He kept nodding."

"Do you remember, Myra? He was going to tell us all something, just before we were attacked by Buckhorn?"

"Don't remind me, dad. I've treated him like a jerk this whole trip. His father just died."

"So maybe he's not the monster you thought he was?"

"He hasn't been the monster, dad."

Half a mile up the trail the meadows of the upper Press Valley opened. All this distance, the smoke was present, but not too thick. As they approached the meadows, the smell grew stronger. Ahead, to the south, over the meadows, smoke concealed the stars.

Myra stopped. Ahead, they saw flames, red dancing light among the trees. The fire was against the slope, over the trail, even burning the grasses of the meadow. Smoke billowed, blacker than night. As they watched, a thick cloud drifted over. William's eyes watered.

Myra turned around and started back. They walked fast. As they walked, the sky brightened. By the time they reached camp the stars were fading and William could see color.

"I thought you said just a minute or two." Tom was in his boots, waiting.

Myra waved back up the trail. "We walked to the valley meadows. The fire that started last night's there, maybe a mile from us. It's growing, probably now covering 20 acres. It's across the trail."

"Hell." Tom's radio sat on a stump. He pointed at the radio. "It was scratchy but I heard it. This trail's closed. That fire down at the Lillian Crossing is 150 acres, right on the trail, up high before the trail drops to the bridge."

Now the sky was light. Sarah sat by the fire ring with Sergei. She had packed all her and Myra's gear, including their sleeping bags and tent. Tom had done the same with his pack and William's gear.

William could see everyone was ready to go, but go where? Overhead and west, the rising sun caught the top of Dodger Point ridge. A pillar of smoke rose from the fire there. Down by the river smoke tendrils drifted through the trees, faint but clear. South, above the trees, William could see the column of smoke from the fire up by the meadow.

Sarah watched the four adults.

"Let me see the map, Tom," Myra said.

Tom handed her his map. She put away her headlamp and sat near Sarah.

Sarah squinted at the map. "Are we trapped?"

"If by trapped, Sarah, you mean unable to get out of here on trails, I think maybe we might be. We can't go ahead to Whiskey Bend because five miles that way is the Lillian fire. We can't go back south to the Hayden Pass Trail or Low Divide because of the fire that started last night a mile behind us." Myra pointed to Dodger Point ridge. "We could try the Dodger Point trail, which leaves the river near Elkhorn, but that fire up there looks to be right over the trail where it traverses the ridge."

Sarah said nothing. Sergei rose and came over to stand by Tom.

Tom turned to Myra. "What do we do, Myra? Didn't you

duck some fires when you did the Pacific Crest Trail last summer?"

"Don't remind me, Tom. At least here we know where the fires are. Last summer I smelled smoke and had no idea. Go forward? Go back? Climb off trail? It was scary."

Tom watched Myra trace a line with her finger on the map. "We're going have to go off trail, aren't we?"

"We could just sit somewhere down here, maybe Elkhorn, hope these fires go out. I'm pretty sure they won't burn all the way to there."

"Been a damn dry summer."

"I know, Tom. Despite the rain when those thunderstorms went through. Even if none of these fires gets close, the smoke will get thick here."

William bent his knees, two or three times. He knew with a pack on his back they would hurt.

"Look." Myra had the map on her knees. Tom and William bent over her shoulder. Sarah looked on from one side, Sergei the other.

"We're here, a mile south of Elkhorn. See? On each side of this river, steep high ridges. There's the trail up Dodger Point ridge, west, a mile ahead, but there's a fire up there. The smoke would be deadly." Myra pointed across the river, up the slope of Dodger Point, at the thick smoke rising. Then she pointed east. "But if we go east, off trail, behind Elkhorn, where we camped coming in, that ridge seems less steep, and there's a source of water. See?"

The map showed a slope east of Elkhorn rising four thousand feet. This was the ridge that separated the Lillian River from the Elwha River. If they climbed that slope, they would eventually come to an unnamed lake just west and 500 feet below Windfall Peak.

Tom traced the ridgeline from Windfall Peak east toward

Mt. Lillian and Grand Peak.

"Myra have you ever been on this ridge? Is it even possible?"

"I don't know, but it's away from the fires." Myra folded the map, handing it to Tom. "We stay down here, it's smoke and no way out. We hike to that lake, we'll have water, no fires, and a way to escape. It may take a couple days and some time, but if we bushwhack over to Grand Valley there are people, rangers, and help."

Sergei put on his pack. "William, you told me you would show me your park, but you failed to mention I would be attacked and then trapped by fires. Now it seems we must flee these fires and then find our way across unknown cliffs to safety." Sergei studied Myra. She studied him back. "I have confidence in Myra."

Myra gave a half smile. William, recognizing her slightly nervous smile, understood she was unsure of the route out of here. Sergei beamed. Sarah pointed at Sergei.

"Myra, when he smiles he looks like Thrower. He doesn't have the ears, though." Sarah crossed her eyes at Sergei.

Sergei nodded. "When I was a boy my father called me Dumbo, for Dumbo the elephant, from an old American story book. I hated that name. My ears were big, then."

"He grew into them, though, didn't he, Myra?"

"Maybe, Sarah." Myra was a little red in the face.

They followed Myra as she led them down the trail. The smoke was with them, drifting in strands through the trees, bitter.

They came down the trail in the hazy smoke and crossed the small meadow, passing the stump where Sarah had drawn the bear. They entered the larger meadow with the shelter and stopped to grab some breakfast. Sergei and Sarah went to the river for water. Tom pulled out his stove.

William was sweating. This day was going to be hot. The

sky was clear, or would have been but for the yellow streaks of smoke up high.

Myra had the map out. Sarah sketched in her book.

Sergei squatted by Sarah. "Sarah you say I smile like Thrower. Do I look like Thrower?"

"When you're not smiling, you don't look much like him. Thin Hair. When you don't smile you look a little like Thin Hair." Sarah turned to William. "Watcher could have been you, William, if he had your eye, and you were thinner."

Sergei peered at Sarah's sketch. She was drawing Tom. It was a good drawing, catching the flash of light off his glasses as he bent to a pot of boiling water.

Tom raised his head. "Sarah you should draw those people. The people you were with." Sarah said nothing. "Do you miss Thrower? Watcher? Bright Eyes?"

Sarah stopped drawing and gazed at Tom with suspicion. "They were real." Sarah spoke softly. "I mean, I know what you think. I miss them. I liked it back there. It was hard, but I liked it."

Tom set the pot of oatmeal aside and sat next to Sarah. He reached out and adjusted Sarah's hat, which had fallen to the side across her face. "You miss Thrower the most, don't you?"

"He taught me to throw." Sarah didn't move away when Tom adjusted her hat.

"He taught you well," Sergei said. "We all owe him a great debt of thanks."

Myra folded the map. Tears welled in Sarah's eyes. Sergei and Tom both reached for the pot of oatmeal and the bowls at the same time.

"Are we sure about this, Myra?" William asked. Somebody had to ask. They were surrounded by smoke, blocked from moving on trails, about to launch off on a killer climb to an uncertain route home. "Is this wise?"

"We can stay here, I guess." Myra was uncertain.

Sergei waved his hands through the air. The smoke wasn't thick enough to swirl, but it could be seen. "Isn't the rule when you get lost, to stay in place? I know we're not lost, but if we stayed here, wouldn't rangers find us?"

"I think it's a tough call." Tom was looking at the map. "We stay here, we're in smoke just waiting for those fires to come get us."

"Or, the fires may go out," William said, doubtful.

"You ready to count on that, dad?"

"Not really."

Myra traced the route up the ridge. "I think it's a coin toss."

"Coin toss? What is that?"

"Sergei, that's an expression. Tossing a coin to decide what to do."

"I don't want to be the one to decide, Myra."

"None of us do, Sergei."

They began eating their oatmeal. In the end they all were looking at Myra. She folded the map and pointed.

"If we go high, right there, that's where we'd start." She was pointing to the slope behind where Sarah had been practicing with the thrower. Sarah followed Myra's arm as it swung up and to the left, indicating their path.

"That's where the bear went, Myra." Sarah squinted, pointing.

"What?" Sergei asked.

"The bear I saw, it went up that hill. It went right the way Myra pointed, exactly." Then Sarah stood, oatmeal forgotten, excited. "Yes. It stopped three times, and peered back at me. It was as if it was trying to show me something, or get me to follow." Sarah turned to face William. "William, it went exactly there. It was showing us. It was showing us what to do. The bear was telling us to climb to this Windfall Peak. I'm certain." Sarah faced the slope as if watching an animal work its way uphill.

Myra thrust the map in her pocket, lips tight. William believed Myra was uneasy about the choice to climb the ridge. He was uneasy, too. "Are you sure, Sarah?"

"Why else would it have stopped, William?" Sarah kept looking up the slope.

"It's just as good a sign as any, Myra," William said.

"You're enjoying this, dad." Myra was irritated. William said nothing. Sarah grinned.

They filled every container with water. The sun, now rising over the ridge, beat on the brown meadow. The smoke drifted, across the grass, through the trees.

They shouldered their packs. William steeled his heart for the ordeal to come.

"Sarah," Myra said, "you lead off, but don't get ahead of us, all right? You start, you show us. Follow where your bear went, exactly."

"It was showing us, Myra."

Sarah led off. Sergei and Tom fell in. They all went across the meadow, passing the tree where Sarah had thrown darts.

Myra took her father's arm. "Dad, take it easy. This is going to be tough. Slow and steady. We've got all day and we'll take all day. I'll stay with you, bring up the rear. Sergei can keep Sarah in sight, call her back if she goes ahead." William adjusted his pack. Myra tightened her grip. "Dad, remember last spring, after Sarah saw the bear, you reminded me I had told Sarah this was a place of magic, history and legend?"

"I remember."

"And then what did you say?"

William thought back. "I said, 'Are we taking Sarah on this trip or is she taking us?'"

"Well, she's taking us, dad. Hell, she's been taking us since she appeared at Tom's door in May." Myra always scrunched her brow when she was thinking hard. "Know what else, dad?

It seems Sergei, maybe even Tom, believe Sarah more than I do, and I'm the local, here."

"Myra, I think Sarah would say they're of the people, too."

They crossed the meadow and started up the steep slope past hemlocks, spruces, firs, and the occasional cedar. They were slow. The air was smoky. Sarah seemed least affected of any of them. She forged ahead, tall pack lurching. The line she followed angled north and east, rising toward the prow of the ridge. Beyond this ridgeline, the ground fell steeply to the outlet stream from the unnamed lake. It would be a difficult walk down a steep slope to get water, and a harder walk coming back, but William knew they would soon use up the water they had. Already they all were sweating.

Myra called to Sarah and told her to keep going as she was until she reached the gentle crest of this prow. She should then turn right and start directly up the crest. Studying the map, it seemed a straight hike all the way on this crest to the unnamed lake.

What the map did not show were the three-foot high ledges scattered everywhere, or the steeper sections where they had to place their feet carefully to avoid slipping back. They climbed slowly. Within minutes the sound of the river, below, disappeared. Now it was silent but for the calls of thrushes and jays and the sound of dragonflies hovering over devil's club.

They came upon a large section of fallen trees, piled on top of each other, the 150-foot trunks in chaotic positions. They tried to work up through the first fall they came to and were nearly lost under trees and limbs. It was almost impossible to move with the packs on and it was even harder to remove them and try to pass them hand-to-hand over the big logs.

Sarah delivered judgment. "Gross."

It took an hour to get through the fallen trees. When they did, William estimated they had climbed only 400 vertical feet, yet half the morning was gone. He was scratched, running with sweat, and becoming pissed off because his hips hurt and his feet hurt and they were going to hurt more. Myra stayed by William and helped when she could, but everyone was fully engaged with their own gear, just getting beyond the fallen trees.

William noticed that Tom's left knee had begun to bother him. Tom had been all right coming down the trail from Bear Valley, but working uphill was hard. He slowed, now walking back with William while Sarah and Sergei led the way. Myra moved back and forth, directing Sarah, looking at the map, sometimes waiting for Tom and William.

When they broke through the fallen trees, they stopped. Sarah threw off her pack and sat, drinking water. She was sweaty and mopping her neck. Sergei had found a log on the ground against which he dropped his pack, then leaned against it, sitting, comfortable. Myra was on the ground, her feet down in a root ball hole, the fallen tree stretching away into the forest. Tom dropped his pack, collapsed, and William collapsed with him.

"I can see why there's no trail up here. Jesus." Tom pushed back his thinning hair. "We'll need all the daylight, this day, if this keeps on."

Looking ahead, up the slope, it appeared more open. There were rhododendrons everywhere. West, through the trees, Dodger Point ridge rose. Well up on the ridge they could see smoke and fire. It was still above, and distant.

"We'll rest 10 minutes." Myra was holding her watch.

Sergei leaned against his log. His shirt was black with sweat. "I have been thinking." He spoke with his eyes closed, head back, resting.

"What? We can all rest here and you're going to carry all our gear and go get help?" Sarah sounded hopeful. Sergei cocked one eye open. He shook his head.

"No. I have been thinking, and I am hoping my new friends William and Tom, both sailors most familiar with Northern Pacific waters, will help."

"It's been years since I've been at sea, Sergei." Tom was now on his back, hat over his eyes.

Sergei sat up. "If we assume the people who lived near the mountains that smoke lived in the same land, Kamchatka, that we Koryaks eventually came to occupy, which has several active volcanoes, that appears a reasonable starting point for Sarah's journey."

Nobody said anything. Myra eyed Sergei. Sergei waited. Tom cleared his throat.

"Could they start by May?" Tom asked. "Remember, she said they needed to be at the headland by the longest day moon, right Sarah? That's late June. Be pretty sketchy, starting a boat journey in early May that far north. Hell, the ice is hardly gone by then." Tom spoke without moving his hat.

Sergei scratched his chin. "But, Tom, at that time there was land north of Kamchatka where the Bering Sea is now. It was the land bridge. The sea ice would have been north of the land bridge. They would have been following the southern coast, against the Pacific. I think they could have left that early easily. Didn't you say, Sarah, you were taken when there was ice still on the sea of grass?"

Sarah, watching Sergei and Tom talk, blinked, swallowing. Myra began to shake her head. William reached over, placed his hand on her wrist. He thought he understood what Sergei was doing. Sergei had seen that Sarah doubted her own sanity because nobody around her had even tried to verify what she had said.

"So these people went in this skin boat from Kamchatka and reached St. Paul Island, except then it was a headland, by the summer solstice," Sergei said. "When the sun rose between the twin peaks. Could they travel that distance in a month, William?"

William had been picturing the route his ship had taken from Petropavlosk to St. Paul. "They'd have to travel over 900 miles. Doable, I think. Averaging 30-40 miles a day? Those skin boats could be paddled four, five miles an hour all day, I'm thinking."

"Carrying wives and bone tools. Something these people tried every five years," Tom said.

"Yes, Tom. Possibly the same bone that became the atlatl we have now lost." Sergei nodded as he spoke.

"What are you doing, Sergei?" Myra was becoming angry.

"It's data, Myra." Sergei brushed off his shirt. "Perhaps, a legend? Didn't you accuse me of ignoring legends?" Myra said nothing. "Then the new people and their one log canoe, which had travelled three months to reach St. Paul, went back, east and south, to a place where they said people once were. They stopped there, and then travelled again. When they arrived it was almost the equinox moon, late September. Three months. People can travel a long way in that period of time. Round trip, six months."

"Where do you think they went, Sergei? Haida Gwaii? One of the Alaskan islands?" Tom was on his back, talking to the sky.

"William, could they have travelled all the way to here, in that time?"

"Here? You mean, the Olympic Peninsula, here?" Myra twisted around to face Sergei. "What?"

Sergei put the stick aside and began to unroll his fingers, one at a time, as he talked. "They sailed south, then west for a time, then made a turn and sailed east, even north of east. Then after several days they came to this Place People Once

Were, a refuge among the ice. William? Tom?"

Tom scratched his head. "Jesus. They followed the 50-meter line from St. Paul south to the Aleutian chain, then west for a bit to where the deeper water came. They turned, just before Dutch, and started back along the edge toward Kodiak. That's east, even east by north. Maybe the refuge was there. Kodiak."

"Maybe a little farther, maybe Prince of Wales Island," William pictured the chart of the Gulf of Alaska that hung in the ship's mess. "That large island lies east and south of Prince William Sound, which would have been a long crossing of open water after the islands west of the sound."

Sergei kept unrolling fingers. "Then they started south, passing islands, passing the Queen Charlottes, passing Vancouver Island. Along the coast, with the lower sea level, they would have encountered lots of barrier islands, which they used. Remember, there was once a large glacier against the west side of Vancouver Island and in the Strait of Juan de Fuca. That could have been the snout of the ice bear." Sergei pointed west, toward Dodger Point and Mount Olympus beyond. "The two-eared mountain they saw coming south? Could it have been Mount Olympus here on this peninsula? I have read that there is evidence the western slope of this peninsula was a refuge during maximum ice times. The green slopes and open land protected by the mountains, was it the west side of this peninsula? Was this the refuge among the ice?"

Tom sat up. "The smoking mountain Sarah saw at the end of her journey? It could have been Mount Baker, when it was still active. It's exactly west of the middle of the Strait of Juan de Fuca."

Myra examined Sergei. "You're the strangest scientist I ever met."

Sarah now stood. She faced down the slope toward the

Elwha, silent below them. "The river we came to, where I saw the salmon in the water, where I hit my head, was it that river down there?" She pointed.

"That's a long damn way to ride a canoe." Tom was shaking his head. "It's 3,000 miles, that headland to here, following the coast."

Minutes passed. Sergei sat up.

"Myra, you actually confirmed everything for me back on the meadow where Sarah saw the bear. Remember? You said the Asian mammoths were North American animals that had crossed the land bridge more than 60 thousand years ago, east to west, replacing the Siberian mammoths." Myra nodded cautiously. "I tried to tell you then, but you didn't want to hear what I had to say. Then when I tried to bring it up a second time, we were attacked. Maybe it was for the best, because now we have heard Sarah's entire story." Sergei wore the strangest expression. "As I told you, we could not date that sliver. But I did do a DNA test. The results seemed impossible. They made no sense. Now, after hearing Sarah's story, maybe they do."

"What do you mean?" asked Myra.

"The sliver tested as bone from a Siberian mammoth. Not a North American mammoth or the Russian mammoth derived from the North American mammoth. It was the original Siberian mammoth, extinct since at least 60 thousand years ago. That means the atlatl we lost was carved and brought here from Siberia at least that long ago. At least 60 thousand years. To here." Nobody said anything. Sergei was watching them. He stood and stretched. "It could have been a glacial refuge here, right here, on the Olympic Peninsula, in the dark time after the Toba eruption, 75 thousand years ago, when ancient people, not yet modern, came together to create us. Right here. That is, if Sarah's story is true."

Sarah gazed toward the river, then north. Tom whistled.

Myra shouldered her pack. "We've got a long damn way still to climb. We better get going." She faced Sergei. "Sarah's story is not the kind of data you can use in a paper, Sergei."

"But Tom's atlatl would have been, had we saved it."

"We don't have it. We have nothing. Nothing. "

"I saw and held that bone thrower, Myra. So did we all. That is data."

"It's gone, Sergei. This theory will never be tested."

"But think about it, Myra." Sergei's teeth flashed. "The data we all did see, and touch, doesn't it prove your legends might be true? I would give anything to prove such a theory. Anything. Right now the data argues against this, but we all had something in our hands that might have changed things. We all saw it. Held it. Maybe there is more data to be found."

"It would have to be an uncontestable, datable, perfect find, Sergei." William noticed that Myra was looking at Sergei with affection for the first time. "I don't need data to know our legends are true, Sergei, but thank you. Of course we have always been here. As I have said."

"That's when modern humans began, Myra." Sergei was gazing toward the Elwha below, then Myra. He lifted his pack. "We are cousins. All of us."

"That's kissing cousins, Myra." Sarah poked Myra's leg.

"Shut up, Sarah." Myra hoisted her pack and strode off.

"She really likes you, Sergei." Sarah pulled on her pack.

"She hates me."

"You're a man. You don't know anything. I know that and I'm not even a woman yet."

Sergei and Sarah followed Myra up the hill.

Tom stood and watched them, then said to William, "We gonna get there, 'Eye?"

"One step at a time, Tom."

"You know, 'Eye, a big canoe like that, handled right, with

a strong wind astern, could probably sail 150-200 miles a day. From here to Alaska and then on to St. Paul might be possible. I think the trip out to the headland, starting probably in early April from here, that's the harder leg of the journey."

Ahead, the others worked uphill. It was hot. They would need water before early afternoon.

"I'm really glad Sarah appeared at your house last spring, Tom."

"I was pissed at you, 'Eye, when you suggested we bring Sarah out here last May, but now I'm glad you opened your big ugly mouth." Tom, sweating, cleaned his glasses, then looked up. "And it seems Sarah went on a journey of her own. What's Sergei say? You need data? For a nuts and bolts guy like me, Sarah's story has all the data I can ask for. I believe her, you know."

"Then tell her, Tom."

They struggled on, always upward. They reached the crest of the ridge, which fell from the peak above them back down to the Elwha. Down the slope to the left might be water, but it was a long way. The footing was better, but still slow. The small ledges, the rocks, the branches, forced them to try to rise step by step straight up the hill, or work in angles, first to the left, then the right, making switchbacks to lessen the slope.

They came to another big blow down, trees piled across the crest of the ridge for hundreds of feet. They had to work down the slope to the left, off the crest, to pass beyond the logs and trees. By the time they were low enough to get around the ends of the trees, they were as close to the outlet stream as they were going to get, so Sarah and Sergei went off in search of water, carrying bottles and the water bag. The sun was bright, even through the trees, and the air smoky. When Sergei and Sarah returned with water, they drank, then filled their bottles.

They climbed. They stopped after an hour, took water, rested. They stopped again an hour later, rested again. When they stopped, they spoke little. They simply dropped their packs and sprawled where they could, breathing, trying to drink, trying to find energy. Tom's knee had become increasingly stiff. William was sure if Tom seized up he would be in big trouble.

It was mid afternoon when they first broke into alpine

➤

meadows after fighting through 200 yards of chest-high, thick, tightly-clustered bushes. It was tedious and slow going. Sergei had been in the lead, and he suddenly found himself facing an opening, a narrow slide chute, piled with rocks. The rocks were large and clustered, rising at a 20-degree angle up the ridge. As they rested in the sun and heat, large flies appeared from nowhere and attacked.

They followed the chute upward at a steep angle 200 feet until the angle changed and the slope led to a broad gentle basin beneath the lip of another climb, beyond which William was sure the unnamed lake lay. When they emerged from the chute into the basin, they staggered 100 yards further up, then went left 50 yards, and stopped. Here the grass was green, the ground smoother, and they were in the open. They dropped their packs.

"The outlet for the lake must be over that rise," Sergei said, pointing north. Higher in the basin, east, William could see a stream emerge over the lip, then drop in a cascade, disappear, then reappear further down, where it dropped in a longer fall.

William was happy to take off his pack. The wind cooled his face. He heard birds and saw an eagle, high above.

To the west lay the peaks and glaciers of the Bailey Range, and beyond that, white and huge, Mount Olympus. Below, the Elwha valley stretched northwest to the sea. To the right, dropping away, the Lillian valley led west to join the Elwha. The Lillian fire was clear, a pall of smoke still covering a large area down in the valley. Framed by the distant opening of the Elwha Valley, they could see the sheen of the Strait of Juan de Fuca, even the pale blue mountains of Vancouver Island beyond.

Further up the basin, two black bears grazed, bush by bush.

"You were right, William." Sergei was sitting, looking west, hand shading his eyes. "This is a beautiful land."

"Your church. Right, dad?" Myra also shaded her eyes.

They had only 300 feet to climb to pass over the lip above and find a level spot by the lake. William could hear, faintly, a waterfall, the outlet stream, tumbling off the ledge separating the upper basin, where they were, from the lower basin below. Maybe he would swim in the lake. They had miles yet to go, days of cross-country travel in steep unknown country, but they were beyond the fires, above most of the smoke, and surrounded by heartbreakingly beautiful country.

Overhead, high up, the eagle continued to circle.

William closed his eyes. They all dozed. The eagle cried, twice.

William opened his eyes.

North, behind the rise of land before him, not 30 yards distant, the biggest bear he had ever seen rose. It faced him, motionless. Somewhere above, and higher, he heard a thrashing scramble and he knew without looking that the black bears above them feeding on berries were rushing away as fast as they could go.

This bear was huge, with an enormous head and long arms. It craned its neck, looking at him. Its fur was long and mottled, a kind of piebald pattern. As William stared, absolutely motionless, he smelled a rank, strong odor, not of today's world. This animal, standing on the knoll 30 yards away, was the same short face bear Sarah had drawn in May. This was what Sarah and her comrades had faced during her journey, bears just like this one, swimming to the island, hungry for salmon yet no salmon to eat. It was the most terrifying yet beautiful animal he had ever seen.

William slowly turned his head toward the others. Tom and Sergei were lying in the sun, eyes closed, perhaps asleep, but Sarah and Myra were sitting, silent, facing the bear. He looked again at the bear.

Its fur shone in the sun. For a long moment it towered, looking, watching. Its head bobbed, once. Then it shook itself and turned, disappearing from sight, behind the rise, headed toward the waterfall and the lower basin.

William glanced over at Myra. She was motionless. Sarah's eyes were glistening. One tear slowly tracked down her cheek. The bear was gone. William somehow knew, watching Sarah, they would not see it again.

Tom and Sergei sat up. Tom dusted off his shirt. Sergei, seeing Sarah, Myra and William's expression, inhaled, sharp.

"You saw it. Didn't you? The bear."

Myra nodded, swallowing.

William said nothing. Thank you, grandmother.

Sarah spoke to Sergei. "The bear has shown us. The Marking Place, the people's sacred place, it must be here. Somewhere in this basin."

Tom rose and went to sit next to Sarah. He placed his arm across her thin shoulders. "Sarah, I make you this promise. We will return, next year. We'll go to Bear Valley and see if we can find another fossil thrower. And then we'll come up here, to find this Marking Place, from your story. And next year, maybe, I'll see this bear."

The eagle flew toward Windfall Peak.

The afternoon light was golden. North and west, beyond the opening where the river flowed, distant, Vancouver Island pointed toward Haida Gwaii, the Bering Sea, the Siberian shore, and the rest of the world.

AFTERWORD

When I first moved to Seattle in 1990 I found myself negotiating agreements with local Tribes to enable commercial shipping activity to coexist with treaty-guaranteed fishing rights in Seattle Harbor. I learned all the Tribes' legends state they have been in the Pacific Northwest forever. Always. This conflicts with current archeological dogma, which holds that humans first arrived in North America at the end of the most recent ice age, 12 to 15 thousand years ago. Being contrary, I wondered, could such legends be true? And, if true, how so?

This became my question. Years came and went, then more years. When I could, I did research, studies of geology and ice movements, ice age refuges, and dozens of books and papers about the origins and spread of modern humans. I have my own ideas about human travel based on my years at sea and recent archeological evidence of ancient seafaring. I was always in the Olympic Mountains, on the peninsula, exploring. The common belief holds that the native people avoided the interior, but this is not so. There are sites deep in the wilderness, several thousand years old. I am convinced some of the high alpine trails were first trod by human feet during the time of the great ice.

Stories are what make us human. The ability to tell a story is a means to remember, to pass culture generation to generation, to learn and hold memory. How did we humans come to be storytellers? What happened? *Strong Heart* suggests what may have happened, and where, and even how. Mostly, though, this is just a story.

Special thanks to Lyn Coffin and all my fellow classmates in her class at the University of Washington, Literary Fiction 1, in 2013-2014. Pete Wise, one of those classmates, was a terrific editor. Ethan Yarbrough, of Iron Twine Press, took a huge chance, because he believed, and his advice and counsel have been invaluable.

An author writes, but friends, family members, teachers, and classmates make a story real through their comments, suggestions, and reactions. In the end they have as much to do with whatever works as the author. Many people helped with this tale, too many to list here, but I would be remiss if I didn't mention my wife, Randa Williams, who was always patient yet encouraging, and Wade Watson, Gerry Quigley, Peggy Schlein, Sarah Schlein, Adam Miller, John Wiggin, Ruth Moulton, Dick Livingston, Teri Johnson, Oskar Sheldon and his Sheridan friend Eric Southworth, Len Richards, Patrick and Monica Fairbairn and Beth Richards, who all first saw this tale back in 2014 and gave me much needed encouragement when I needed it most. To those many others who later gave feedback, and there were many, thank you, too. It seems it takes a village to tell a story.

This tale was written in Bellingham, Seattle, and deep in the Olympics with my trusty battered notebook, then revised when I was working aboard the vessels MV *President Truman*, *Gilliland*, and *Shughart*. Special thanks to Vince O'Halloran and my shipmates at the Sailor's Union of the Pacific for giving me an effective vehicle for spinning a yarn – seagoing work gives time ashore between gigs on ships to write, and time while at sea to ponder. It turns out you need both.

Charlie Sheldon

ABOUT THE AUTHOR

Charlie and a replica of a Short-face bear at the Royal Museum, Victoria, British Columbia.

Charlie Sheldon studied at Yale University and the University of Massachusetts, where he received a Master's Degree in Wildlife Biology and Resource Management. He then went to sea as a commercial fisherman off New England, fishing for cod, haddock, hake, lobster, red crab, squid, and swordfish. Active in the fight for the 200-mile Fisheries Conservation Zone, he later worked as a consultant for Fishery Management Councils, developing fishery management plans and then engaging in gear development projects to develop more selective fisheries. He spent 28 years working for seaports (New York, Seattle, and Bellingham, WA) as a project and construction manager and later as an executive, including habitat cleanup projects and working with Puget Sound Tribes to reduce tribal fishing conflicts. Later he returned to sea, shipping out with the Sailor's Union of the Pacific as an Ordinary Seaman, Able Bodied Seaman, and Bosun. His last gig was as bosun aboard USNS *Shughart*, New Orleans to New York, in 2016. Always a writer, he published *Fat Chance* with Felony and Mayhem Press in 2005. He began working on ideas for *Strong Heart*, his tale about the Olympic Mountains, the Pacific coast, and human origins long, long ago and began serious research in 2010. These days he hikes in the Olympics whenever he can, cooks for his wife, and continues to write tales in Ballard, Washington.